THE WEREWOLF OF WALL STREET

Pereset Press Books by Gary Greenberg

The Moses Mystery: The Egyptian Origins of the Jewish People

King David Versus Israel:
How A Hebrew Tyrant Hated by the Israelites Became a Biblical Hero

Also by Gary Greenberg

101 Myths of the Bible: How Ancient Scribes Invented Biblical History

The Judas Brief: Who Really Killed Jesus?

Manetho: A Study in Egyptian Chronology

Books by Jerome Tucille

Dillerland

Gallo Be Thy Name

Alan Shrugged

It Usually Begins With Ayn Rand

It Still Begins With Ayn Rand

Rupert Murdoch

Trump

Kingdom: The Story of the Hunts of Texas

Others

The Werewolf of Wall Street

Gary Greenberg and Jerome Tuccille

PERESET PRESS
New York, NY

A Pereset Press Book

All inquiries should be addressed to:
Pereset Press
P. O. Box 25
New York, NY 10008
Info@peresetpress.com

This book was originally published under the title *War of the Werewolf.*

First Pereset Press printing in 2009.
ISBN:978-0-9814966-2-7

Part I
1990

CHAPTER ONE

Alex Mallum had a problem: he needed to reach the LA airport before the German's bonecrushers figured out he stiffed their boss for one hundred and sixty grand, and now he regretted his decision to take the scenic route along the northern California coast. His blood-red Alfa Romeo snaked along the narrow twisting highway carved high into the jagged cliffs. No barrier stood guard along the narrow shoulder at the cliff's edge. Way below, angry waves pounded against the rocky shore. The sleek convertible tenaciously hugged the asphalt as Mallum raced around sudden sharp turns and into long rolling banks.

Overhead, storm clouds sailed rapidly across the night sky. The crystal light of the full moon disappeared behind the dark clouds, leaving only the car's headlights to penetrate the black void that hid the road. Flashes of lightning briefly illuminated the coastline, and then quickly vanished into the void. Blasts of thunder boomed against the mountain walls.

Rain started to fall, a few drops at first, slowly building into a light drizzle. Mallum pulled to the side of the road, lifted the soft roof out of its compartment, locked it into place, and then sped back onto the highway. Twenty minutes later the drizzle thickened into a solid downpour. Cursing his luck, Mallum let up on the accelerator, cutting his speed by half. If this rain didn't taper off soon there was no way he could reach the airport in time. Mallum was scared. The German would hurt him—hurt him so badly that he would beg for death. And the German would grant his wish, in his own sweet time.

Beads of sweat gathered on Mallum's forehead. His palm tapped nervously against the steering wheel and little drops of moisture trickled down his cheeks. He could not sit still, could not help fidgeting in his seat as he winced his way through the sheets of water deluging the windshield. The wipers swept them away, but managed only to leave a blurry smear. The rubber blades whined across the glass, fueling his frustration. His foot pressed harder on the accelerator, picking up speed against his better judgment. The road was slippery and the tires skidded sideways, closer to the precipice. Again he slowed down, slammed his fist onto the dashboard and cursed his luck.

The skyburst lasted a full hour longer before it stopped. Mallum uttered a long slow sigh, and alternately increased and decreased his speed to accommodate the snaking road, which was still slick from the rain. He had not seen a single other vehicle during the hours he had been racing down the coast. Isolation heightened his panic. The darkness, the emptiness were eerie enough without this fear. Then, suddenly, there were headlights up ahead. Just the beams were visible, meaning the approaching vehicle had to be rounding a bend. Mallum moved to the edge to give the driver sufficient space to make the turn.

As he veered left following the bank of the road, the headlights were in his eyes. The high bright lights temporarily blinded him. An instant later he saw the truck, a pickup, tearing around the bend three-quarters of the way into his lane. There was no room on the right, just the precipice and the drop off into darkness. Mallum swung to the left, cutting in front of the truck as he aimed for the wider shoulder along the mountain wall. The pickup never slowed. Its right front fender slammed into the rear of the Alfa Romeo, spinning it out of control. Mallum hit his brakes, skidding toward the mountain wall as the truck continued past. He swerved to avoid a frontal crash into the rocky embankment, and heard the shrill horrific scream of metal scraping along the rock. A stream of sparks illuminated the blackness as the Alfa scraped along the rugged craggy stone.

It all took place in seconds, but in Mallum's fevered state it seemed like eternity. Directly ahead, a large outcropping of rock blocked his path. Mallum slammed down on the brake, and then skidded abruptly across the highway toward the far edge. He deliberately picked up speed to generate friction on the road, and twisted the steering wheel left, back toward the mountain wall. Now he swerved back and forth from left to right, struggling to hold the middle ground between the deadly precipice and the towering rocky embankment. The crash had knocked out his left headlight, and his view of the road was even more obscure than before. Too late, he noticed a downhill leftward curve, and before he knew it he was on the far shoulder along the edge traveling much too fast.

He was going over the edge; he knew it in his soul, when he heard the pop. A tire blew. The Alfa swerved toward the left, then cut back in the opposite direction toward the cliff. He hit the brake as hard as he could but the Alfa kept on sliding. Mallum screamed. He threw his arms across his face and braced against the steering wheel.

The right front tire went over first, but the left side of the car smacked into a tree on the edge of the cliff. The entire windshield shattered in on him as the Alfa slammed to a halt. Mallum's body surged forward, his head banged into something hard and unyielding, but the seatbelt kept him from flying out through open space. He touched a painful spot on his head, removed his hand and saw blood on his fingertips. He reached into his pocket for a handkerchief to dab the wound, and his shifting weight caused the car to rock in place.

Mallum stopped squirming. His mind began to clear and he looked around. The Alfa was perched halfway out over the edge of the cliff. He had to get out—slowly, calmly, without disturbing the vehicle. He gripped the door handle on the driver's side and tried to turn it, but the door was stuck. He rolled down the window, reached overhead and unlocked the convertible roof. With extreme care, he pushed it back and eased himself up, ever so slowly, out of his seat, over the top of the left side of the car.

Mallum stood on solid ground. He was shaky, dizzy, so he leaned against the tree until the sensation passed. Then he looked closely at the tree trunk that now formed an integral part of the car's grille. He also noticed his left front tire was bent at an unnatural angle to the ground. Without thinking, he poked it with the toe of his shoe. He turned and saw one of his star-shaped hubcaps lying twisted in the middle of the road. He walked over and picked it up, then rubbed it clean with the sleeve of his sports jacket. He took out his handkerchief and buffed the metal. He placed it under his arm and returned to survey the wreckage of his car.

It was beyond recognition—his blood-red Alfa Romeo Spider Veloce, with glove-soft leather seats, digital electronic ignition for easy starting in any kind of weather, electronic multi-point fuel injection system automatically adjusted by a microcomputer several times a second to ensure a perfectly running engine—now a useless pile of twisted scrap metal sitting on the edge of a cliff.

He loved that car, the one possession he treasured. Mallum traced his finger along the hand-stitched leather seat, fighting back the tears. Tears for what? His treasure? Himself? The Alfa was shattered, and so was what remained of his life. He lowered himself to the ground and rested his back against the tree. A great pall of depression, loneliness, unhappiness descended upon him. Mallum studied his reflection in the hubcap and saw the rivulet of blood rolling down his cheek. He buried his head in his arms and gave in to the weariness and the feeling of complete despair.

"Damn!" His voice was a croak, choked with grief. "I just can't catch a break."

Composure regained, Mallum stood up and walked over to the edge of the cliff. He stared down at the churning waters crashing against the rocky shore below. I wonder, he thought, if jumping off could be anywhere as painful as anything the German could do to me. What was that old line about a coward dying a thousand deaths, a hero dying but once? One simple jump, then eternal peace and no pain.

He almost persuaded himself to do it, but then had second thoughts. With my luck I'd bounce off the rocks, break every bone in my body, and land on some bushes. If the German found me like that, crying in agony, he'd probably just laugh and leave me there to die a slow agonizing death. Screw it! I'm not jumping.

Mallum turned to leave but as he stepped away his foot landed on a loose rock. His ankle twisted and he stumbled backwards, rolling over the cliff's edge but luckily managing to grab hold of some shrubbery as he fell over the side. He held on to the deeply-rooted bushes with all his strength, his body dangling over the foaming sea.

"Give me a break!" he screamed. "Just this once." His voice faded to a whimper. "I'm not greedy. Just one break is all I ask."

He tried to haul himself up but was unable to lift his weight. Perspiration flowed from every pore; his hands grew damp and started to slip along the shrub. Straining every muscle in his body, he swung his legs back and forth, widening the arc with every swing until he had built enough momentum. He put everything he had into one final lunge. His left leg cleared the top, giving him the leverage he needed to belly himself onto the shoulder's edge.

Mallum crawled forward on hands and knees to the middle of the road, then rolled over and stared into the tar-black sky. "Thank you, God," he said softly, forgetting his atheistic predilection, if only for the moment. "I owe you one."

He stood up and walked over to fetch the flashlight from the glove compartment. Gingerly, he reached across from the driver's side without putting weight on the vehicle until he found it with his fingers. He flicked it on but nothing happened. Of course not. Nothing else had gone right for him lately; why should this? Mallum hurled it to the ground with all his strength, and then watched the light pop on with the impact. Shaking his head from side to side, half smiling and half crying, he aimed the beam down the road. Instantly, the light cut out once more. This time he banged the flashlight against everything in sight—the tree, the car, the mountain—to no avail. He flung it away for good over the side of the cliff.

He had to move on, but not before he got rid of the car. The German would recognize the distinctive vehicle immediately, even in its battered state. He would know he was alive somewhere in the vicinity, perhaps hobbling off down the road after his accident. Mallum planted his feet against the ground and braced his shoulder into the back of the car. It required a bit more strength than he imagined, but the Alfa rolled slowly toward the edge and toppled over into the abyss. He watched it bang along the rocky palisade and crash into the churning waters below. The trunk of the vehicle remained visible above the boiling surf. Good, he thought. If the German finds it first, maybe he'll think I'm dead.

A chilly wind suddenly blew in off the ocean. Mallum turned up the collar of his sports jacket and wrapped the coat around himself, hugging it tightly across his chest. He looked down and saw the hubcap lying on the road. This, too, he kicked over the side. How far was he from LA now? Still over two hundred miles, he guessed. He continued south along the curving road even though there was no chance whatsoever of getting to the airport in time. His best bet now would be to find a place to stay for the night.

After about a half mile, Mallum's ankle began to throb. Apparently he had strained it slightly when he tripped on the rock. Walking became increasingly difficult, so he sat down on the side of the road. He knew he couldn't remain there long, knew that every moment he hesitated he ran the risk of being seen by the German who was most probably in pursuit. The pickup truck was the only vehicle he had seen in hours. With his luck, the next one that came along would be the German's—him and his goons racing him down the coastline to keep him from reaching the airport. Mallum got up and tried to walk again.

The wind grew colder and brisker. By midnight the pain in his ankle was excruciating; walking any further was out of the question. The cold wind became damper, bringing moisture in off the ocean. The dampness turned to rain, the rain into a downpour. Within seconds he was drenched to the skin and freezing. The water poured down his face in a ceaseless cascade. His nose was running, his throat felt raspy. He began to sneeze without letup. Hopeless. Utterly, utterly hopeless. His life was over, he had hit bottom. No way out. If only I had the guts, he thought, I would end it all right now.

Sick, feverish, drained of energy, terrible pain jolting his entire body, Mallum was ready to pack it in. If he didn't have the courage to hurl himself off the cliff, he could simply refuse to go on. He could collapse onto the side of the road, slip into unconsciousness, and refuse to get up again. Just lie down and die. Like an old dog. He was thinking of doing exactly that when he looked ahead, through the rain and the darkness, and thought he saw a light. Was it merely his fevered imagination? Or was it real? Hobbling closer, he believed he could make out the shape of a large old building, perhaps an inn. Mallum screamed and ran ahead on his throbbing ankle. The pain slowed him down but he kept on moving, hobbling with all the strength he could muster.

He reached the front of the building. The sign over the doorway read:

PENTAGRAM PUB AND INN.

Mallum howled. "Can you believe it?" he shouted. "Right out of a damned Wolf Man movie." He shook his head and laughed. Only in California, he thought.

Mallum turned the handle, pushed the door open, and fell forward, face down onto the hardwood floor.

CHAPTER TWO

Dolph Hauptmann, a.k.a. "the German," sat in his usual booth at Jammie's, a San Francisco restaurant popular with people on the make—former military officers who had recently moved into the corporate world; networking young professionals looking for a big score; former government officials between administrations. The German looked every inch the stereotypical Aryan sadist. His hair was blond and closely cropped. His eyes shone with blue fire. A thick wound that might have been taken for a dueling scar in an earlier age ran down his left cheek.

Keeping him company were his two chief lieutenants, Vinnie Raposo and Cowboy, brutal enforcers who had risen to the top of their highly competitive profession. Raposo, unusually short and slim with jet-black greasy hair, took his profession seriously. Rumor had it that he once dressed up as a nun in order to get close enough to a troublesome bishop to stick a shiv in his ribs. Cowboy, blond like his boss but with longer and more stylish hair, simply enjoyed the work. Tall and muscular, with tattoos etched heavily on both arms, he looked like an ex-biker who had found his true calling breaking kneecaps for the German.

"He ain't gonna show," Raposo said as he mindlessly swirled a swizzle stick in his untouched scotch and soda.

"He'll show," the German said. He seemed unconcerned. "He don't, his father-in-law will. Not to worry."

"Yeah, not to worry," the Cowboy echoed his boss. How he idolized the man. The German had brains, a real head on his shoulders. Cowboy wanted to be just like him, and would be, just as soon as he got his act together.

"I ain't worried," Raposo said. "It's your money. I just don't understand how come you gave him all that credit in the first place." He was referring to the one hundred and sixty thousand dollars Alex Mallum had lost that afternoon when all eight of his long shots failed to finish in the money.

The German stared at Raposo with what passed for a smile on his scarred face. "You still don't get it," he said. "That's because you got a fuckin' cobblestone for a head. All rock and no brains. Even Cowboy over here can figure that one out, right, Cowboy?"

"Right as rain, boss," Cowboy said.

"Ask yourself who Mallum's father-in-law is," the German said. "Peter Dante. Who is Peter Dante? Only the chief executive officer of Palliser Dynamics, one of the largest fuckin' defense contractors in the country. You think he can afford to have the word get out that his son-in-law owes money to the boys? You think he'll let that one go by? Either way we get paid, either by that schmuck Mallum or by Dante. It's all the same to me, ain't that right, Cowboy?"

"Right on, boss. You hit the nail right on the head," Cowboy said.

"So me and John Wayne over here might as well go home," Raposo said, half sneering. "That means we don't get to do no work tonight."

"What's the matter?" The German laughed. "That blade burning a hole in your pocket?"

Now Raposo laughed. "I got it right here just in case," he said, patting the right hip pocket of his Jacket.

Cowboy extended his right hand and pretended to pull the trigger of an invisible gun. "Not so fast," he said. "You ain't havin' all the fun by yourself, little man."

"I'll show you who's little, you dumb fuck," Raposo said. He braced his hands against the table and started to slide back.

"Cool it!" the German said.

"He ain't talkin' to me like that," Raposo said. Cowboy laughed and Raposo started to rise again.

"Cool it I said! Wipe that stupid grin off your face, Cowboy. You two don t stop giving me grief, I go to the zoo and hire a couple orangutans instead. They're just as smart as you two and they don't talk back."

Raposo and Cowboy glowered at each other a moment longer, then lost interest in the game. They didn't have much fear for anyone or anything in the world except the German. He gave them both the chills whenever he stared at them with those crazy blue eyes.

Suddenly, there was a commotion at the door. The three of them looked over and saw the maitre d' and a passel of waiters ushering in a portly gray-haired gentleman in a double-breasted blue suit. It was Peter Dante, and with him were three men—one black man with a shaved head, another black with Jherri curls, and a short, blocky white man. The four of them were escorted through the lounge, past the German and his boys, back into the dining room.

"That's Jimmy Bones with him," Cowboy said, referring to the big black man with the shaved head. "Last I heard he was in Mozambique startin' a revolution all by himself."

"He works for Dante now," the German said. "The pay's a lot better."

"Yeah, well, Mallum ain't gonna show, that's for sure. So whatta we gonna do now?" Raposo said.

The German's eyes were blue currents flashing brighter with every second. "We sit tight for a few minutes," he said, "then we go pay a visit." He revealed nothing of himself to the others, but inside he was seething over being stood up by that miserable punk Mallum, and snubbed by Dante and his guard dogs who had strode by him without so much as a nod of recognition. Stiffed by a scumbag and snubbed by his big-shot father-in-law. Somebody was going to pay.

The German sipped his gin and tonic, and then he put his glass down and nodded at the others. They all rose together, the two goons following their boss as he headed back through the lounge into the dining room.

"Mister Dante," Hauptmann said, extending his right hand toward the industrialist. "You know me. Dolph Hauptmann. So how come you don't say hello?"

Dante stared at the hand for a full five seconds before looking up at the German. "Hello," he said without accepting the handshake. Bristling, the German balled his hand into a fist and lowered it to his side.

"So what can I do for you?" Dante said.

"Your scumbag son-in-law owes me a hundred and sixty grand," the German said. "I come over to collect the debt."

"I don't know anything about it." Dante lowered his eyes and studied the menu.

"Alex put twenty grand each on eight long shots today. Poor fuck couldn't tell a pony from a porcupine. Lost every single race. Said if he didn't come around to pay off, I should see you about it. I was you, I'd keep a closer watch on that boy before he gets himself in deeper."

Dante pried his eyes away from the menu, stared up at the German, and then burst out laughing. His three companions joined in with him as though he had just told the funniest joke they ever heard.

"Alex is a dumb gambler," Dante said. "But you know what's dumber? Some bookie that'd trust him for one hundred and sixty thousand dollars. And what's even dumber than that is you thinking I'm going to pay it off for him. That's the funniest, dumbest thing I ever heard." Dante roared with laughter again, his companions joining in with even more gusto than before.

The German's face smoldered, burning slowly into a deep scarlet fire. "Laugh now, Dante," he said. "You won't think it's so funny when the press gets word that Peter Dante's son-in-law is in hock to the boys. That's not gonna sit too well with your connections in Washington."

"Now that's not funny." Dante stared at the German without expression, his face a frozen mask. "That sounds like a threat and threats I don't find funny. You're a fool, Hauptmann. Your information's out of date. My daughter divorced that loser Mallum six months ago. Finally came to her senses. If you think you've got leverage on me with him, you re a bigger fool than I thought you were."

Dante had him and the German knew it. He had called his bluff and won. His choices were limited. The German could back down and lose face completely, or he could strike at Dante with the only weapon he had left. He lunged forward but, before he could reach Dante, Jimmy Bones reached out and caught his arm. The German was locked in a vise. He glared at Jimmy Bones, his face burning red and his neck bulging with purple veins. Hauptmann was big and tall, but Jimmy Bones had three inches and thirty pounds on him.

"Get your hands off me, boy, or I'll pound you flatter than your Aunt Jemima's favorite pancake." The two men stood eyeball-to-eyeball for a long, tense moment.

"Jimmy, Jimmy." Dante broke the tension. "Mind your manners. You don't want to put your hands on Mister Hauptmann, do you?"

"No, Mister Dante."

"Release him then." Jimmy Bones let go of Hauptmann. He turned away, walked three steps, then whirled on one foot with blazing speed and smashed his adversary's jaw with the heel of the other foot. The German dropped to the floor as though he had been struck by lightning. Cowboy reached for his gun first, Vinnie a split second later. Neither was fast enough. Dante's other two bodyguards already had theirs drawn, pointed in their faces. A pall of silence fell over the room as the diners looked on, too shocked to utter a sound.

"That's better, Jimmy," Dante said. "Why should you get your hands all dirty touching filth like that before you eat?" He turned to Cowboy and Raposo. "Your boss is very rude, disturbing peaceful people having supper and minding their own business. Why don't you monkeys drag him out of here before Mister Bones loses his temper?"

The fear was a palpable thing in their eyes. They were afraid for themselves, but it was more than that. The sight of their fallen leader, the invincible German who only had to look at men to make them tremble, crumpled like a rag doll on the restaurant floor, had shattered their own sense of invulnerability. Cowboy bent over, placed one arm behind the German's back and a hand around his wrist, and helped him to his feet. He and Raposo half carried and half dragged him back to their booth in the lounge. They eased him onto the padded bench and hovered above him like two unlikely nurses who didn't quite know what to do.

"You okay, boss?" Raposo said, his voice an anxious rasp. The German didn't answer. Raposo walked over to the bar and got half a tumbler full of bourbon. He brought it back and tilted it under the German's mouth. The German clutched it in his hand and sipped it slowly. He did this for several minutes, catching his breath and sipping the bourbon. Finally, he sat up and rubbed his aching jaw, feeling it more than rubbing it to see if anything was broken. He thought he had been kicked by a horse. Nobody had ever hit him that hard before. Through clenched teeth, his jawbone grinding like broken glass, he spoke through the pain. "Alex Mallum dies. Find him. Hurt him. Kill him. Now."

CHAPTER THREE

The man behind the bar was enormously fat. His bushy black eyebrows and unruly black beard looked like a costume set—the kind you wear on Halloween. The barroom was dimly lit. Scattered throughout were a few empty tables and chairs made of rough-hewn wood. Thunder crashed outside, rocking the walls and the very foundation of the earth. It was, the bartender thought, a night from hell.

He stood behind the bar, polishing glasses and wiping down the bar for the night. He thought he heard a feeble whimper, but looked around and saw nothing. He attributed it to the storm. Through the corner of his eye he saw the door swing open wildly, letting in wind and rain and frightening crashes of thunder and lighting in the distance. He felt a rush of wind and saw something fall down near the door. It looked like a pile of rags, a stack of dirty laundry.

The barman threw up the swinging gate and walked with some trepidation toward the door. What in hell did this storm blow in? As he came closer he saw it was a human form, a man, one of the sorriest specimens of humanity he had seen in his entire life. He approached the stranger and stood above him, eyeing him more closely. Gradually, the man looked up. His eyes were wild and scared, shot through with panic. He opened his mouth to speak.

"Please! Help me," he said

Good Lord, the bartender thought. The poor lad's half dead already. Realizing that there was no danger to himself, he reached down to help the stranger up. With some difficulty for a man his size, he escorted him to a table near the fireplace. The fire had been banked down, but there were still a few smoldering embers glowing red in the dark hearth. The night was cold and damp and the stranger shivered in his saturated clothing.

"Do you . . . d-do you have a dry blanket?" the stranger stuttered.

"Right away," the bartender said. "I'll fix you right up."

He went back behind the bar, poured the stranger a shot of whiskey, and then tapped a bell three times in rapid succession. "Drink up," he said, handing him the whiskey. The stranger took it in both hands, shivering with the cold, and gulped it down. A moment later, a gorgeous young woman appeared through an inner doorway. She had a cascade of lush blonde hair spilling over her shoulders. Her face was deeply tanned, and she was wearing a loosely fitting light-blue ankle-length skirt and a flouncy white blouse. She looked at the stranger and smiled.

"Did you want me, father?" Her voice had a melodious lilt, sweet and warm and comforting.

"Tanya darling. This poor man just blew in from the storm. Fetch some dry towels and a blanket from the closet. And bring him a terrycloth robe as well. Quickly, darling, before he comes down with pneumonia."

He turned back to the stranger. "Just hang on a little bit longer. We'll have you good as new in no time."

"Thank you," the stranger said. The whiskey seemed to have done him some good. "I . . . I've got to get to an airport right away. Or a train. It's very important that I continue on my way."

The bartender laughed sharply. "Not at this time of night," he said. "There's a bus station about forty-five minutes from here, but nothing's running until morning. How did you get here without a car anyway?"

"My car's wrecked. I hit a tree a few miles up the road. Almost went off the cliff with it. Lucky to be alive. Hardly a scratch at all, except for this ankle. God! It hurts like hell from all the walking."

"Let Tanya take a look at it. She's a wonderful nurse. Hands that heal. A gift she inherited from the old country. What's your name, stranger?"

"Alex Mallum."

"I'm Lothar and my daughter is Tanya."

Alex winced visibly. "Lothar? Is that German?" he said feebly.

"No. Why?" The barman looked at him oddly. "Not German at all. Eastern European actually. Romania."

"Sorry," Alex said. "I've nothing against Germans. It's just that . . . " He decided to let it go. "I'm happy to be here. Thank you for your kindness."

"Let me get you another drink. And some food. You must be starving."

"I hate to put you through any more trouble."

"Nonsense. I'm an innkeeper. That's my job, making strangers feel at home. Here, start with these and Tanya will fix up a sandwich for you."

Lothar put a bowl of peanuts in front of Alex and watched him as he gulped them hungrily. Tanya returned with an armful of towels, a blanket, and a thick terrycloth bathrobe. "Here you go," she said. "Let me show you to your room."

Alex tried to stand, but pain shot through his entire body when he put weight on his injured ankle. He collapsed back onto the chair.

"You're hurt." Tanya spoke with genuine concern. "Here, let me." She took a towel and wrapped it around his head, drying his hair vigorously. "Help me carry him to his room, Father," she said. "We've got to get him out of these clothes." They each grabbed one of Alex's arms and helped him to his feet. Alex limped along as best he could, sniffing the strange flowery aroma that Tanya exuded. Was that perfume? Or was it her? Whatever the case, he found it almost intoxicating.

They guided Alex to the bed and sat him down. Tanya removed his jacket and handed it to her father who left the room, then returned a moment later with the robe and towels.

"Can you fix Alex something to eat, Tanya?" he said. "He must be starving."

"I'll do that now while you help him change."

With Lothar's help, Alex removed his wet clothes, toweled himself dry, and slipped into the warm robe. Lothar produced a pair of sandals and picked up the soggy clothing. "Almost as good as new," he said. "Let me help you back to the bar."

Together they returned to the front room. Tanya had already set a place for Alex and was sitting at the table waiting for him. The dish contained a cold roast beef sandwich and potato salad.

"What would you like to drink?" she said.

"A beer would be great. Whatever you have on tap is fine."

Alex bit into the sandwich. The meat was lean and tender, coated with a delicious tangy sauce that he failed to recognize. When Tanya returned he asked her what it was.

"An old family recipe. Do you like it?"

"Very much. The potato salad is also wonderful. Did you make that too?"

Tanya nodded yes and smiled—a warm, dimpled, marvelous smile that melted Alex's heart. He was ravenously hungry and devoured his meal in short order, washing it down with the long draft of crisp, ice-cold beer. His meal had been simple, yet oddly satisfying. He couldn't remember the last time he had taken so much pleasure in such basic food.

"God that hit the spot." He patted his stomach, as contented as he had been in ages.

"Now that you've eaten, let me take a look at that ankle." Tanya lifted his foot onto her lap. She smiled gently at Alex's embarrassed attempt to keep his robe from opening up, exposing his nakedness underneath. With the fingers of both hands she probed his ankle, his heel, calf, and sole of his foot. Alex winced slightly with pain but tried not to show it.

"I've something that will help," she said. Tanya slid out from under his foot and rested it on her chair. "I'll be right back." Lothar finished his mopping-up operations at the bar, stretched his arms and yawned. "Time to turn in," he said. "It's been a long day. You're in good hands with Tanya. Sleep well and I'll help you get going in the morning."

Alex thanked him for his hospitality and said goodnight. Tanya returned a moment later, carrying a bowl filled with a pasty concoction and some bandages. She took her seat and placed Alex's foot back on her lap. "This is just what the doctor ordered," she said. She rubbed the mixture onto his ankle and kneaded it into the skin. Instantly, it produced a warm tingling sensation that worked its way right through the bone. Tanya wrapped the ankle with gauze. The warmth climbed up Alex's leg and traveled throughout his entire body, totally enveloping him. He sat back in his chair, more relaxed than he could remember being in his life. He rested his head onto the back of his chair, and remained there half-entranced as time seemed to disappear. It was as though he had been transported into a different dimension, void of time, sense, or feeling. Suddenly, the sensation was gone. The warmth disappeared and he was back in the room with Tanya smiling before him.

"What happened?" he said.

"Feel better?"

"Oh . . . I guess so." Alex focused his attention back on his injured ankle, but felt nothing, no discomfort, no pain. "I think the pain is gone," he said, noticing also that the scratch marks had disappeared. How curious!

"Stand up."

Alex placed his good foot on the floor, pressed his palms against the tabletop, and lifted himself slowly. Carefully, he lowered the bandaged foot and tested it with his weight. Nothing. It appeared to be completely healed.

"Incredible. What was in that stuff?"

Tanya smiled, pleased with his reaction. "An old family poultice. It has healing power."

"Magic, that's what it is. I'd like to learn some more about these family recipes of yours. Where did your father say you were from again?"

"Eastern Europe. What they used to call Transylvania, in Romania."

Transylvania, he repeated to himself. That probably explains the hokey theme. "This stuff is dynamite," Alex responded. "You ought to bottle it, make a fortune."

Tanya stood up, her face aglow with a brilliant golden smile that set Alex's heart on fire. Whatever was going on tonight, whoever these people were, it was nothing less than magic as far as he was concerned. Warmth, friendship, great food and drink, and the healing magic of a gorgeous young woman—it was magnificently unreal, yet here he was experiencing all of it. He was not dreaming. It was about time he caught a break. Maybe his luck had finally turned around.

"Come." Tanya took him by the hand. "Now that your ankle is better, you can dance with me. It's not often I have the opportunity to dance out here."

Alex froze for just an instant. "I'm not very good at it."

"You'll do just fine." She led him over to the jukebox on the far side of the bar. "Pick out something nice and slow. Anyone can do a slow dance. All you have to do is hold me."

Alex needed no further encouragement. Any excuse to hold this enchanting creature would do. Memories of his ex-wife Danielle and their painful divorce, which had tormented him until this night, faded wraithlike into the ether.

He studied the lineup of songs on the jukebox, searching for a slow number. He realized immediately that he need not have worried. The selection was curious to say the least: *Blue Moon, Moon over Miami, Moonlight Becomes You.* What was it with this moon business? These people had come up with a nutty theme for a pub, to put it mildly. He took another look at Tanya standing beside him, so ravishing in her beauty and freshness, in her perfect innocence. So what if she's a little strange? Nobody's perfect, he reasoned.

Alex selected *Blue Moon*, which turned out to be the original slow version, not the rock 'n roll knockoff that came later. He turned to face Tanya and almost swooned. Did she know he didn't have a thing on underneath his robe? Did she care? He had all he could do to keep his erection from poking through the opening. She put her arm around his neck and he almost fainted. They held each other tightly, and moved slowly to the music. Her perfume—her powerful, flowery aroma, whatever it was—wafted upward and consumed him. By the time the song was over he felt as though he had died and gone to heaven. Could heaven be better than this?

Tanya selected *Moonlight Becomes You* for their next dance. She came to him, hugged him even more tightly than before, and he could feel her warm breath against his neck. Alex's heart beat faster; a feverish heat spread throughout his body. He felt Tanya's lips nibbling his earlobe. His breathing came in gulps now. Faster and faster. Dizziness overwhelmed him and he began to stagger.

Tanya backed away and felt his temples with her fingertips. "You poor dear," she said. "You're exhausted after your ordeal. Let's get you to bed." She massaged his temples more firmly. "Come, let me help you to your room. You can take a hot shower while I turn down your bedclothes."

Alex was beyond protesting. He was feverish, his heart was racing, his breathing grew increasingly labored. He felt that he was at the point of collapse. Tanya led him in his quasi-hypnotic state out of the barroom toward his room. Nurse, friend, doting caregiver, enchantress—Tanya was all of that and more.

In his room, she ushered him into the bathroom. "A shower will refresh you," she said. "When you come out, our bed will be ready. You'll sleep like a baby tonight."

"*Our* bed?" Alex repeated shyly. Tanya smiled.

Alex shed his bathrobe and stepped into the shower stall. He turned the faucet and adjusted the water temperature. As he showered he still had difficulty slowing down his heart. What was going on here? Would she be there when he was done, smiling with radiant innocence as she tucked him into bed? He finished quickly, toweled himself dry, stepped over to the sink and studied his visage in the mirror. My God! He was a wreck. His cheeks were stubbled with a prickly growth of beard, the whites of his eyes were streaked with red.

He lathered his cheeks with shaving cream provided by the inn, and shaved himself with the complimentary safety razor. Next he splashed himself with cologne, put his bathrobe back on and prepared to reenter the bedroom, not knowing what to expect.

He was relieved to find that nothing had changed. Tanya was standing beside the bed, the sheets pulled down, motioning for him to climb in. Incredibly, she walked over to him and untied the belt of his bathrobe. The robe fell open, exposing him in all his glory. There was nothing he could do about hiding his maleness now; it protruded before him, the most visible object in the room, in his own mind at least. Tanya slipped beside him and slid the robe from his shoulders.

Obediently, he allowed himself to be guided downward toward the mattress. He rolled onto his back, staring up at this dazzling goddess who had taken command of his life with such bewitching authority. Alex melted. He was beside himself with desire, lust, possibly even a glimmer of love. Such intoxicating beauty. She was rare, a precious treasure, all but hidden out here away from the bustle of civilization. And now she was his, completely his, to savor and enjoy.

Tanya reached behind and pulled her blouse up over her head. Her breasts were perfection itself—smooth and round and without a visible flaw. Alex felt himself grow faint. A heavy drowsiness descended upon him. Please Dear God, don't let me fall asleep now. Let me stay awake a half-hour longer. Permit me to bathe myself in the mystery and magic and loveliness of this woman before I slip into unconsciousness.

Despite his efforts, Alex could not keep his eyelids from closing shut. It was a drowsiness heavier than any he had ever known. In a moment he was transported; it was more than merely sleep. It was deeper and more hypnotic than sleep. He descended into a dreamworld. For one bizarre moment he dreamed of Tanya beside him. But she was not the ravishing beauty of waking life. She was hideously deformed.

Her glistening perfect white teeth were not teeth at all, but razor-sharp fangs. Saliva oozed down her wrinkled cheeks. Her brilliant blue eyes consumed him with the blazing fires of hell.

Alex struggled to wake himself out of this nightmare. Please return me to the real world, to the real Tanya with all her pure, pristine beauty. But he could not awaken. The Tanya beside him in his dreamworld was monstrous, a hideous and deformed creature from the lower depths of the Inferno. This monster snuggled beside him. She lowered her jaws into the crook of his neck and sank her fangs into his flesh. His body grew taut. Alex struggled to cry out, but no sounds would come. His eyes stared at the ceiling and it appeared to spin in circles, faster and faster.

Then he went numb. His vision failed. He tried to get up and walk, but the nightmare refused to release him. He tumbled to the floor. As he lay there in a pool of his own blood that ran freely from his neck, an image of his ex-wife Danielle fixed itself in his mind. He saw her clearly before him, laughing as he lay there in helpless distress. Then his energy drained away and the vision faded. His consciousness, ever so mercifully, ebbed away into the blackness.

CHAPTER FOUR

The storm had rumbled out to sea long before dawn. The noonday sun sat high above, illuminating a clear blue sky glowing with promise. Its golden rays filled the bedroom where Alex lay motionless, except for the slow rhythmic pulsing of his chest. The heat built up slowly in the room, filling it with stagnant air. Perspiration glistened on his body and he tossed and turned uncomfortably. He awakened with a sense of his own discomfort. His eyes popped open and took in the surroundings. With a sudden lurch, he bolted upright and searched his room for traces of his nightmare. But there was nothing; everything appeared to be normal.

Alex sat alone in the room. In his mind he recalled the horrific vision of the night before: lovely Tanya, pure and innocent as virgin snow, transformed into a hideous monster before his eyes. How horrifying it all was. How real it seemed. He felt his throat for a sign of injury where he imagined her fangs sinking in, but he detected nothing unusual. Against the wall, opposite the foot of the bed, he saw a mirror hanging above a redwood dresser. He jumped out of bed to see what he could find.

He tilted his head this way and that, searching his neck for some evidence that his fevered brain had not invented the whole episode. Nothing. Not a single scratch, not a cut or blotch of any kind. How can anything seem so real, he wondered, and yet be only a dream? And if it had been just a nightmare, what then had really happened? There was no lovemaking that he could recall. Damn it! He had so been looking forward to it. The entire evening was a dream: Tanya; the food; the healing elixir; dancing; her apparently innocent yet hypnotically seductive way with him. Then he showered, returned to the bedroom and watched her undress him, saw her unveil the most perfectly flawless breasts he had ever seen. All of it followed by a horrific nightmare!

How could he not remember making love to such a desirable young woman? Was it likely that he would have been overcome by sleep at such a delectable moment? What was the magic, the power she had used to enthrall him? Could he have been consumed by a nightmare at such a critical moment in the evening? His sense of timing had never been the best, but this was ridiculous—even for him.

Once again Alex ran his fingers along his throat in search of clues; once again, nothing. Then—something. Nothing visible, no scratch or mark, but his throat felt dry and he experienced a thirst more intense than he had ever felt. He needed a drink, a long cool drink to relieve the discomfort.

He turned from the mirror and was about to step into the bathroom, when something caught his eye. There on the pillow! He stooped over to get a better look and saw—or was it his imagination playing tricks on him again?—a faded brown stain that looked as though it could be dried blood. It was a tiny spot, no more than just a speck, but enough to send a jolt through his body. He stared at it for a long moment. Possibly it was blood; but it might also have been a faint discoloration in the fabric itself. There was no way to be sure.

The beat of his heart quickened, and he fought to hold back the panic mounting inside. He fought to contain his emotions and got them under control. The fear was there, but he was able to function rationally. Was he being observed, or was he feeling paranoid after his experience of the night before? He walked over to the window and looked outside. The sun shone brightly, the landscape sparkled with life and energy, the day could not have been more lovely. Everything was normal; he had nothing to be afraid of except his own seething imagination.

The thirst overwhelmed him. Alex walked into the bathroom and saw his clothes on hangers suspended from the shower rod. They appeared to be washed and ironed. They smelled fresh and they were dry to the touch. He dressed hurriedly, then bent over the sink and turned on the cold water. It flowed freely, a nourishing elixir from heaven itself. Alex drank in mouthful after mouthful until his stomach swelled. His thirst abated substantially, but not completely. He wanted to drink more but he felt bloated. He had drunk enough for the moment. He washed his hands and face and felt his cheeks. They were still smooth from his shave the night before, so he decided to let it pass. He patted his face with cologne, combed his hair, and prepared to face the day—whatever it held in store for him.

Lothar was sitting at one of the tables in the barroom when Alex walked in. Beside him was a misshapen fat hag, an old crone with a deeply pockmarked face and wild frizzy white hair. She wore a tattered bathrobe and a pair of old, dirty gray sneakers. Her elbows were propped on the table in front of her as she slurped coffee across her toothless gums.

"Good morning, sir," she said. "I hope you slept well last night." Her voice was hoarse, and she spoke with the same slight accent, largely unidentifiable, that Lothar had.

"G-Good morning." Alex's expression registered confusion. Who was this woman? Where did she come from? "I don't believe I met you last night."

The woman laughed coarsely, a nasty cackle more than a laugh. Lothar joined in with a gusty guffaw of his own. "I shouldn't wonder," the crone said, "seeing's the shape you was in last night. Treated him like our own son, we did, and that's the thanks we get."

Lothar smiled broadly and extended his right hand. "Don't mind her," he said. "She's feeling out of sorts this morning. We're happy to see you looking like a new man today. Last night you were half dead and we didn't know whether you'd last the night. Allow me to reintroduce ourselves. I'm Lothar and this is my wife Tanya. And you're Alex, as I recall you said. Is that right?"

Alex shook Lothar's hand absent-mindedly. His face, he knew, registered complete shock. "Tanya did you say? Did you say your wife's name was Tanya?"

"You heard him right," the crone answered for her husband. "Don't remember anything, I'll bet, the state you was in."

Alex stared at the two of them with open disbelief. "The s-same name as your daughter? Where is she—Tanya—the one I met last night I mean?"

"Off his head completely, ain't he?" The old hag eyed him evilly, scowling up at him over her cup as she slurped her coffee noisily.

Lothar waved her into silence and smiled up at Alex. "You were running a high fever last night, son. If it wasn't such a terrible night we would have called for a doctor. We have no daughter. Tanya and I have been childless throughout our marriage."

"That's the thanks we get for taking in strangers," the hag said, scolding Alex. "Me with my bad back and all. Carrying you into the bedroom with Lothar after you fainted by the fireplace. Putting you to sleep. Listening to you yelling half the night about somebody called the German, somebody else called Danielle. There's no gratitude in this lifetime, let me tell you."

"Now, now, Tanya," Lothar said. "The lad was running a fever. It's not his fault."

"I distinctly remember meeting Tanya your daughter last night. She was young, blonde, absolutely beautiful. We danced over there by the jukebox after you went to bed. With all due respect, the Tanya I met looked nothing at all like your wife here."

"Insulting me to my own face, right here in my own home." The crone slammed her cup down on the table. Suddenly, her face crumbled and she began to weep openly with her face hanging down onto her withered chest.

Lothar reached over and patted her hand gently. "Take it easy, darling," he said. "Alex doesn't mean it like that. The lad's in shock, that's all."

"I'm terribly sorry." Alex patted her on the shoulder.

Anger and fear gave way to shame. How could he have been so thoughtless, so-so unfeeling and so selfish?

"There, darling," Lothar said. "Alex isn't like that really. He's just in shock is all it is. A bit of the fever left over in him. A hearty breakfast and he'll be completely restored. It was a horrible ordeal he went through. That terrible storm. Lost his car over the side of the mountain and almost went over with it. It's a wonder he survived to tell us about it."

Lothar stood up and put his hand on Alex's shoulder. "Sit down, son. Let me get you a cup of coffee and some rolls. You've had a terrible night, but look at you now. Almost a complete recovery. We'll have you back in tiptop shape before you know it."

Alex sat down in a trance. Could he actually have imagined the entire evening: dancing with the gorgeous blonde Tanya; hobbling off with her to his room; seeing her unveil herself to him as he slipped into bed? Then his frightful nightmare?

He looked at the crone, still weeping beside him. "I'm terribly sorry. I . . . I didn't mean it like that. It was thoughtless of me. It's just that . . . " What was it? He wasn't sure what was going on?

The hag wiped her eyes with a wrinkled handkerchief that she pulled from the sleeve of her bathrobe. "It's a hard life," she said, "living way out here with nobody to talk to most of the time. Then you take in an occasional stranger who treats you like rubbish. It can get awfully lonely at times, let me tell you."

Lothar returned with a piping hot cup of coffee and a platter of warm rolls that smelled as though they were fresh from the oven. "Eat up, son," he said. "Then we'll see what we can do about getting you some transportation to wherever it is you're going."

Alex stared at the coffee and rolls and suddenly felt his thirst return with a vengeance. "Could I trouble you for some cold water? My throat's awfully sore and dry. I was thirsty as hell when I woke up." Alex thought he saw Lothar shoot an angry glance in his wife's direction.

"I'll get it," the crone said. Her disposition had improved considerably. She smiled at Alex with a motherly warmth and rose to her feet with surprising energy. Alex watched her go to the bar and fill a frosted mug with clear, cold water. She placed it on the table in front of him and stood there while he drained it in one swig. His overpowering thirst receded, but the soreness in his throat remained. The crone returned to the bar and busied herself with routine chores. Alex rubbed the soreness in his throat, which now seemed to be concentrated in one small section instead of spread throughout as it was earlier. He left his coffee and rolls untouched.

"Feeling better?" Lothar said.

"Much. I don't know how to pay you for your hospitality. I . . . I barely have enough money for a bus ticket and some pocket change, and my wallet and credit cards got lost with—"

"No, no, please." Lothar waved him into silence. "We're only too happy to help you."

"No, really. Just as soon as I get back on my feet, I want to send you a check. I insist."

Lothar smiled. It doesn't matter, he seemed to say with genuine kindness. "Don't rub your throat like that. You might injure it."

"Yes, strange. I never . . . anyway, it doesn't hurt as much as before."

"Well, if I'm going to drive you to the bus station we'd better get going."

Yes, the bus station. He remembered that all right from the night before. He hadn't dreamed or imagined that. How could everything else be such a jumble? How could he be lucid about some things and delirious about others? While Lothar went into the back to fetch a jacket, Alex sauntered over to the jukebox to check out the music. Everything was as he remembered it: the strange selections he had danced to—or did he?—with a lovely blonde named Tanya. *Moonlight Becomes You, Moon Over Miami*. His memory was clear on that, but supposedly he had imagined everything else.

He turned and saw the old lady studying him from behind the bar. There was a glint in her eye, a sharpness, not altogether unfriendly, but yet—he didn't know what. Something weird was going on here. It was time to leave, just get the hell out and put the entire episode, dream, nightmare—whatever it was—behind him. Lothar returned, a big smile flashing through his bushy beard. Alex said goodbye to Tanya, if that was her name, and followed Lothar to the front door.

Before they stepped out into the sunshine, the sound of a car door slamming broke the silence. Alex put his hand on Lothar' s shoulder and pulled him back. "Hold on a second," he said. He stepped over to the window, pulled the curtain aside an inch and looked outside. In the parking lot in front he saw a Cadillac convertible. A large, muscular, blond man stood beside it on the driver's side, and on the other side—a short, thin, dark-haired man with crazy eyes exited from the passenger seat. Alex recognized them both, Cowboy and Vinnie Raposo. There was no doubt as to why they were here.

CHAPTER FIVE

Alex felt his gut tighten. Panic seized him and he could feel himself growing faint. "Oh God, oh God, oh God," he cried.

"What is it?" Lothar regarded him curiously.

"Please. You've got to help me. Those men outside. I can't explain now, but don't let them know I'm here. They want to kill me."

Before Lothar could respond, Alex ran across the room, past the bar, and back down the hallway into the room he had slept in the night before. He closed the door noiselessly behind him, locked it, and pressed his ear against the wooden panel. The first sound he heard was knocking on the front door, followed by Lothar yelling that he was coming.

"Hiya, pops." The door muffled the voice, but Alex was sure it was Raposo's.

"Hello," Lothar said.

"We're looking for a friend of ours. Somebody spotted his wrecked car nearby. We wanna find him, make sure he's okay. Here's his picture, maybe you seen him. Five feet five or six, black hair, thin, clean-shaven. Recognize'm?"

A moment's silence, then, "Yes, that looks like Alex."

"Right, right. You seen 'm then. Know where we can find 'm now? We're really worried he might be hurt."

"He was in bad shape when he came in here last night. Ranting out of his head that somebody wanted to kill him, even insulted my poor sick wife over there."

The bastard's going to give me away, Alex thought. He searched the room for an escape route—possibly the window that opened onto the side of the building. If he had to, he might be able to slip out there without being seen.

Alex heard Raposo laugh, a phony, hearty laugh. "Sounds like good old Alex," he said.

"He was delirious with a fever. We calmed him down, gave him something to eat, and then he left."

Alex breathed a sigh of relief.

"Know where we can find him now, pops?"

"After a while this truck driver came by. Said he was going to San Diego and Alex asked him for a lift. Gave him twenty bucks and said he'd pay for the gas. Said he had to leave real fast before these people, whoever they were, found him."

"That's Alex for you," Raposo said. "I tol'm his dick was gonna cause 'm grief some day. All it is, is this guy caught 'm in bed with his wife. Told Alex he was goin' to kill'm. But it's all blown over now. He's running away for nothing. The guys back home're having a good laugh over this. We gotta find Alex and tell 'm it's okay. What kinda truck'd you say he left in?"

"Big old fruit truck, full of watermelons I think. Must be all the way down to San Diego by now."

"Thanks, pop. You've been a big help." Raposo pulled out his cell phone and called in a message. "He went to San Diego on a watermelon truck. We're on our way now. Any word from the spotters at LAX?" A brief silent pause was followed by shuffling at the door, a couple of distant voices outside in the parking lot, and the sound of an engine coming alive and the squeal of tires peeling off at high speed.

He unlocked the door and stepped outside. Lothar was just coming down the hallway into the barroom. "I can't thank you enough," Alex said.

"I don't know what's going on." Lothar was scowling, his face dark with anger. "But I know what I don't like. I don't like that little one calling me pops. Who does he think he is?"

"They want to kill me."

"How so?"

"Their boss has this idea that I owe him a hundred and sixty grand. It has to do with some horse races, but it's a big misunderstanding."

"I don't approve of gambling," Lothar scolded. "But I like violence less." He stared at Alex accusingly for several seconds. Finally, he seemed to have reached a decision. "Come, I will help you once more. We will get you on a bus."

Lothar fetched his keys from behind the bar and told Alex to follow him out back. Alex turned to say goodbye to—to Lothar's wife; somehow he could not get himself to call her Tanya—and as he turned toward her, he saw her staring at him with a tear rolling down her wrinkled cheek. She looked at him silently, with an expression of genuine fondness in her eyes. Something within him stirred. There was a bond there, a closeness that gave him a shiver. He had no idea what it meant, but he knew he wanted no part of it. He turned away abruptly and followed Lothar out of the inn. The car door on the passenger side of Lothar's ancient blue Volkswagen Beetle was open, waiting for him to climb in. Somehow, Lothar had managed to wedge his gargantuan bulk behind the steering wheel.

"Off we go, son," Lothar said with fatherly affection. "It's time to hit the road."
Tanya stood at the door, watching as the two drove off.

"Poor Alex. What have I done?" she whispered to herself, patting her teary eyes with a tissue. "Ludwig will never forgive me. He'll be so angry. Should I call and tell him what happened? Better not. I don't think I could face him."

Alex rested his head against the backrest of his seat and closed his eyes. With ten hours on the road now since his narrow escape from the German's search party, he felt more relaxed. He needed to put the threat out of his mind, and the best way to do that was by thinking of Danielle, his ex-wife. How he loved her still, despite all that had happened.

That was the hardest part about leaving California, not seeing her anymore. He knew now that there was no chance of reconciliation, but the dream that they might one day get together persisted nonetheless. Just seeing her around town from time to time, talking to her about old concerns, helped fuel his fantasy. Escaping to New York now would bring the dream to an end, but it would also put an end to his nightmarish fear of the German.

He had met Danielle Dante during their undergraduate days at Harvard. He had organized a campus protest against the inclusion of South African stocks in the school's investment portfolio, back before Mandela came to power and the white racist regime still controlled everything. She had been a feminist leader concerned about the lack of women on his steering committee. They worked out an accommodation, and soon they were organizing more demonstrations together on other issues of mutual concern. Her campus celebrity was further enhanced by the fact that she was the daughter of Peter Dante, chairman of Palliser Dynamics, the largest defense contractor in the country.

Following graduation, they moved in together and continued their political activism. Alex achieved notoriety as a member of the San Francisco Six, a group of radicals charged with the murder of several students and soldiers in the bombing of a campus ROTC recruitment meeting. The six publicly denied any involvement in the explosions, but the widespread belief that they were guilty made them martyrs of the left. Like the Chicago Seven trial years earlier, this trial also evolved into a celebrated media event, with the press lionizing the defendants and excoriating the judge for his sarcastic judicial demeanor and alleged "bias" against them. Alex and his confederates, true to form, taunted the judge in court as a "right-wing tool of the political establishment" and entertained everyone in attendance with their own kind of political theater. The judge eventually had them bound and gagged, a sight that reinforced the medias' contention that the Court planned to railroad the San Francisco Six for political reasons.

The jury acquitted them in the end, but the judge sentenced them to lengthy jail terms for their "contemptuous behavior" in court, despite the verdict. In response to the sentences for contempt, the six defendants, four males and two females, turned their backs on the judge and collectively flipped him six full moons. The judge sputtered and shouted obscenities at them. Then, suddenly, he grasped his chest and began to shudder. Slowly he sunk to the ground, the odor of bodily fluids and excrement filling the courtroom. It was a heart attack, and two hours later the judge was dead. A subsequent appeal, citing numerous instances of judicial misconduct, resulted in a vacating of the contempt charges and no one served time. Alex emerged as the most celebrated of the group, and basked in the ensuing publicity, dutifully making his appearance in an endless round of radio and television talk shows. During one debate with a well-known conservative columnist on the subject of national health care, Alex ignited an American flag and his opponent physically attacked him. His incendiary actions triggered a congressional debate about broadcasting regulations concerning the limits of freedom of speech on the public airwaves. The proposed new legislation became known as the "Ax Alex" bill.

Danielle took her place as a leader of feminist causes, and enjoyed literary success as the author of *Missiles and Misogynists*, a "seminal work," according to the *New York Times*. The book remained on the bestseller lists for over sixteen months and gained a reputation on college campuses as "the New Testament" of the feminist movement, a natural successor to Betty Friedan's *The Feminine Mystique*. Alex and Danielle enjoyed their mutual and somewhat codependent status as the King and Queen of the modern counterculture movement for several years, until communism fell apart in the former Soviet Union and Eastern Europe, changing the political landscape all over the globe. The radical left had pretty much shriveled and died out, except for pockets of professors and student teaching assistants on the elite campuses. Alex and Danielle never thought they were that far left themselves, but deep down in the recesses of their souls they were somewhat saddened to see the Berlin Wall fall as Capitalist West Germany gobbled up Socialist East Germany. Danielle's next book was a resounding flop, and Alex's high-paid invitations to speak dried up.

With their political cause receding from the public spotlight—and their money running out—Danielle turned to her father for financial support. Peter Dante was nothing if not a tough and shrewd negotiator who rarely let an opportunity pass him by. He saw at once a chance to reclaim his daughter from the "wrong side of the political fence," as far as he was concerned, and emasculate his son-in-law's political "extremism." Peter threw them a lifeline in the form of a lucrative job offer for Alex, provided they legalize their relationship and adopt at least a semblance of middle class existence. The fiery couple swallowed hard, and decided to accept. Alex never considered, when he assumed the post of vice president of Public Relations for Palliser Dynamics, that he might be selling out. He told himself and his former comrades on the barricades that he had joined the system to subvert it from within. He assuaged his conscience by directing a generous portion of his salary to the causes he loved so dearly.

Few of his former allies bought that line, however. They accused him of handing out Twinkies to homeless people while he and Danielle lived high on the hog like Country Club Republicans. Alex and Danielle responded by moving a little closer to the center—fashionably left of center, as it were—and showered their largess more and more on liberal candidates for public office. After serving as the campaign coordinator for several successful Democratic candidates for the California state legislature, the powers-that-be tapped Alex to run for the seat being vacated by the retiring congressman in his district.

While Alex worked the coffee and cocktail circuits day and night for votes, Danielle directed her own energies and talents to daily journalism. She traveled the world interviewing heads of state and other dignitaries, and developed a reputation for her civilized and reasonable discussion of the issues that pleased many and offended no one. Some of her old followers thought she had become a trifle vacuous. Vacuous or not, sell-out or not, Alex's and Danielle's separate but equal careers pulled them further and further apart. Weeks went by without them crossing paths, sometimes months as he mined traditional party strongholds for votes and Danielle hopscotched the globe in her new nonconfrontational style. While many admired her impartiality toward democratically elected leaders and feral terrorists alike, others who knew her when she was a rebel with a cause found it maddening. Reading her articles and watching her interviews on television (which was the only time Alex got to see her), Alex could not help but wonder if she had turned into a closet Republican.

It came to a boil one night when Alex, nursing his bruises after a rough day on the campaign trail, turned on the tube to see his lovely wife being interviewed on a popular public affairs program. Danielle—*his* Danielle, the visionary radical who had (wo)manned the barricades with him for so many years—announced that she had shifted her political allegiance to the Republican Party. "The Democrats have grown stale and hidebound, refusing to cross the bridge into the twenty-first century," she intoned in exquisitely crafted syllables. "This new generation of post-millennium Republicans is offering far more progressive programs on the key issues of the day, and I've decided to direct my energy where it will count the most."

"But, Ms. Dante, Ms. Dante . . . " The stunned host, sensing a scoop, could scarcely control his excitement. "Your husband, Alex Mallum, is running for Congress as a Democrat himself this year. How will this new allegiance of yours affect your support of him?"

"Alex?" Danielle arched her brows, as though she had some difficulty placing the name. "Alex and I learned a long time ago not to let politics get in the way of our marriage."

"But you are supporting him, are you not?"

"Alex would be the last person in the world to expect me to endorse him for personal reasons," Danielle answered without a second's delay. "I intend to evaluate both candidates' positions on the issues and make my decision accordingly. The fact that Alex and I are husband and wife has no bearing whatsoever on matters of public policy. Alex wouldn't ask me to go against my conscience for him, nor would I expect that of him."

Alex was stunned. Blindsided! By his own wife! How could she do this to me? After all we've been through? Immediately, his phone started ringing off the hook. He started to get up to answer it, then decided to let the machine record the messages. Everybody in the world wanted to talk to him—the media, leaders of his party, his own campaign manager. His political star, shining so brightly just a few short hours ago, was suddenly falling to earth where it would soon burn up in the atmosphere. It had taken him years to get where he was, and his wife had destroyed him in three minutes on prime time television. Why, Danielle? Why did you do this to me?

He got his answer the following night, when Danielle returned home for the first time in weeks. Alex was sitting on the floor in the den building a pyramid with empty beer cans when she came in.

"Good Lord! Don't tell me you drank all those," she said, her voice laden with unmistakable disdain.

"Why did you do it, Danielle? You've ruined me. Couldn't you at least have discussed it with me first?"

"There's nothing to discuss, Alex. You and I have always formed our political opinions independently, and it's no different now than it ever was. We just don't see things the same way any longer."

"The same way! We're not even close. You've done a complete one-eighty from one side of the political spectrum to the other."

"People change. You have too."

"I admit I've toned down some of my positions, rhetoric mostly, but you! You're not even recognizable anymore. You've renounced everything you ever stood for. I don't understand how . . . I get it. It's your father, isn't it? Your father and his money."

"That's insulting, beneath contempt. I won't discuss this any further if that's your attitude."

"Jeez, Danielle! Think of how it looks for me. The wife of the Democratic candidate for congress in one of California's most liberal districts switching allegiance to the other side. Couldn't you at least have waited until after the campaign?"

"Under the circumstances, I really don't think so."

"What circumstances?"

"You won't be burdened much longer with an uncooperative wife. I'm filing for divorce, Alex." Danielle lit a cigarette, something she hadn't done in years, to keep her hands from betraying her emotions. "I want this to be as amicable as possible, and I do want us to remain friends. But our marriage is over."

Alex was in shock. Yes, their marriage had gone stale. Yes, they were apart more than they were together lately. But he still *loved* her! That had not changed. It was nothing they couldn't repair once this damned campaign was over. "I'm stunned! I can't believe this. Are you telling me you don't love me anymore?"

Danielle dragged on her cigarette, stared at him and then looked away without speaking.

"Is there someone else? There must be. You've found someone else, haven't you?"

She mashed out her cigarette and faced him squarely. "Yes there is, since you asked. I don't have to tell you things haven't been going well for us for a long time now. You're married to . . . to that damned movement of yours. I need more than that, Alex! I want more."

"Who is it? Can you tell me that?"

"Jake Edwards."

"My opponent? You can't be serious!" Alex rose unsteadily to his feet, and then almost keeled over from dizziness. He held his head with both hands to regain his balance. "My opponent, Danielle? This will absolutely destroy me. Can you imagine how ludicrous I'll look when this gets out?"

"All you're concerned about is your damned public image," she said.

"That's not true. I love you. I always have. And now you not only betray me, but you humiliate me as well." He searched her eyes for some sign that she was joking with him, but found nothing there. He was looking into the cold, glittering eyes of a woman he did not recognize.

She walked toward the door, and then turned and said, "My lawyer will be in touch with you tomorrow."

It was all downhill after that for Alex Mallum. A week later the Democratic Congressional Campaign threw its support behind his rival in the primary—a corrupt former state senator who had been running so far behind Alex in the polls that no one had given him a chance to win. His father-in-law fired him from his job at Palliser. The house they lived in belonged to Peter Dante, so Alex's share of the divorce settlement came to only twenty thousand dollars and his beloved Alfa Romeo, which Danielle allowed him to keep.

Alex had nothing. The friends from his marriage with Danielle refused to take his phone calls, and his old comrades from the "movement" days had long ago dispersed to parts unknown. He turned to alcohol for comfort and was arrested three times in one month for driving while intoxicated. The third time, after he nearly hit a pedestrian on the sidewalk, the judge told Alex's lawyer that he would put him away for five years to keep him off the streets. The lawyer convinced Alex that he could buy off the judge for ten grand—five for the judge and five for the lawyer—and Alex went along despite the fact that the payoff would leave him almost broke.

This, too, backfired when the three of them were caught in the act and led away in handcuffs. Alex spent the rest of his settlement on bail, and was released from jail the next day pending trial in two weeks. Alex assessed his situation and concluded that he was about as badly off as he could possibly be. His credit cards were charged to the limit, and he had less than a thousand dollars left to his name. If he waited around for the trial, he would almost surely be looking at several years behind bars. Not a rosy picture. It didn't take him long to reach a decision; he would go underground and hide, preferably in New York City where he could blend into the polyglot street life without being noticed. But first he needed a stake—something to tide him over until he got back on his feet.

With nowhere to turn for funds, he concocted his fanciful scheme to strike it rich at the track. Twenty thousand each on the eight longest shots of the day. He needed only one to come in first and pay off for him. There's always *one* long shot that comes home in a day of racing, he reasoned. He would rather have done business with Attila the Hun than with the German, but circumstances left him with little other choice; no one else would extend him credit. Alex felt he was overdue for a break, but if things did not work out the way he planned, the German was the last person in the world you wanted to owe money to. Alex took out an insurance policy in the form of an advance booking on a flight from Los Angeles to New York City. He would be at the airport waiting for the race results. If fate was good to him, he would head north, collect his winnings, and pay the German back. If not, he was flying east.

But a storm intervened and changed his plans. It destroyed his Alfa and kept him from reaching the airport. He had lost every one of his bets with the German and, instead of flying to New York at supersonic speed, he was inching along a twisting highway on a Greyhound bus.

I'm not in good shape, Alex thought, looking out the window at the passing scenery. Definitely not prime condition. I'm still alive, but some things are better than life—like a painless death.

Part II
1996

CHAPTER SIX

Moonlight becomes you. Blue moon, I saw you standing alone. How long had he been in New York City now? Six years already, but time had lost all meaning. Six years and still he had not been able to get those lyrics out of his mind. They popped into his head at the strangest times, in his dreams, during the day when he was shopping or performing some routine chore, often when he least expected it. He might be thinking about the outcome of a baseball game, for example, when all of a sudden, without warning, he found himself humming the tune to one of the songs he danced to at the inn that night, or mouthing the words to himself.

This was not normal. Then again, what was normal these days? Certainly not him or his life, certainly not the country he lived in. And not this weather either. New York was abysmally hot with the temperature hovering over a hundred for days at a time and the humidity right behind it. The air was foul and stagnant. His apartment in the East Village was oppressive. After his third shower of the day, he felt as though he had stepped back into a tropical rain forest and the perspiration poured freely down his body.

Alex wiped himself dry, threw on shorts and a T-shirt, walked over to the radio and turned it on. A seventy-five percent chance of precipitation, the announcer said. Even the meteorologists were making book on the weather. So much for science. He checked himself in the mirror—thick black beard to camouflage his face, dark shades, black sweatband around his head, black T-shirt and black shorts despite the weather—just another innocuous dropout in the East Village crowd. Even his mother wouldn't recognize him, let alone some muscle-bound baboons from California looking to break his legs.

The street in front of his apartment was strewn with the usual litter, human and otherwise. Junkies sat wall-eyed on the front stoop, winos lay against the building alongside over-filled garbage pails, dread-locked Rastas sold joints openly on the sidewalk, street kids with squeegees hustled change by cleaning windshields, rats big as dogs scurried among the garbage, gorging themselves without restraint. A heavy blend of dog-shit, urine, and other exudations hung with an almost physical presence in the air. It was summer in New York.

Alex stopped at the candy store on the corner, bought himself one of the few remaining authentic egg creams available anywhere in the world, and scanned the magazine rack. The cover of Fortune caught his eye immediately. There, staring back at him as though he didn't have a worry in the world—what did he have to worry about anyway?—was the handsome, powerful, buccaneer face of Luke Fenris. Unlike earlier waves of money-hucksters who floated between Wall Street, the Hamptons, Washington, and prison, Fenris shunned the public spotlight. In an age when most moneyed celebrities, anxious to prove they had the common touch, talked about everything from the type of underwear they wore to the quality of the drugs they experimented with, Fenris remained silent. His public resume had more missing pieces than a discarded jigsaw puzzle. Where exactly had he come from? No one knew. He remained a mystery despite his high-profile business deals, his billions, his astonishing focus on corporate integrity coupled with a frightening single-minded ruthlessness. The public admired him as a can-do guy who could get things done, without understanding exactly what he did. He was a strong leader for sure, at a time when leadership was in scarce supply. The public was hungry for someone to step forward and clean up the mess, restore the nation to greatness. Fenris, the man of mystery, seemed to fit the role. Talk of a third-party Fenris for President Campaign frequently dominated the Sunday morning pundit circuses.

Alex harbored an instinctive loathing for the man; on the surface at least, he appeared to represent everything Alex had fought against all his life. Something about Fenris gave him the chills. Give a man like that too much power and you could wind up with a dictator—the wrong kind of dictator. On the other hand, there was something about him that Alex admired; Fenris appeared to be, as far as anyone could tell, an implacable enemy of Peter Dante. Was the enemy of my enemy my friend? Or was he just as dangerous? Alex guessed he was just as bad as Dante, but with his own agenda in mind. He flipped through the article, finished his egg cream, and then put the magazine back on the rack. It was time to move on.

Down on St. Marks, past the sushi bars, the Indian restaurants, the cappuccino joints, the second-hand clothing stores, the Greek tavernas, the rundown bars, was a six-story building with a sign out front. The sign read, CHESS A-GO-GO, a fixture from the sixties, and Alex entered beneath it and walked up to the top floor. For some time now he had been trying with limited success to recreate from memory the moves of a grand master that he had been following in the newspapers. Perhaps tonight would be different.

He sat down at a table, ordered coffee, and studied the board in front of him. He looked up when the waiter arrived and noticed a young woman sitting directly across from him. She was somewhat plump, with black hair topped by a black beret. Her attire was all military chic—camouflage fatigues, boots, a jacket with epaulets—the favorite outfit of leftist militants. She had decorated each wrist with a tattoo bracelet and sported the fashionable ring through her eyebrow. She wasn't much to look at, Alex thought, but something about her lively green eyes sparkled and attracted him. He was about to turn away when he saw the title of a book she was reading—*I'm OK! You're Out $29.95*. A big best seller of the season, it was written by some contra-touchy-feely shrink who believed that too much openness and communication was destroying the social fabric.

Alex absorbed himself in his game simulation until he finally hit an impasse and threw his hands up in disgust. He had barely touched his coffee and it was now ice cold as he lifted it to his lips. He checked his watch and saw that he had been at it for almost an hour, so absorbed in his game that he had lost track of time. Perhaps that's what he liked about it. It passed time quickly for him, and took his mind off his problems.

He looked up for a moment at the sound of a nearby movement and saw the woman with the outfit staring at him. She had her book in her hand and sipped coffee, studying him as if she were trying to make a decision about something. Not that bad looking, he thought, but definitely not his type. What kind of a statement was she trying to make with her Banana Republic guerrilla costume? Whatever it was, he wasn't buying it. Then again, who was he to talk with his East Village Night Fighter's rig? To hell with it; it wasn't worth it. Alex turned away, not wanting to engage with her.

"Care for a game?"

Alex looked back. She was talking to him. "Uh, sure. Why not?" He motioned toward the seat across from him. "Alex Maltese," he said when she sat down.

"Maltese?" She continued to eye him curiously. "Interesting. I'm Sally Milano." She picked up two pawns, one of each color, and shuffled them in her hands. She held out two closed fists and said, "Pick a color."

They played intently for half an hour, barely speaking a word to each other. The advantage shifted back and forth several times until Sally finally beat him. Alex was pissed but tried not to show it. "You're good," he said, "really good."

"I'm okay." She laughed at him.

"Okay?" Alex could not help laughing himself. "You're also out twenty-nine ninety-five."

They both laughed at that. "Did you read it?" she said.

"Flipped through it."

"What'd you think?"

"Parts of it are fun, especially the part about women deliberately losing to men in games like chess and tennis to make them feel good. But most of it is basic crap. I mean, this country's in the toilet right now. People are starving, homeless, unemployed, sick. The environment's a pigsty. A woman's right to get an abortion is being challenged. Everything's a mess, there's no justice anywhere. The right wing's back in control. And this stupid shrink comes along with a book on how to improve your relationships by reviving the old romanticism. I mean, come on! Talk about pabulum for the masses. We need a revolution in this country, not garbage like that."

A light seemed to go on in Sally's eyes. She kept staring at Alex disconcertingly, her jaw dropping an inch at a time. "What did you say your last name was?"

"Maltese. Why?" Alex felt his heart shrivel. His defense system was on full alert.

"You looked familiar before, but I couldn't put my finger on it. You reminded me of somebody."

"Really?"

"Yeah. Alex . . . Alex . . ." She worked the name around in her head. "Didn't you use to live in California? Weren't you one of the San Francisco Six? And you married that feminist. Alex and . . . yeah, Danielle? You're Alex Mallum, right?"

"You've got me confused with somebody else." Alex was frantic. Recognized after all this time in New York. Because of some stupid, chance encounter in a chess club. What was he supposed to do, hide in his apartment all the time? Turn himself into a complete hermit? He had to go out for fresh air—*fresh* air?—once in a while.

"Are you sure?" Sally persisted. "I mean, underneath your beard and all you look just like him."

"I know who you're talking about. And I've been mistaken for him before. But I'm not him, all right?"

"I didn't mean to, you know, invade your privacy or anything. If you say you're not him, that's fine with me. I used to live out there myself back then. I remember Alex Mallum when he was running in the Democratic primary for Congress. The way he took on the establishment and all. He and Danielle were, like, my ideal if you know what I mean. They were the Golden Couple, the stars of the radical movement. And then, all of a sudden, he just disappeared. Danielle defected or something after she made a lot of money, and everything just seemed to dissolve after that. I always wondered what happened to him."

"Sally, listen to me very carefully, please." Alex was quivering. He had all he could do to keep his hands from dancing on the table, so he folded them in his lap. "I know who Alex Mallum is. I sympathize with his ideas, too, but I don't think we should be talking about him in public like this. He's a fugitive from justice and you never know who's listening in." Alex looked quickly from left to right to emphasize his point. "I'm very upset that you think I'm him."

"I would never do anything to betray the ideas he stood for or put him in danger. He was, like, my ideal."

"His life could be in real danger, and it's not just his politics. As I remember, he got himself in trouble with some loan-sharks who were also out to get him."

"How do you know so much about him?"

He had to think about that a minute. Why didn't she just shut up and leave him alone? "I used to live in California myself at the time."

She squinted through her thick lenses and studied him, not buying a word. "Yes, well, if you say you're not him, that's just fine. But even if you were, your secret would be safe with me. I'm part of an underground movement myself, and we've all taken an oath to protect one another no matter what. So if your name is Alex Maltese, that's cool. Nobody'll ask any questions."

He was going to protest at first, then checked himself. Like it or not, his life was intertwined with hers now; he could not risk alienating her. Maybe she could be of use to him somehow. She seemed sincere. She had looked up to him at one time. Could he trust her? He had to. He had no choice, unless he wanted to pack up and race off to another city. Even then, it was only a matter of time before someone else discovered his true identity. Only a matter of time—always time. And next time he might not be so fortunate as to be unmasked by someone like Sally Milano. He made his decision.

"Why don't we get out of here?" he said. "Are you hungry? Let's get something to eat."

They went to a deli around the corner and ordered sandwiches. When they finished eating, Sally asked, "Do you like Raw Shark?"

Alex made a face. "I can't stand sushi. Everything's polluted now."

"No. Raw Shark, the rock group. They're playing down at the Bleeding Ulcer tonight."

Jesus, Alex thought. I'm really out of it these days. "Sure," he said. "Sounds like fun."

"They do slam dancing there, an awesome mosh-pit." Sally said. "It's group sharing and great exercise at the same time."

The lounge was six blocks away on a side street in the Alphabet City area. Down a litter-strewn alley filled with overflowing garbage pails they found a metal door. They went inside and encountered a bald-headed man, six-four, two-fifty, wearing a metal-studded black leather jacket, sitting on a stool in front of a gate made of chicken wire and wood. He had six stud earrings all in a row in his right ear. He sat there nonchalantly, cleaning his fingernails with a hunting knife.

"Sally, sweetheart," the bald man said. He stopped cleaning his nails and replaced the knife in a leather sheath on his belt. He took Sally's hands in his and gave her a bear hug. "Long time no see."

"What's shakin', Stallion?" Sally kissed him on the cheek. "How's your mom? Still on the killer weed?"

"Been off it two months now. Turned into a real bitch on wheels. I liked her better when she was doin' two packs a day."

"Give her my love, will you?"

"You bet. Hey, who's the geek?" He stared malevolently at Alex.

"Be nice, Stallion. This is my friend Alex."

"No offense, dude. Just watchin' out for Miss Sally here." He extended his right hand palm up.

"No offense taken." Alex slapped his palm, paid the cover charge for both of them, and Stallion let them by. Inside he whispered to Sally. "That's one mean looking son of a bitch."

"Stallion?" Sally laughed. "You're right. He runs the Gay Vigilante Patrol, a volunteer group that protects gays from frat-boy attacks, and they can be one tough bunch of head-crunchers when they have to. Real good people, though. Come on, let's dance."

CHAPTER SEVEN

Alex winced. Noise shattered the air. Wave after wave of piercing din reverberated back and forth, splitting eardrums, slicing into the brain. Bedlam ruled on the dance floor. The crowd was packed solid, wiggling and vibrating with anarchic abandon. There wasn't an inch of air space in the teeming mass.

Sally hopped and bounced in front of Alex. She raised her arms over her head and leaped like a mad woman. Alex tried to join in, but had trouble getting into the swing of it. He smiled lamely and tapped his foot on the floor, holding his arms rigid down his side. After a while he was carried away by the frenzy of the mob. He was a cork on a roiling sea, tossed and thrown back and forth as though he had no will of his own. The leaping and prancing grew more violent with each passing second. Dancers bumped into one another deliberately with sideways leaps, deranged acrobats out of hell. They crashed and slammed and bumped and rammed, spilling beer all over each other and on the floor. The din was unnerving, chaotic. Men and women floating on a sea of hands raised above their heads drifted across the hall like flotsam in the waves. Conversation was out of the question. Alex felt out of it, but Sally was in a trance as she slammed into the hurtling forms around her without regard for safety or decorum. Then, abruptly as it all began, it ended. The music—music?—stopped, leaving a deafening silence in its wake. The dancers screamed, some tossed beer bottles onto the stage in an apparent sign of appreciation.

Then Raw Shark came out and the place erupted all over again. Four males in leather jackets and tattooed bare chests took the stage, along with one female wearing a black leather miniskirt and matching halter. The woman, Miranda, wore her hair in an eighteen-inch spiky Mohawk with alternating white, purple, green, and orange stripes. Two of the males sported long multi-colored locks, another was shaved bald, and the fourth had long blond, shoulder-length hair. The bald male also wore a baseball catcher's mask while one of the colorful hairdos had a razor blade dangling from his left ear lobe, and the other wore large gold hoop earrings on each ear and three crucifixes around his neck. The blond wore a simple red headband and a single red stud in his right ear. All five wore nose-rings and had their fingernails painted in different colors.

They took their places with their instruments; the one with the catcher's mask played drums, two others pounded electronic guitars, Miranda shook a tambourine. The blond went over to the microphone and flicked his metal-studded tongue at the audience. Next he wiggled it to the tip of his nose and the crowd screamed. He then removed a switchblade from his pocket, snapped it open, raised it above his head and yelled, "Life sucks! I want to die!" With the mob roaring approval, he drew the knife along his left wrist, producing a thin red line. He licked it as the audience gasped. "Anybody thirsty?" he howled. Blood poured freely down his arm, dripping onto the floor, and a deathly pall filled the room. Then the blond laughed, wiped the red streak clean and raised it high to show the crowd it was all a big joke. Everyone heaved a collective sigh of relief and Raw Shark launched into its first number.

Electronic blasts thundered through the club once again as the mob resumed its slam dancing. Raw Shark sang of teenage suicide and a paean to the chainsaw. With the mob whipped into a frenzy once again, the group launched into its new hit, rapidly climbing up the charts:

> *I wanna kill a celebrity.*
> *Shoot the bosses in the factory.*
> *Drop a nuke on Washington, D.C.*
> *What's wrong with peace, love, and harmoneeeeee?*
>
> *Hitler's the hero of history.*
> *Stalin's good enough for me.*
> *Hang all those who wanna be free.*
> *What's wrong with peace, love, and harmoneeeeee?*
>
> *Fascist America is a tragedy.*
> *Socialism is a comedy.*
> *Your vote don't count in a democracy.*
> *What's wrong with peace, love, and harmoneeeeee?*

The audience exploded in cheers as Raw Shark finished what the music media dubbed "The New National Anthem." One of the guitarists responded by smashing the drummer across his catcher's mask with his guitar, splintering it beyond repair. The drummer rolled backward, leaped up and ran to the front of the stage, jumped off into the arms of six roaring fans and sent them sprawling onto the floor. Some of the crowd charged the stage, but were repelled by the musicians who kicked them in the face and hammered them with their instruments.

A free-for-all ensued. Beer bottles flew through the air, smashed into walls and onto the stage, bodies slammed into one another not in dance this time, but in a freewheeling punchout. Alex had enough. He grabbed Sally's hand and dragged her toward the exit. "But Alex!" She shouted as he sliced through the breeches.

On the way out, four women wearing black lipstick on their whitewashed faces tried to tackle Alex. He dodged around them as they screamed, "Cut off his dick! Chauvinist Fuckmonster! White Male Cuntmaster!" Alex charged past them, Sally in tow. Stallion was still manning the gate as Alex lurched by.

"Party poopers!" Stallion bellowed with laughter. "Gutless hetero cuntlapper!"

Stallion's taunting laughter followed them into the street. Alex dragged Sally down the alley and didn't stop until they had reached the main thoroughfare. Exhausted, quaking with fear, he collapsed onto the stoop of a dilapidated brownstone and tried to catch his breath. If Sally was traumatized by the experience, she was showing none of it. Her face glistened with perspiration, her eyes were wide with electric excitement, and she brimmed over with something resembling a contact high.

"God that was wild! I've never seen it so . . . so alive!"

Alex looked up, not quite able to believe her exuberance. "You liked that?"

"Well . . . yeah. Didn't you?"

"About as much as I'd like to see another outbreak of the bubonic plague. I'd rather have open heart surgery without an anesthetic than go through that again."

"Oh you. You're just feeling down because of all the hassles you've been through. It's a good thing I ran into you, you know that? You need a real pick-me-up, something to put a little spark back in your life. Come on. I've got just the medicine for you."

"Where're we going?"

"Back to my place. Don't argue. You need a lift . . . and I mean, like right now!"

Sally grabbed his arm and practically lifted him off the stoop. Alex was still in a daze, and he let Sally lead him through the grimy streets that resembled a combat zone more than anything else toward her apartment.

"Where we going?" he asked again.

"My place."

"I mean, like where?" He tried to hide his irritation.

"Not far. Over by Rivington."

"Oh yeah." He started to tell her he lived not far from there, near C and Houston, and then thought better of it. What she didn't know wouldn't hurt her, and what she did know could hurt him. He decided to keep her on a need-to-know basis, for the time being at least.

Sally lived on the top floor of a six-story walk-up, a dilapidated tenement that had clearly seen better days. The climb left them both out of breath. Walking up was part of the ordeal, entering her apartment was the rest of it. Like most city dwellers she had the place locked up as though it were a vault at Chase Manhattan. Three locks barricaded the door. Inside stood a four-foot long police bar anchored into the floor that she propped back against the door. Then she turned an assortment of knobs that slid two steel bolts into place. Finally, she secured the knob on the door chain into its slot.

Alex shook his head in wonderment. He had to go through more or less the same procedure each time he entered and exited his own digs. It was a simple fact of life, the way people had to live if they valued their lives and property. He checked out her apartment—a tiny studio with a bathtub in the kitchen. A wooden plank laid on top turned it into the kitchen table. A mattress on the floor with two pillows served as her bedroom, a chair in the corner the living room.

Two cats peered down at him from the top of her refrigerator. One was gray and white and slim, the other brown, black, and fat. They leapt down to get a closer look at him, but as they approached, sniffing at his ankles, they both recoiled, arched their backs and moved away toward their food bowls.

"Fidel! Che!" Sally scolded. "That's not very friendly. What's wrong with you?"

"It's not them. It's me," Alex said. "Cats don't seem to take to me. I don't know why." At least not since California, Alex thought. Strange too. He and Danielle had always been cat lovers, and had a menagerie of them as pets at one time or another.

"That's rude! Just for that you can wait for your dinner."

"Don't punish them on my account."

"They can wait until I make us coffee. I've got this great Jamaican roast. People say they put ganja in it, but I think they're full of it. Tastes good though."

Sally put on water to boil and Alex watched her cats frolic in the far corner of the room. Their reaction troubled him, but he tried not to show it. He had always loved animals, particularly cats, and gotten along with them. But these past few years for some reason they seemed to circle wide around him, sometimes even hissed at him. While Sally busied herself at the stove, he decided to make another pass at them. He walked over to where they were grumbling at their bowls and leaned over to pet the fat one. Without warning, the cat lunged and bit his hand, drawing blood. Alex yelled out.

"What happened?"

"He bit me."

"Fidel?"

"The fat one. I tried to pet him and he just lunged up and bit me."

Sally stared wide-eyed at her pets. "What's gotten into you? They're never like this. I'm sorry, Alex. Let me get you a Band-Aid."

"It's nothing, just a scratch." Alex shook his head, mystified. "I didn't eat any garlic tonight. Do I have B.O. or something?"

Sally stared at the cats, then at Alex. "They're always so warm and affectionate. It's just not like them."

"It's me I guess. Household pets and little children scream at the sight of me. Now you know why I can never run for public office."

Sally lathered his wound with iodine and covered it with a bandage. The water came to a boil and Sally prepared two cups of steaming black coffee for both of them. She scooped some peanut butter into the cats' bowls—their dinner apparently. "It's organic," she said by way of explanation, then went over and sat down on her mattress. Alex joined her. He noticed an astrology magazine on the floor beside the makeshift bed.

"You don't believe in that stuff, do you?"

"Just for fun. Let's see." She picked it up and thumbed through it. "What sign are you?"

"Scorpio."

"Really?" She stared at him as though that had some significance. "It says here, 'In the light of the full moon'—that's tomorrow by the way—'Venus will enter the house of Mars. A period of turbulence will follow and . . . ' "

Alex started to shake uncontrollably. He had to put down his cup of coffee to keep it from spilling. His hands quaked and his stomach heaved with violent spasms. A wave of nausea almost overwhelmed him, then subsided.

"Alex! Are you all right?" Her face was a study of deep concern mixed with fear.

"I . . . I don't know what came over me. Sorry." He pressed his palms against his temples to still the anxiety. "Maybe . . . maybe it's a delayed reaction to Raw Shark. I think I just need some sleep. I'm really bushed."

"Do you want to just lie back here and close your eyes? You look so . . . so pale and—"

"Thanks, but I . . . I probably ought to be going. It's getting late and—"

"Alex!" Sally took both his hands in hers and looked directly into his eyes. "You're not worried about, you know, about me mistaking you for Alex Mallum tonight, are you? I mean, I want you to know that whoever you are, it's perfectly all right with me. I wouldn't dream of even mentioning it to anyone."

"No, it's not that. I believe you when you say that." He eyed her steadily. Could he really trust her to keep her mouth shut?

"I mean, why would I do anything to hurt Alex Mallum? He and Danielle were the absolute neatest couple."

I thought so, too, Alex thought, rubbing his eyes. But Danielle had other ideas. My beautiful Danielle. She found a new religion—Peter Dante-style religion. So much for keeping the faith. What was Danielle doing tonight? Right this minute?

Whose arms was she enfolded in? The very thought of her—and his incredible loss—twisted like a knife inside him.

"I can't believe they got a divorce," Sally said, as though reading his thoughts.

"Well it happens to the best of us." Alex was getting nervous again.

"I guess we shouldn't keep talking about them." Sally bit her lip.

Great idea, Alex thought. Let's not talk about it at all. My whole life was turned upside down six short years ago, and it still tears me up inside whenever I think about what happened. It might be good to talk to someone about it. Some day. But not now. And not with her. What did he know about her anyway? She was just someone he ran into at a chess club, someone who was as idealistic as he was a few years back. But did that mean he could trust her?

"I'd better go," he said. "It's getting late and I'd better go home and get some sleep."

Sally looked concerned for a long moment. Then she said, "You don't have to go outside in the jungle at this hour. Why don't you lay back and get a few hours sleep here? I promise not to attack you, okay?" She smiled, sisterly, patting his hand. "You'll feel better after some sleep."

Alex was about to resist, then decided against it. Drowsiness descended on him like a heavy dark curtain. He could barely keep his eyes open. He rested his head down on the mattress, and in an instant he flew away into the world of his own dark dreams.

He awakened first in the morning. He got up quietly, walked down to the corner deli and bought Cheerios and milk, and a bag of Fancy Feeds for the cats. By the time Sally woke up, Fidel and Che were purring warmly, rubbing against his legs as he sprinkled cat food in their bowls.

"I see you made some friends," Sally said.

"I'm a different man today. Amazing what a good night's sleep can do. There's cereal and milk up here for you. I got to cut out to work, but look. Here's my phone number on the counter and I got yours off the phone. Let's stay in touch, okay?"

"Alex?"

"Yeah?"

"I will see you again? I mean, don't say yes if you don't want to."

Alex hesitated a second. His mind worked on overdrive. He'd better stay close to her, keep her as a friend. Besides, she wasn't so bad after all. "You kidding? After I made up with your cats and all? Of course I want to see you."

Sally smiled.

"I'll call you later from work." An instant later he bounded down the stairs to the street, wondering what in the world was happening to his life.

CHAPTER EIGHT

Luke Fenris strode through the long, marbled lobby of Xanadu Towers, Manhattan's posh new condominium complex. The doorman, who looked more like a general in a South American army, jumped out of his seat and opened the heavy glass door for him. Fenris stepped into a blast furnace. The heat was blistering as he looked west, toward the corner of Fifth and Fifty-third, and then turned back toward the doorman.

"Sure is a hot one, Mr. Fenris." The doorman wiped his forehead with a handkerchief. "You'd think it would cool off now that it's evening, wouldn't you, sir?"

"Sure would, Estaban. I'm expecting my car any moment. Would you please tell Martin I'll be waiting on the Fifth Avenue side of the building for him." Fenris pulled a twenty from his pocket and handed it to Estaban. He watched the doorman smile appreciatively, bowing slightly in deference, as he pocketed it. "Buy yourself a cold one."

"Thank you, sir."

Loyalty carried a premium, but it was well worth paying for. Fenris turned north at the corner and walked to the middle of the block, in front of the massive bronze and pink marble facade that framed the entrance to an eight-story atrium with several tiers of outrageously expensive shops enclosing an ice-skating rink. The rink was encircled by a fence decorated with ornate gold trim. On the outside was a tree-lined plaza adjoining an outdoor cafe.

Fenris checked his watch, then walked north three blocks, examining the elegant window displays inside the shops and boutiques. Moments later he returned to the entrance of his building. The heat was overpowering, but you could not tell that by observing Luke Fenris. He looked to be completely in control, almost cool inside his dark blue, wool, summer-weight suit, yellow cotton, button-down shirt, red and yellow-striped silk tie, calf-length blue-cotton stockings, and shiny black wingtips. His blond hair was immaculately combed, with not a strand out of place. His passport gave the color of his eyes as blue, but they were more like glinting chips of ice. The overall portrait was of a strikingly handsome man, thoroughly self-absorbed in his unruffled precision—almost like a superior being from a distant planet.

While he waited in front of his building, a thin African male with tan pants and a gaily-colored pullover shirt set up shop on the corner. He placed a blanket on the sidewalk and loaded handbags from a cart onto it. He was joined by another African associate who exhibited an array of expensive looking watches—knockoffs, no doubt, of the genuine articles on display in the upscale boutiques along the avenue. Three more of their countrymen—Senegalese, Fenris guessed—arrived with wares of their own: belts, sunglasses, necklaces, earrings, and assorted junk.

"Bastards," Fenris muttered to himself. "They've even got Fifth Avenue looking like a filthy Moroccan souk."

At that moment his car arrived. Martin pulled the black Cadillac limousine over to the curb alongside the mini-bazaar on the sidewalk. He got out and opened the door for Fenris who approached with a deliberate stride across the blanket of cheap jewelry, crushing some of it under his feet.

"Hey, man! Watch it," shouted the tall burly African. At two hundred and twenty pounds he was perhaps thirty pounds heavier than Luke Fenris, who carried his weight on a lean, six-feet-two-inch frame. "What you think you doin', man?" He grabbed Fenris by the arm and tried to throw him off the blanket. With startling speed, Fenris's free hand darted out and seized the peddler's thick wrist. He bent his arm back and down, forcing the man to his knees.

"This street is for pedestrian traffic, not for trash that clutters up the sidewalk." Fenris's lips barely moved. His words came out in a frightening hiss through clenched teeth.

The peddler tried to twist himself free, but Fenris's grip was an iron vise around his wrist. The vise grew tighter, bruising the bone, and the street vendor started to whimper. "You're hurting me, man. Please. I didn't mean to offend you. I'm just trying to make a buck." The peddler noticed a sudden dark red glow appear in his captor's eye, and a chill raced through his body.

"Make it somewhere else. This is my street, my sidewalk, my home. Now beat it." Fenris released the man, kicked the rest of his trinkets into the street, and got into his limo. Martin, also of African descent, closed the door, turned to the peddlers and said in his lilting West Indian accent, "I'd do what he says if I were you. Next time he might not be in such a good mood," then slid in behind the wheel.

"Drop me off at the South Ferry Heliport." Fenris checked his watch. "Make sure you pick me up at three A.M. sharp. You can use the car in the meantime."

"Thank you, sir."

Fenris's copter landed at JFK almost simultaneously with the arrival of Peter Dante's jet. The aircraft taxied in to the Palliser hangar as Fenris stepped down onto the tarmac. He looked up and saw Danielle exit the plane first, her father right behind her. His eyes drank in her beauty, her own special quality that seemed to glow more brightly with each passing day. Most women were diminished by widowhood; the death of a loved one, particularly one's lifemate, leaves a shadow that is never quite extinguished. Not so with Danielle. She appeared to come more fully into bloom after the mysterious, unexpected death of her second husband only eighteen months earlier.

Peter Dante held back a step and beamed as his daughter bounded ahead into Fenris's arms. "Darling," she almost gasped. She devoured him with her lips and molded her body into his. "God, I missed you."

Fenris held her, breathed in her perfume, her very essence for a long moment, then released her and shook Dante's hand.

"Good to see you, Luke."

"Likewise. Trip okay?"

"Why complain?"

"What have you been up to?"

"The usual bullshit. Work, work, and more work. How about you?"

Fenris shrugged and curled his lips in what passed for a smile. "Pretty much the same."

"So what's all the urgency about? What's with this sudden, big meeting tonight?"

"You'll find out soon enough." Fenris took Danielle's hand and kissed her again. Dante knew enough not to press him. If there was one man he looked up to and feared in the entire country, it was Luke Fenris, his relationship with his daughter notwithstanding. Every time you thought you had a handle on Luke, got to know him a little bit, the man had a chilling way of cutting you down to size. Truth be told, there was something about this man he hoped would be his future son-in-law that scared him half to death.

"Well, it's your party, Luke," Dante said. "I'm sure you got a good reason for it. Lead the way."

Dante was a lot more concerned than he let on during the half-hour copter ride to South Hampton. It wasn't Luke's toughness, his ruthlessness, that troubled him. Those were traits that he admired, indeed, had cultivated in himself. It was the mystery surrounding Luke Fenris that bothered Peter Dante more than anything. He had emerged from nowhere, in the space of a few short years, as the most successful financial shark in the country. Where did Fenris come from? Who had ever heard of him? Dante put a team of private detectives to work doing a background check, and all they came up with were blanks. Fenris had obliterated his entire background, erupting spontaneously it seemed, and beating the best business sharks at their own game.

Dante wouldn't even have minded that so much if he hadn't heard rumors that Fenris had targeted Palliser Dynamics for a hostile takeover. Fenris had a reputation for moving in on big, top-heavy conglomerates that subsisted primarily on government contracts, stripping them of corporate fat, and turning them into lean and hungry, competitive enterprises. Just as Dante had prepared his defenses to ward off a possible attack, Fenris made his move—not on Dante's company as he feared, but on his daughter Danielle instead. At first Dante was alarmed. But the more he thought about it, the more he liked the idea. What a partnership that would make—Dante and Fenris! Between the two of them, with their combined fortunes and all the power wealth could buy, they could become a financial jugger-naut with hefty influence over several key industries. Hell, the two of them together would constitute a formidable economic team that would be difficult for anyone else to contend against. The combination would be dynamic. And Danielle was his insurance that the merger would work. Instead of being subsumed by Fenris, they would come together as relatives and partners.

As for Danielle, she needed no encouragement from her father. She had listened to common sense and dumped that pinko Mallum before it was too late. After that, she handled the sudden "disappearance" of her second husband like a real trooper. Thank God! The little bastard got religion after getting elected to office with Dante's money, and could no longer be trusted. Dante did what he thought necessary, even though he felt uneasy about Danielle's reaction. Then Fenris came along and solved that potential problem; she fell head over heels in love with the swaggering pirate at first sight. Dante thought about that for a full two and a half seconds before giving the match his tacit blessing.

So here he was, sitting in a chopper on his way out to the Hamptons alongside some bastard who had the power to cut his balls off if he felt like it. It was like sitting next to an eight-hundred-pound gorilla that had its hands wrapped around your nuts. It didn't hurt now because he wasn't squeezing. But any time he wanted to, he could turn you into a soprano. Dante didn't like the feeling, but for now at least he didn't have much choice. Meanwhile, he had a meeting to get through—a meeting at which Luke Fenris and his buccaneer buddy Carl Navi would be holding all of the aces.

The chopper settled down onto the Navi estate, the most priceless gem among all those dotting the coastline along Billionaire's Row. Navi, himself, was one of the richest men in the world and he wanted everyone to know it. His sixty-room mansion ensconced on ten acres of prime waterfront property had hosted the most lavish and well-attended parties in this part of the world. The rich and famous from every walk of life—industry, politics, royalty, theater, art, real estate—fought like teenagers for invitations, which themselves were a barometer of who was currently in or out of fashion. Tonight's shindig was no exception. However, in addition to the usual throngs of A-list power merchants, twenty-five of Luke Fenris's closest and dearest financial backers would also be in attendance.

Fenris exited from the helicopter first, then held Danielle's hand as she touched her slippered feet to earth. Her eyes sparkled in the darkness as they swept the heavens. "God, Luke. Look at that full moon. And those lights out on the water. Can we walk along the beach for a few minutes before you go in? I won't get to see you at all once those vultures get hold of you."

Fenris thought for a second. "Sure," he said, and turned to Dante. "Peter, why don't you go in and tell Carl I'll be along in a few minutes."

Dante smiled, kissed his daughter on the cheek and winked at her, then walked from the helipad up the lawn toward Carl Navi who was waiting with his entourage on the veranda. A full hour later, Fenris sauntered in to the grand ballroom, Danielle on his arm. They passed through large oak doors engraved with bears. The ballroom itself was done up like a medieval hall. Multicolored banners were festooned from the ceiling. Antique tapestries draped across the walls depicted various stages of a deer hunt. Along the floor suits of armor stood guard at their posts. A full orchestra played classical music on the balcony overhead. Beneath them was a display of crossbows, swords, lances, cudgels, spiked hammers, and other medieval weapons.

Dante was the first to see them come in. Fenris observed him approaching through the crowd. He reached down into a glass museum case and started to remove a gold scabbard clustered with variegated jewels. He changed his mind, closed the case, and took down an Arab scimitar from the wall instead. Dante was smiling broadly as he walked up, then stopped dead in his tracks while the color drained from his face. Without warning, Fenris had raised the scimitar and pointed the tip at Dante's throat. If Dante had not slammed on the brakes he would have walked right into it.

"Jesus, Luke! That's not funny."

Fenris observed the smaller man, beads of perspiration spontaneously erupting on his forehead and upper lip, without smiling. He remained silent for a full ten seconds, the tip of the scimitar frozen in the air an inch from Dante's Adam's apple.

Finally he said, "Nasty little item, isn't it? Probably a lot more effective than those dud missiles you foist on Uncle Sam and some of our allies, wouldn't you say?" He put the weapon back on the wall and curled the ends of his lips upward in a facsimile smile.

Dante's eyes were wide with something akin to terror, which he attempted to hide as best he could. "You . . . you got a strange sense of humor, Luke. It's gonna take some getting used to." Dante's eyes flitted to his daughter who looked back and forth at both of them quizzically, trying to fathom the elaborate joke.

"Navi and the others are waiting, Luke," Dante said. "You ready to come in now?"

"I'll be along in a minute, Peter."

"Well, right then." Dante shifted from foot to foot, like a schoolboy not quite knowing what to do next. "So I'll go tell them you're coming along."

"Do that, Peter. We'll make a decent little administrator out of you yet."

"I think you shook up daddy," Danielle said after her father left.

"Just having a little joke."

A waitress in medieval peasant garb approached them with a tray of drinks. Fenris accepted a Perrier for himself and a glass of white wine for Danielle. Another came by with a platter of shrimp, crabmeat puffballs, and other hors d'oeuvres. Danielle took a shrimp and Fenris waved her away impatiently.

"Time to go in," he said. "Sorry to leave you, but I'll see you later."

As he was about to kiss her goodbye, a middle-aged blonde in a black strapless evening dress with a diamond necklace and matching earrings rushed up to him. Her hair was stiff as though it were made of spun polyester, and her face radiated an innocuous smile.

"Mr. Fenris!" She extended her right hand outward.

"Yes?" He did not take it.

"Oh . . . uh, I'm Jeanette Davenport. I believe you know my husband Mark with Davenport, Williams, Oransky, and Devereaux. He's one of your bankers."

Used to be, Fenris thought. I've no use for people who talk business with their wives. "What about him?"

"Well, I didn't want to talk to you about him actually." Her frozen smile grew more uncertain in the face of Luke's unfriendliness. "It's about my upcoming charity ball at the Waldorf to aid the homeless. I was hoping you might help cosponsor it."

"I'm late for a meeting." Fenris started to move away.

"But, it's for a good cause, Mr. Fenris. We're trying to raise money to build shelters for the homeless."

"Sorry. I don't participate in public events."

"Perhaps you'd be interested in sponsoring a table then. It's only five thousand dollars and this promises to be the most meaningful social affair of the season."

"Not interested."

"Tickets for you and . . . Ms. Dante . . . then?" She looked hopefully at Danielle.

"I don't mean to be rude, but I am running late."

The woman fingered her necklace nervously, her composure all but shattered. Surely he must be joking; no one ever spoke to her this way. "But . . . all of the most prominent people are getting involved in one way or another. Mr. Dante, Mr. Navi, the ambass—"

"Let me be blunt, Mrs. Davenport. I don't want homeless people in New York. Now, if you want to build shelters in Utah or Wyoming for residentially-challenged citizens, I'd be only too happy to lend a hand."

There was no longer any question of maintaining her dignity now. She stared at Fenris with an expression that was equal parts shock, alarm, and confusion.

"Your husband's one of my former bankers, so he'll understand these figures. It costs three times as much to house someone in New York as it does in the Southwest. We can remove three times as many filthy, disease-ridden swine off the streets for the same dollar outlay if we ship them to the desert."

Mrs. Davenport was nearly in a swoon. Danielle reached out a hand to steady her out of fear she might collapse onto the floor. She opened her mouth to speak; a whisper came out. "Mr. Fenris. You . . . your sense of humor is quite . . . quite—"

"I don't make jokes, Mrs. Davenport. Never. I'm deadly serious when I tell you that I am willing to underwrite the entire cost of erecting several exact duplicates of Grand Central Station in the middle of Wyoming in order to house your unfortunate friends. I'll even include steam vents and overflowing garbage pails to make your cherished derelicts feel at home."

Again the woman looked at Danielle for encouragement, but found none there. She turned back uncertainly to Fenris. "Surely, the Southwest has problems enough of its own." She chuckled nervously.

"Wyoming's not a concern of mine, New York is. New York is where I live. However, I'm willing to make you another offer. You own the estate two lots down, sixty-five rooms on six acres. You also own a fifteen-room apartment on Park Avenue between Sixty-sixth and Sixty-seventh. I'll convert your estate into a shelter for three thousand of your beloved homeless and redesign your apartment to accommodate another one hundred. You and your husband get to keep one of the bedrooms for yourselves."

Enough was enough. The man's rudeness, to say nothing of his unspeakable social conscience, was well beyond the pale. Someone needed to put him in his place—notwithstanding her husband's business relationship with him. "I find it difficult to believe you're serious, Mr. Fenris. But if you are, I'm afraid I find your . . . your attitude toward those less fortunate than ourselves to be totally unacceptable."

"If you feel you have an obligation toward them, that's all the more reason why you should be willing to share what you have and take them in yourself. My offer is a generous one. I'm willing to pay the cost of remodeling your homes, which I estimate to be about five million dollars. Or, perhaps your social conscience doesn't reach that far. Perhaps you feel you've done enough by housing these miserable wretches in some filthy structure you wouldn't dream of living in yourself. Good evening, Mrs. Davenport. I have a meeting to attend."

This time Fenris would not be detained. He smiled at Danielle, then wheeled around and strode away. The woman glared after him, her eyes glinting with unconcealed rage. "Just whom does he think he's talking to?" she said to Danielle. "Does he always treat people like this?"

"Yes," Danielle said. "But that's only a small part of his charm."

CHAPTER NINE

Despite their sharply contrasting styles, Carl Navi and Luke Fenris had been inseparable business partners for the past five years. That was something else that concerned Peter Dante as he sat at the conference table with the others, awaiting Luke's arrival. The two of them together comprised a formidable team—a team that sometimes had Dante feeling as though he were odd-man-out whenever he happened to be in the same room with them.

Navi, the playboy scion of a wealthy Lebanese family of merchants, was an inveterate social animal. His parties were legendary; he was seen in all the right places with all the right people, active in all the major charitable events. He was a master manipulator who played both sides of the political fence, raising money for politicians across the entire ideological spectrum. Fenris on the other hand, aside from being a man without an apparent past, was Navi's polar opposite socially. The newspapers and magazines were filled with speculative articles about him because of his incredible success, but he gave no interviews and deliberately kept as low a profile as possible. He rarely appeared at events such as the one he was attending tonight.

The closest the media had ever come to cracking the impregnable wall of secrecy Fenris had constructed took place two years earlier. Fenris launched an attack on the Fortunato restaurant empire—a highly profitable chain of steakhouses that was reportedly a mob front. Rumor had it that Tony Fortunato, heir apparent to his father's kingdom, did not look kindly upon this unprecedented incursion into his family's dominion. Before Fortunato the Younger could take suitable action, however, six of his most powerful underbosses were found in a back alley in Little Italy in uncharacteristic repose; their throats had been torn out, and what was left of their faces and bodies had been flayed open with claw-like slashes. Tony Fortunato himself disappeared from the scene the following day when he did a jackknife off the roof of a hotel he owned in midtown Manhattan. Some say it was remorse over the demise of his fallen compadres; more cynical observers claimed that his dive had been involuntary.

The combined forces of the media and law enforcement agencies of various levels of government were unsuccessful in solving the mysteries of the atrocities. Luke Fenris was mentioned frequently as the primary suspect, but no one could come up with a shred of evidence leading to him. It was as though the murders and "suicide" had taken place in a vacuum, as it were. The absence of fingerprints, clues, witnesses, or any incriminating evidence was as baffling as it was horrifying. After a while the public lost interest in the deaths of a bunch of goons who, most people felt, only got what they deserved. The country had more pressing things to worry about. Perhaps the one most concerned about what had happened was Peter Dante. Fenris's power seemed to be boundless. The man was untouchable. He could take on anybody, beat them decisively, and then move on to his next victim.

Even Carl Navi, one of the wealthiest and most well-connected men in the world, owed Fenris an immeasurable debt, which was the cement that held their partnership together. Five years earlier Navi had found himself thwarted in an attempt to take over Parcel Industries, a multinational conglomerate headquartered in New York City. Fenris, a virtual unknown at the time with no solid financial backing, was occupied himself in an attempt to buy a fledgling computer software firm that was being run into the ground by three brilliant, but financially unsophisticated whiz kids. Fenris knew they had developed a powerful software firewall and encryption technique that could revolutionize the e-commerce industry, but they didn't know a flow chart from a spreadsheet and were in danger of going belly-up. Fenris needed fifty-five million dollars to buy the firm right out from under them, but he was fifty-four million nine hundred and ninety-nine thousand dollars short. That's where Navi came in.

Through a combination of uncompromising arrogance and dazzling financial logic, Fenris convinced him that, if he backed him in his own venture, Fenris could provide Navi with the means to complete his own deal. Navi had his numbers-crunchers check the figures and they added up. The fifty-five million was only walking-around money for him; even if Fenris failed to deliver on his end of the bargain, Navi could arrange to take control of the computer company himself, which would make a fine addition to his ever-expanding empire.

In the end, Fenris delivered as he said he would—and the manner in which he did so elicited an outpouring of admiration for the handsome young pirate that Navi hadn't felt in years. Clearly, Fenris would be a force to be reckoned with for years to come, and Navi wanted to have him on his side. It came to a head one afternoon when Navi brought his protégé along to a board meeting of Parcel Industries, his target company. He introduced Fenris to Darren Ames, CEO of Parcel, and Fenris wasted no time in insulting the dapper, middle-aged executive.

"Your boy here could use a lesson in manners." Ames frowned at Navi.

"Save the etiquette lesson for later," Fenris said. "I came here to talk business."

Ames checked his watch. "Yeah, well you've got five minutes to get my attention."

"All I need is three. We came here to take over your company. Your annual 10-K filings with the SEC have more holes than a city block in lower Manhattan and I've got the figures to prove it. Personally, if it were up to me, I'd throw you and all your accomplices out on the street. But Carl here says you're an old friend and he asked me to soften the deal. So here it is. We don't blow the whistle on you. In exchange, you sell us controlling interest in your company. You and your board get to stay on two more years before disappearing into the sunset with your reputations intact."

Ames made no pretense at self-control. He exploded and jabbed his finger in the air, in front of Fenris's chest. "Who the fuck do you think you are, coming in here and insulting me with demands like that? Carl! Where did you find this cowboy anyway?" he said to Navi, but continuing to glare at Fenris. "You bring him in here and let him insult me like that? Get him out of here before I have him thrown out!"

"His offer is very generous, Darren. I think you should listen to him."

"I've heard enough. Get him out of here!"

"You haven't heard anything," Navi said. "Your company's losing millions, thanks to you, and you've been covering it up. You've been cooking the books, Darren. Your financials read like a bad crime novel. Unless you want to spend the next ten years in Club Fed, I suggest you go along."

"Bullshit! What have you got? The Bel Air Group offered me fifty percent more than your best offer so far, and I turned them down."

"No more," Fenris said.

"What do you mean 'No more'?"

"Exactly that. Your deal is off the table. They've thrown their support behind Carl and me."

"Fuck you! I spoke to Jeffrey Hart only two days ago and their offer is solid."

"Call him again. I faxed him a full report on your company yesterday. He wanted to turn it over to his lawyers, but I convinced him to throw his hat in with us instead."

"You're bluffing!"

"Call him like he says," Navi said.

Ames continued to glare at Fenris, but there was a flicker of fear in his eyes as he moved toward the telephone. In a minute he reached his party. "Jeff? Darren here. Just wanted to sound you out a little further on your offer. As you mentioned the other—what?—withheld information from you?—I assure you, Jeff—Now wait a minute, there's no call for a lawsuit. Let me explain—Yes, yes, there is a minor patent infringement claim against us, but there's not a chance in hell—The collapse of our second source on our Intel-killer chip? Jeff, for God's sake, don't fly off the handle on—What dry well in Texas?—Well shit, I thought you knew about that—"

Navi let him squirm a moment or two longer, then removed the receiver from his hand, raised it to his lips and said, "Jeffrey, this is Carl. I truly appreciate your cooperation. No, I don't think we'll have any trouble either. I'll call you later."

The rest was a routine mopping-up operation. The paperwork was done, signatures affixed to their proper places, and the deal was set. The most frightening business partnership—as far as Peter Dante was concerned—was a *fait accompli*. Fenris was the domestic arm of the operation, Navi handled overseas. Fenris by himself would have been bad enough. But Navi/Fenris was a powerhouse no adversary could go up against and survive. Between the two of them, they controlled five Fortune 500 companies, two of them among the top ten. Dante felt his stomach heave as Fenris entered the conference room. An equal partner, he thought. That's all I want to be. And Danielle, thank God, is my ace in the hole.

Fenris looked around impatiently at the assemblage; besides Navi and Dante, twenty-five of the most influential business and financial leaders in the country—eighteen men and seven women – were present. "This location isn't secure," Fenris said.

"Relax, Luke." Navi smiled as he walked over to one of the bookcases and pulled aside a panel. Behind it were ten numbered buttons. Navi removed a small plastic card from his suit pocket, inserted it into a slot above the buttons, and punched out a five-digit code. The entire wall slid sideways slowly, uncovering an even larger room than the one they were in. In it was a large, gleaming ebony conference table surrounded by black leather swivel chairs. There was also an impressive array of telephones, computer terminals, printers, large television screens, and other electronic wizardry that made the room look like the control center of the Starship Enterprise. Navi gestured grandly and said, "Gentlemen and women, shall we begin?" They all took seats around the table while Fenris walked to the front and waited for them to settle in.

"I'm going to speak for just a few minutes," he said. "I want you all to hear me out in full, then I'll take your questions."

A silence that was almost a physical presence fell among them. Fenris waited for the last murmur to die down, and then began.

"America is dying. It's just a question of time before it collapses beneath its own elephantine bureaucracy, its own inertia. And the media are primarily to blame. It keeps pushing its own left-wing agenda, manufacturing one crisis after another— AIDS, global warming, homelessness, gun control, crime, drugs, the environment, health care, jobs, you name it. If a problem doesn't exist, the media elite will invent one as an excuse to push for higher taxes, more entitlements, more bureaucracy, and more government spending, all of which drain the productive forces of our nation. When the liberal programs don't work, the media find some bureaucratic or corporate scapegoat and call for more of the same. If only they could keep on raising taxes and expanding the size of government, they think, our problems will go away.

"We already have too many people on welfare and in our public schools, but when we try to keep illegal immigrants off the welfare roles and out of the schools, what do the media have to say about that? It's cruel and heartless, they cry, to exclude these people from our society. So let's tear down our borders, let everybody in who wants to come in, and give them everything we've got. Oppose this recipe for financial collapse and the media tag you as a racist.

"The people who control the media today like to portray themselves as fair, honest, and objective. We know they're not. Journalism has been replaced by unadulterated editorializing, and the dominant message we're bombarded with is 'collectivism is good and capitalism and individual freedom are evil.' The media practice thought control, which is the source of total power.

"Ladies and gentlemen, I am here to tell you tonight that this situation can only get worse unless we take effective action. Now, all of you here have become very rich and fat and comfortable—thanks to Carl and myself. We've cut the deals and brought all of you in on them, and our fortunes are secure. No matter what kind of a quagmire we've got in this country, all of us are in a position to buy our own safety. To a great extent we've prospered by subverting the democratic process and putting our own people in office. However, this state of affairs can't continue indefinitely. The system is breaking down.

"I've brought you here tonight to ask you to join me in making a revolution. I've worked out a plan, but before I go into it, I need to tell you that what I say from this point on is strictly in confidence. There's criminal risk involved. You're going to be asked to risk your wealth, your comfort, your security to make a revolution that will guarantee a better world for all of us to live in when it's over. To accomplish this I require your complete loyalty and confidence. Those who can't make that commitment now are free to leave—in fact, you must leave. Because if you stay . . . ," Fenris paused and looked everyone individually in the eye to emphasize his point, " . . . you stay from this moment on, there's no turning back. Those who leave will be cut of from any future dealings with Carl and myself but, other than that, there will be no recrimina- tions. Those who remain will not be permitted to back out later."

Fenris folded his arms across his chest and listened to the murmurings, watched the faces dart back and forth in animated discussion as they debated among themselves. Three minutes later the voices died down, the fidgeting stopped. Silence returned. No one had left the room.

"That's it then," Fenris said. "You're all in, you're all totally committed to our enterprise. To ensure the success of our revolution, we're going to seize control of the American media. The media control the agenda, decide what the key issues are, create our heroes and our villains, decide what is good and evil—in short, the media decide how people think and what they think about.

"Quite simply, I mean to take control of that power for myself—ourselves. The reality is, neither political party can be trusted. No matter who gets in, they all pander to the collectivist special interest groups and let the media call the shots. It's just a question of degree, which party can spend the most on which stupid entitlement program. In my . . . in *our* hands, ladies and gentlemen, we can use the power of the media to create the kind of society we all dream of living in. Imagine a society, a world, in which we liberate productive taxpayers from the leeches who sap our creativity and our strength. Imagine a civilized world governed by a true Pax Americana, a world where thuggish Third World dictators disappear and free up the productive forces of their people. This is the broad picture I wanted to paint. Now let's get down to specifics."

Fenris planted his palms on the shimmering ebony conference table and leaned forward. "Any questions so far?"

"I have one." Marie Winkler, president of Winkler International, a major telecommunications and high-tech company, looked around at the others as she formulated her remarks. "We all know you're a man of remarkable resources and ability, Luke. But what you're proposing seems so . . . so ambitious shall we say. The media, Luke? The media aren't a monolithic enterprise, like a single company that you can just take over. It's sprawling, mammoth, diversified. It would be like trying to grab hold of a handful of sand. It's spread out all over the place. Can you do it?"

"That, my friends, is where you come in. Here's the plan." Fenris removed a stack of documents from his briefcase and distributed them around the table. "Note that there are names at the top. Each packet contains individual instructions for each of you. At the end of the meeting you will study them thoroughly and return them to Carl. They cannot leave this room. But before you open them, let me give you a general summary.

"It is illegal for any entity to take control of all the networks and main newsgroups. There is no legitimate way we can publicly unite to buy all the key institutions. But secretly, we can divide ourselves into seemingly independent alliances, with one or the other team buying a key player. These documents outline who belongs to which team and what the targets are. To add a little spice and fun to the deal, I will come on as a corporate raider seeking a network or other operation. The media will raise a stink, until one of the designated teams comes in to rescue the target from my greedy grasp. Each time, of course, my shares will be bought back at an enormous profit as part of the settlement, and that profit will be funneled through one or another of the banks under our control and used to underwrite both sides of each successive foray.

"This brings us to the question of how much will this really cost. A lot less than you think, shockingly less. By way of comparison, Exxon's buyout of Mobil in 1999 cost eighty-two billion dollars. What I'm proposing will cost considerably less.

Several years ago, Capital Cities bought ABC for a mere three-and-a-quarter billion dollars. GE paid six-and-a-half billion for RCA, which owns NBC. The network portion of that deal amounted to less than four billion. CBS recently went for about thirty-seven billion, including their non-broadcast properties. Today, we could probably buy all three networks for about what Exxon paid for Mobil."

Fenris paused a moment to clear his throat, then continued. As far as print is concerned, we're talking about the *New York Times, Washington Post, Dow Jones, Gannett, L. A. Times Syndicate, Time, Newsweek, Associated Press,* a few other key papers here and there, most of them struggling financially. For a few billion more, we can own them all. And we don't even have to put up all the money ourselves. A good deal of that can be borrowed. Throw in the greenmail profits, and I think you begin to see that this is almost a nickel and dime operation."

The voice of Dan Hollings, CEO of Tanner-Voight Industries, one of the largest chemical concerns in the world, rose above the ensuing din. "Luke, you can't be serious. As soon as word got out that you were making a move against—"

Fenris raised his hand for silence, waited a moment for the cacophony to subside, and then spoke without a trace of a smile on his lips. "Word won't get out. You all will make sure of that. This is revolution and failure will be fatal. Let me emphasize 'fatal'. I mean it literally. We all rise or we all fall together. Any problems?"

Several of those present thought they detected an eerie red glow flashing in the depths of Fenris's ice-blue eyes. It was a momentary thing that left as quickly as it came. The entire assemblage sat frozen as a single entity, riveted to their chairs, mesmerized by Fenris's performance. Then, abruptly, his eyes returned to normal, sparkling with blue fire. "Needless to say, all of this has to be accomplished in utmost secrecy. There cannot be even a hint that we are working in concert. Are we all clear on that?"

This time Peter Dante was the first to speak. "I think it's brilliant, Luke. I think we can pull it off. Absolutely."

"There's no question of that, Peter. It's just a matter of executing my plan."

"Forgive me for bringing it up," said Hollings somewhat timidly, "but this *is* illegal, like conspiracy or a violation of RICO or something? We can all wind up in jail."

"Illegal? Of course it's illegal." Fenris studied him with a look of genuine amusement. "Everything is illegal as far as the government is concerned. We have so many rules and regulations on every aspect of our lives, many of which are contradictory, that it's impossible for even the most law-abiding people not to be in violation of some law or another. That's the reason collectivists want so many laws. It gives them arbitrary discretion to go after anyone they don't like, anyone with the wrong political agenda. Take pricing laws for example. If you sell at a price below your competition, you can be indicted for 'predatory' pricing. If you sell for the same price, you could get indicted for price-fixing. And if you charge more than the competition does, you're 'gouging' or engaging in monopolistic practices. All businesses can be prosecuted or harassed into bankruptcy by these laws, but only the politically incorrect will feel the wrath of a politically corrupt Justice Department. Of course what I'm proposing is illegal. So what? It's not immoral. I said in the beginning that there's criminal risk here. We're making a revolution together. We're all totally committed, heart and soul. There's no turning back now, as I made clear earlier." Fenris paused a moment. "Anything else?"

There were no further questions or comments.

"Fine. Study the instructions in your packets and give them back to Carl when you're done. Your individual roles are outlined in detail. I have to leave now, but I'll be in touch shortly."

Carl Navi rose from his chair, inserted his card and slid the wall open for Fenris to leave. Beyond the hearing of the others, he whispered to Navi, "Don't say anything about the rest of the plan for now. Everything in due course."

"Trust me." The shorter man smiled.

Fenris could almost feel Peter Dante's eyes drilling holes in his back as he stepped through the passageway. He knew the man was churning inside with a fear that bordered on panic. An instant later the wall slid back in place behind him. He kissed Danielle goodbye and told her he would see her soon, as soon as he wrapped up a business deal in Brazil. It was a lie but he wasn't quite ready to tell her about his strange disappearances for weeks at a time. Then he was aloft, his black helicopter silhouetted against the full moon high above.

CHAPTER TEN

The large gray wolf stood secreted from the street in the dark shadows of the tenement alleyway, its nose sniffing the air for the scent of danger, its tongue lapping out over its jaw as it panted in the heavy heat. It was hungry and needed to eat. A giggling child on the street caught its attention, and the wolf stalked out from behind a garbage bin and stared into the darkness. A pink rubber ball came bouncing from the street and rolled toward the wolf's feet. The wolf sniffed it, then looked up toward the street. A boy ran into the alley, and stopped close to where the wolf stood watching. The wolf bared its teeth, emitting a soft growl. It didn't move. The boy and the wolf stared at each other, the wolf's eyes glinting in the darkness. Then the boy smiled. He reached forward and touched the wolf's head, rubbed it behind the ears.

"Perro bonito," the boy said as he continued to stroke the wolf's head.

The wolf's tongue lapped the boy's hand, then stopped. It perked up its ears at a new sound from the street.

"Aiyeee!" The wolf heard the shriek first, and then saw the woman running down the alley. "No, Roberto!" She grabbed the boy around the waist and pulled him away. She ran with the boy back toward the street and the wolf trotted behind them.

"Cujo!" The boy looked back, smiling, watching the wolf follow along.

The wolf stopped under a street lamp and looked around as people screamed and ran in all directions, searching for a safe haven. It saw the woman running with the boy across the street and darted after them. The woman tripped on a pothole and lost her balance, cradling the boy in her arms as she fell. The wolf ran up and put its muzzle an inch from her face; a low rumble bubbled up from its throat. The woman's eyes were wide with terror. She tried to scream but no sound came out. The wolf peered into her terror-stricken eyes, leaned forward, and then licked the boy's cheeks. A moment later it galloped off into the night.

The night wore on and the wolf patrolled the neighborhood, hiding furtively in the shadows, slithering along through passages and alleyways. Its hunger deepened. On the corner stoop ahead the wolf saw two young males mumbling incoherently to each other, their heads bobbing up and down on their chests. On the steps beside them lay a hypodermic needle, a spoon, and a long thin rubber tube. The wolf approached and sniffed the syringe, sniffed the boys, then recoiled its head away from the smell of their polluted blood. Its hunger grew into a bloodlust for clean, warm, and healthy life-sustaining fluid.

The search continued throughout the night. In the early hours of the pitch-black morning, the wolf heard the sounds of heels clicking on the pavement. A pleasing flowery scent wafted across its nostrils. The wolf moved on and saw a young, dark-skinned female dressed in a white uniform walking in its direction. Behind her, closing on her quickly and quietly in the darkness, was a young wild-eyed male holding a metal blade in his right hand. Hunter and prey, the wolf intuited. The blood would soon be flowing and it was time for the wolf to strike.

The female stepped off the curb and the stalker grabbed her from behind. He wound his arm tightly around her waist and put the shiny blade to her throat. The wolf growled hungrily in anticipation of warm, healthy blood—the nourishing life force of a young male. The wolf crouched and crawled ahead on its belly. The female screamed and the wolf quickened its pace. From ten feet away the wolf could see the eyes of the young male widen in terror as he shifted his gaze. With flashing speed, the huge gray wolf leapt into the air, slicing the male's knife hand with its claws. It landed on all fours, then turned and saw the knife in the street and the male screaming as he ran away. The wolf bounded after him, leapt again and landed hard on the male's back. The wolf landed on top as they fell. The male reared back, his mouth open in a silent scream as the wolf swiped its claws across his throat. The male lay motionless in the street.

His blood flowed freely in a thick, dark stream. The wolf devoured it as it flowed, its tongue lapping the street dry until it had fully quenched its monstrous thirst. Finally, the wolf finished. It pointed its snout upwards toward the bright full moon, and unleashed a long series of inhuman, blood-curdling howls against the black canopy of the night.

As the wailing subsided, a new sound emerged from the wolf's throat, the ringing of a telephone. Alex Mallum popped awake abruptly, unsure of his surroundings. Gradually, his brain cleared, and the furnishings of his bedroom came more clearly into focus. The window was open, the sun was high and bright, the heat overpowering. The wolf dream again, he thought as he reached for the telephone.

"Alex?"

He grunted.

"Are you okay? Where've you been?"

"Sally?"

"Yes, you creep. Who'd you think? Where've you been keeping yourself anyway?"

"What do you mean? I've been right here since I left you."

"Like hell. I've been calling you for three days. We had a date the other night, remember?"

The other night? What was she talking about? Then it hit him: he had another one of his blackouts.

"I've literally been in a fog for a few days now, Sally. I caught the flu and dosed myself up with some crap that I must be allergic to. Totally knocked me out. I haven't even eaten since I saw you. What . . . what day is it anyway?"

"Well at least you're inventive. I never heard that one before. You stand me up and now I'm supposed to feel sorry for you."

"Look, I'm sorry." Alex rubbed his hand down his face. "I'll tell you what. Give me a few hours to take a shower, grab a bite, and pull myself together. I'll come by for you later, say around seven-thirty or eight. Okay?"

"I don't know if I want to see you. I still think you're a creep."

"Give me a break, will you? I've been sick, still am. I swear."

"Well . . . I don't know." The waver in her voice betrayed her true feelings.

"Give me another chance. Please. I'll make it up to you, I promise."

"I probably shouldn't, you know."

"Say yes, okay?"

"Well, just this once. But if you ever do anything like that to me again, Alex . . . " She left the rest of her thought unfinished.

"Scouts' honor. See you later."

After he hung up, Alex checked his clock and turned on the radio. Eleven A.M., Sunday morning. That meant he had been out for three nights this time. What had he done? Where had he been? Cooped up in his apartment? Or . . . ?

He showered and had his usual Sunday breakfast, bacon and eggs at the Bagel Nosh, then sauntered over to Washington Square Park with the Times. He read it through quickly, observing the usual parade of oddballs between sections, and saved the business section for later. Then he wandered toward the chess tables and scouted up a couple of games. His play was strong this afternoon as he took two out of three and netted ten bucks on side bets.

On the way back to his apartment at the end of the afternoon, Alex thought about the problem of his blackouts. They started soon after he first arrived in New York, lasted two or three days at a time, and recurred every few weeks or so. At first he was alarmed, then dismissed it with a joke, blaming it on an allergy to the city's air or water. Maybe he just needed to withdraw periodically from the frantic pace of life in the Big Apple, something he hadn't yet gotten used to. Before long, however, it became obvious that his blackouts coincided with the appearances of the full moon. It was neither an oddity he could explain nor one he cared to discuss with doctors or therapists. He just accepted it. Like he accepted the dream about Tanya back at that inn in California. The dreams were probably the result of a chemical imbalance, he guessed, something affected by the moon's gravitational pull, like the ebb and flow of the tides. But, he had to admit that the problem had become more alarming. He forgot about the time sequence when he made the date with Sally and it got her angry, something he could ill afford. He had to face up to the fact that something serious was going on. The blackouts and the wolf dreams? Were they related? Did they have anything to do with the night he spent at the Pentagram Pub and Inn? He had caught something out in the rain; he was feverish, out of his head completely. There was that bizarre dream about Tanya and then the shocking reality of the following morning. Perhaps it was time to see a psychiatrist, much as he had always distrusted them. But how could he talk to anyone about his mysterious problems, including his run-in with the mob? No one could be trusted with that information, with the knowledge of his true identity. He had no alternative but to keep his own counsel.

Then there was the question of Sally Milano. She knew who he was. She had recognized him and promised to protect him, and now he had upset her with his mysterious disappearance. If it continued, he risked alienating her altogether and jeopardizing his safety. Once again, he felt his world shaking beneath him.

Alex had a couple of hours to kill before his date with Sally, so he settled onto the sofa and clicked on the television. Sixty-five channels had little to offer except multiple showings of the same movies, tractor pulls and other bizarre sports events, old sit-coms, look-and-sound-alike music videos, and World War II documentaries. He was about to give it up as a lost cause and dive into a book when an interview program came on, hosted by Jane Godiva. She, at least, was easy to look at, so Alex decided to check it out.

"Our guest tonight is Ludwig von Dracula of the Vampire Liberation Front," Godiva said with a broad smile on her gorgeous face. She was reporting from the sidewalk in front of a loft building in Tribeca. The camera followed her as she entered the building and walked up three flights of stairs. Alex was about to turn off the television in disgust—what crap, he thought; the media pretend to be impartial in its coverage and gives air time to screwballs like this. But all it does is divert attention away from the real issues. Radicals like me never got a hearing. Try to have a *serious* discussion of political issues on television, and the media just revert back to the same old establishment agenda. He would have flicked off the set if the sight of Jane Godiva's rump ascending the stairs had not been so riveting.

"Since Mr. Dracula only comes out at night," Godiva was saying as she ascended, "we taped this interview in advance instead of doing our usual live show. Our guest today is a commercial artist, winner of three Clio awards for his work in the advertising industry. Mr. Dracula says he is an honest-to-goodness vampire who has decided to come out of the coffin, so to speak, to put an end to the victimization of vampires. I don't know if he's real or not, but I'm not taking any chances. I've brought with me a crucifix, a clove of garlic, and several sharp wooden stakes. Well, here we are outside his door."

She winked into the camera and knocked. What a travesty, Alex thought. The country's going to hell in a hand-basket, and all we get are documentaries on the latest East Village pop fad, like these phony vampire cults that have taken over some of the best clubs. Talk about pabulum for the masses.

The man who opened the door was boyishly handsome, not yet out of his twenties, with neatly combed blond hair down to his shoulders. He was slim and muscular, dressed in jeans, boots, and a T-shirt. A large button displayed over his heart read: BLOOD *IS* THICKER THAN WATER. He carried a can of beer in his right hand.

"Mr. Dracula?"

"Yo. Come on in." He swept his arm in a grand arc toward the living room. Jane Godiva entered his apartment, and the two of them settled side-by-side on a blue-and-white sofa.

"Excuse me," Dracula said. "Do I smell fresh garlic?"

"Just a small clove under my shirt." The interviewer smiled conspiratorially into the camera.

"Fortunately," Dracula responded, "it isn't chopped and cooked. Otherwise I could have a severe allergic reaction."

"Really?"

"Yes. I suppose you brought along a crucifix and wooden stakes as well?"

"They're no bigger than pencils actually."

"I agreed to do a serious interview with you today, and now it turns out you've decided to treat it like some sort of a freak show with the usual vicious stereotypes before we even get started."

"To be honest with you, Mr. Dracula—

"Ludwig. Call me Ludwig."

"Yes, thank you. To be honest with you, Ludwig, you should be aware that most of our viewers don't believe in vampires. Most people, myself included, assume that such creatures exist only in folklore and in horror films. To begin, how do we know you really are a vampire?"

"I explained to you on the telephone how we've been persecuted for centuries."

"Yes, yes, but how can we be sure? Can you turn into a bat for example?"

"A bat, a wolf, mist. Whatever I want actually."

Godiva turned back to the camera, winked and smiled, then said, "Our viewers would love to see you in action. Why don't you turn into a bat for us?"

"Don't be ridiculous."

"But you said you could."

"If you were interviewing Jesse Jackson, would you ask him to prove he's black by doing a tap dance or shooting hoops?"

"Surely you can't be equating racism with . . . with—?"

"With discrimination against vampires? Yes I am, precisely. Bigotry takes many forms, Jane."

"I don't mean to sound patronizing, Ludwig, but if you're asking us to believe that vampires are real and you're one of them, it's incumbent on you to offer some measure of proof. At least clear up some inconsistencies. Your reflection, for instance."

"My reflection?"

"Yes, I can see it in the mirror there."

Dracula glowered at her with a look that was part pain and part infuriation. "Whatever gave you the idea that I shouldn't have a reflection?"

"Well, in the movies . . . "

"Another example of vampire stereotyping. Did I tell you I was a stealth aircraft? I live and breathe the same as you and, yes, I also have a reflection. I am not an agent of the devil, I don't have a closet full of zombies waiting to conquer the world, I don't shrivel up in front of crucifixes and holy water, and if you drive a stake through my heart, I die just like every other living creature." When he finished, Dracula's eyes were brimming with tears.

"I . . . I didn't mean to offend you." Godiva was wavering now between her playful tone and genuine concern that she may have stepped over the line. "I'm just trying to sort out reality from myth here."

"The reality is that vampires have been persecuted for centuries by religious fanatics. Here, look at this." He pulled a small blue case from the drawer of a side table. He opened it and held four silver crucifixes of various sizes up to the camera. "These were given to my great great grandfather, Vlad von Dracula, by the King of Romania in recognition of his role in driving out the Turkish invaders and liberating the nation many centuries ago."

"*Vlad* von Dracula? *The* Count Dracula?"

"None other. Murdered by Van Helsing and his scurvy band of bigots—*fleder-phobes* if you will—an Old European version of the Ku Klux Klan."

"I . . . I don't quite know what to say."

"Van Helsing was a local bully boy who traveled with a band of hoodlums. My great great grandfather came upon them one night when they were molesting a young woman, and he gave them all a sound thrashing. Van Helsing vowed revenge. One night he and his thugs sneaked into Vlad's castle and drove a stake through his heart. It was he, Van Helsing, who originated some of the most vicious lies about vampires to justify his own dark deed. He whipped the public into such a panic, they even elected him mayor. Until that time vampires had been revered as an honored group in society."

"You're saying that it was this Van—Van—?"

"Van Helsing."

"Van Helsing who started all these stories about vampires and crucifixes and garlic and—"

"Precisely. Let us not forget that Christians, at the time, were the architects of the Crusades, the Inquisition, witch burnings, pogroms against Jews, then later the enslavement of blacks and Indians. They were the ones who went about thrusting crucifixes in everyone's face, demanding surrender. Vampires had long been horrified by Christian fanaticism and violence, worried that they might be next on the list. All they ever wanted was to be left alone to live in peace. Because vampires preferred to keep to themselves and not be swept up in all the fanaticism and hysteria, they were branded as agents of the devil who feared the cross."

"I must say, this is all very enlightening. What do vampires believe in anyway?"

Alex couldn't believe her. Was she actually being taken in by all this lunacy? Jane Godiva? His estimation of her went into free-fall.

"For the most part, we worship Apollo Lycus, patron of the arts and sciences."

"Part of the misunderstanding, Ludwig, is due to the fact that vampires are said to come out only at night, when the rest of the world is sleeping. Can you shed some light on that subject . . . no pun intended?"

"It's unfortunately true. The vampire species suffers from a genetic problem. Even brief exposure to sunlight triggers a cellular breakdown that results in skin cancer."

Jane turned to the camera with a look of bleeding-heart concern on her face. Alex identified with her compassion for victims of bigotry and discrimination, but thought it was misdirected here. He was not at all convinced that Ludwig von Dracula and his fellow vampires were a new "minority" that needed to be protected. He felt it was demeaning to *real* downtrodden minorities to include vampires among their ranks.

"Our guest today looks human in every way, yet he has volunteered to come forward with his story." She turned back to Dracula. "Why are you going public after all these years, Ludwig?"

"Like most persecuted people, I got tired of living a lie, pretending to be something I'm not. I'm a vampire and I'm proud of it. We have a magnificent heritage and culture. It's about time the world knew about our contribution to the arts and sciences. That's why we're sponsoring the 'Open Coffin Art Exhibition,' where several prominent artists will reveal their vampire nature."

"Can you tell our audience who some of the leading vampire artists and scientists are?"

"We all have to decide individually to go public on our own. Personally, I hope that more and more vampires will find the courage to step forward and reveal their true identities. As far as those long dead are concerned, I don't think there's any harm revealing who they were. Among the vampire artists were Beethoven, Michelangelo, Rembrandt, and Goya. Our scientists included Edison, da Vinci, and Archimedes. And, of course, there was my uncle Victor—Victor Frankenstein. Over two centuries ago he discovered the secret of DNA, way ahead of contemporary biologists. He invented gene-splicing in the first place. But the religious fanatics wouldn't leave him alone. They put pressure on the government to suppress his findings, to regulate scientific research. Hence, the Transylvania Science Administration was born. It was impossibly bureaucratic and inefficient, not unlike today.

"Well, Uncle Victor refused to put up with it. He single-handedly organized a strike of vampire scientists in Transylvania, the home of ninety percent of the vampire population. Scientific progress came to a screeching halt. A whispering campaign ensued among the human population, blaming vampires for the breakdown in society. They accused us of practicing witchcraft and black science—manufacturing an army of zombies—artificial humans—to overthrow the government and establish a vampire dictatorship. The demagogues had a field day, stirring up the peasants then standing back and allowing them to burn our homes and kill our people. But many escaped, including my uncle Victor.

"Victor gathered together the remnants of our decimated community and told them, in effect, that they had been responsible for most of the progress and development in the world—increased life expectancy, industrial growth, art and music—and they had asked for nothing in return except to be left alone. He said, 'If humans think they can do without us, let us give them their wish.' He led his followers into seclusion, but over the centuries many continued to do their work— under the guise of human beings. It was safer to just try to 'blend in,' as it were."

Jane was drooling empathy, and Alex wanted to throw up. This was all so preposterous it would have been hilarious if she didn't seem to be taken in by this space cadet.

"You've told us an absolutely harrowing tale, Ludwig," she said. "Yet one more example of human beings' capacity for persecuting those among us whose only crime is that they are 'different.' Now we come to perhaps the most critical part of our discussion. Just what is it your organization is seeking, Ludwig?"

"We demand the rights of survival, Jane, like everyone else. Life, liberty, and . . . nourishment."

"By nourishment you mean—?"

"Blood."

"Blood? Are we talking about—?"

"Human blood. It's the only substance that sustains us. We require it in order to continue our existence."

"Pardon me for sounding obtuse." Jane looked genuinely befuddled now, not wanting to hurt his feelings, but seeking clarification without offending. "But, doesn't that, wouldn't that, I mean, be a violation of human rights?"

"Depends on how you look at it. Is it a violation of animal rights for humans to eat cows, pigs, chickens, fish?"

"But, those are lesser species, Ludwig."

"Well, pardon me for stating the obvious, but on the evolutionary ladder humans stand a few rungs below vampires. Using your logic, if humans have the right to devour cows and pigs, why shouldn't vampires have the same right in the pecking order of things?"

"But we're practically the same species!" Godiva's face registered alarm, fear, shock. Alex Mallum was ready to dive through the screen and slap some sense into her. "Wake up!" he shouted at the screen. "This is a spoof."

"We only look alike," Dracula said. "True, humans look more like vampires than apes look like humans, but that's only on the surface. Humans would have to mutate genetically to advance to the same plane of intelligence as vampires. We have the ability to read minds, transfigure ourselves, the power of telekinesis, humans don't except on a very rudimentary level. Humans believe in butchering their own species as well as subspecies, vampires don't. Having said all that, I want it clearly understood that we are not advocating *killing* human beings, merely sucking a little blood. So what's the big deal?"

Alex had never seen Jane Godiva so rattled. Normally the picture of telegenic aplomb, Dracula had nearly succeeded in reducing her to a quivering wreck.

"But don't people, humans I mean, die from that? Like with puncture wounds on the neck and all?"

"Another nasty stereotype, Jane. My organization is offering a hundred thousand dollars to anyone who can prove a human died from a vampire bite. In every instance where a human body has been found with fang marks, we've been able to demonstrate that death was a result of other causes. As a matter of fact, fang marks actually protect humans. They're signals to other vampires that this human has already been used and should therefore be left alone. We are not so stupid as to deplete our only supply of nourishment. Besides, if the government would legalize private commercial blood banks, the whole blood-sucking issue would be moot."

"Ludwig, I—"

"Luddie. Call me Luddie," he said, resting his hand on top of hers.

"Luddie, I'm sure our viewing audience finds this all as fascinating as I do. But aren't you being somewhat biased yourself?" Godiva, professional that she was, seemed to have regained her composure. "Are you saying that humans should do nothing to protect themselves? Are there no such things as bad vampires who might go out of their way to harm humans?"

"Yes and no. Let me explain. No pureblood vampire would ever intentionally harm another creature. However, over the centuries, there have been some mixed marriages, and therein lies the problem."

"By mixed marriages you mean

"Vampire-human marriages. Vampires have fought against them, but love is a powerful aphrodisiac. In rare instances . . . and I emphasize the word rare . . . the offspring of these unions can inherit dangerous characteristics. These are twofold. First, some of them lose the physical need for blood, while simultaneously possessing a psychological mania to see blood flowing. They usually gravitate towards politics.

"The second and by far rarer group—we believe there are only a handful in existence, living in California—is composed of mutants who experience unusual changes during the three days in which the moon is fullest."

Alex's entire sensory apparatus tingled with these words—three days, full moon. Was there a correlation? For the first time during the entire interview he wondered if there could be a kernel of truth in what this character was saying, fantastic as it sounded.

"This second group," Dracula continued, "can be dangerous and unpredictable. Humans refer to them as werewolves. For some genetic reason they are incapable of reproducing and, therefore, they are the end of their particular bloodlines—with one exception. In the rarest instances—so rare it is statistically insignificant—these so-called werewolves harbor a bacteria in their saliva that can infect the human bloodstream and pass on these traits."

"So there is some danger to humans after all?"

"I assure you, Jane, that we as a species are doing everything in our power to eliminate this threat. Once again I have to emphasize that we are talking about an extremely rare phenomenon, no more than one in ten million if that. Still—"

"I'm afraid I have to cut you off at this point. I wish we had more time to explore this further, but we've got to sign off. Thank you again, Luddie, for a fascinating interview. Those who wish more information on this topic can write to Ludwig von Dracula at the Vampire Liberation Front in New York City or care of this station."

Alex Mallum clicked off the set. He hadn't been this agitated in ages. His seething emotions were tossing him in six directions at the same time. On one hand, he assumed the whole vampire thing was a joke. On the other hand, there was something horrendously wrong with his biological system, something related to the appearance of the full moon; he could no longer deny it or dismiss his mysterious blackouts with jokes.

He checked his watch. It was time to pick up Sally. Against his better judgment, he decided to follow the urging within and drop a note to this Dracula clown. If he was for real, then Alex had to talk to him. How did you compose a letter to a vampire without sounding like a kook? It occurred to him that, if Ludwig knew what he was talking about, he would recognize the names of Lothar and Tanya from California. Why not simply say that he had a message from them and let it go at that?

When he finished, he bounded down the stairs, dropped the letter in the corner mailbox, and then hurried off to meet Sally.

CHAPTER ELEVEN

"So, you did show up after all."

"Sally, I said I was sorry. I feel like a normal human being again for the first time in days."

Despite her admonishing tone, Alex could tell she had forgiven him and was just making a face-saving point. Once again she was dressed for combat—beret, fatigues, lace-up boots. He thought her get-up bordered on the ridiculous, but he let it go. We all have our—peculiarities, shall we say?

He was happy to see her cats slithering around his legs again, instead of hissing at him and looking to draw blood. It was a further sign that things had returned to normal, whatever that meant these days. They purred and preened as he opened up some cans of expensive chow he had brought along to win them over. It worked.

"So, where to?" he said to Sally.

"I have a CRUSH meeting tonight and I thought maybe you could come along.

"CRUSH?"

"Committee to Rescue United States Humankind."

"Sounds impressive. What are we being rescued from?"

"Fascism. We want to do what's right and decent. We're small now but growing, Alex."

"How small is small?"

"Nine now but—"

"Nine?"

"Don't laugh, all right? I know that sounds silly to you after all the support you used to have, but—maybe if you came to the meeting you could give us some inspiration and special insights."

"Sally! What are you talking about?"

"I'm sorry. I just can't get it out of my head that you're Alex Mallum no matter what you say. Anyway, we need to make a revolution.'

Alex decided against further reprimand and tried to talk her out of her fantasy. "Still. Nine people, Sally. For God's sake."

"We've got to start someplace, Alex!" She put her hands on her hips and glowered at him. "I mean, like, if each member brings in one new member a month, and they all bring in one new member a month, in like two years we'll have a whole army. I mean, is that crazy or what?"

Alex heaved a sigh of exasperation. What was the point in arguing? Or denying who he was since she obviously didn't believe his protests? "Sally, listen. I've got to be careful."

She put her hands on his shoulders and looked directly into his eyes. "I promised you," she said. "To me a promise is a promise, a sacred oath like. No one will know who you really are. You're just there as a friend of mine, okay? Please."

"Shit!" He looked away.

"You've already changed your name. You can't hide in your apartment forever. I mean, you've got to go out and meet people sometime. You've got to continue to fight for what you believe in one way or another. Alex, if I'm not making any sense tell me to shut up right now."

He was trapped. He had to keep tabs on her, stay close to her, make sure she didn't betray him. Already he was beginning to feel like her prisoner. It was an absurd position to be in, but he had no alternative. Nine people! Nine maniacs trying to make a revolution. What the hell! How much harm could they do?

"Lead the way," he said.

The headquarters of the revolution was in a six-story tenement a few blocks away. CRUSH's office was on the top floor and, naturally enough, the building had no elevator. It seemed that nobody Alex knew these days lived below the fifth or sixth floor in a walk-up apartment building. As he suspected, the premises were more suited for rodent habitation than for human. The only reason the city hadn't condemned it was because no one cared anymore.

Sally introduced him to the others as Alex Maltese. The first one he shook hands with was five feet tall and well over two hundred pounds—so fat, in fact, that he could barely raise himself off the floor. His unruly beard all but obscured the front of his stained T-shirt, and exploded outward in every conceivable direction. But his beard was well groomed in comparison to his hair, which resembled a dead raccoon that had been left out in the rain for a couple of weeks.

"Meet Pinto," Sally said.

Pinto grunted, eyed Alex suspiciously, offered him a limp hand, and said, "You're not one of them fuckin' Sparticists, are you?"

"No," Alex calmly replied, suppressing a strong desire to giggle. Apparently incoherent factionalism was still alive and well on the left. He slipped his hand out from his interlocutor's wet grasp.

"Didn't think so. You look more like some sort of mealy-mouthed Trotskyite." Pinto stared straight at Alex's eyes to see if he got a rise out of him.

The group's leading theoretician, Alex thought to himself, and let out a soft sigh.

"My great granduncle helped plan Trotsky's assassination," Pinto added, still looking to see if he could get Alex's goat.

Sally pulled Alex away before Pinto could press on any further and introduced him to the other members.

"Okay, let's get started now," someone called out.

"Not yet," said a cadaverous woman with dark, frizzy hair and wire-frame glasses. "Kirk ain't here yet."

"Fuck him, Sharonna," Pinto said. "He knows what time we called the meeting for. That whimpering Maoist mother can't get here on time, we start without him."

In unison, everyone present began screaming at everyone else, debating the finer points of whether or not they should commence their meeting. The debate raged on for a full twenty minutes until a tall, red-haired man arrived wearing jeans and a white sweatshirt, and carrying a large can of beer. "Yo, sorry I'm late, gang," said Kirk.

Pinto glared at him as though he were a piece of rubbish blown in by the wind. "You know, man, you got to develop some revolutionary discipline. Who the fuck are you anyway?"

"Stuff it, you over-privileged Zapatista. I had some business to take care of."

"Who you tellin' to stuff it, mother? You fuckin' I.R.A. asshole!" Pinto charged Kirk, grabbed him around the waist and hoisted his thin frame into the air. Kirk hammered at him with his beer can as they crashed around the apartment.

Finally, a muscular black man with a trimmed beard, bald head, and gold earring grabbed both of them around the neck and said, "For Malcom's sake, dammit! Chill, bro, Chill before I bust some heads."

"I'm cool," Kirk said.

"Me too, Kenyatta. Leggo my fuckin' neck you pseudo-Leninist thug."

Kenyatta released his stranglehold, stared at both of them to be sure they didn't renew hostilities, then said, "Now we begin, 'less somebody got an objection. Jennifer, you go first with the treasurer's report."

A short thin woman with brown hair pulled back into a bun, wearing granny-glasses, hoop earrings and bracelets up to her elbows, rose to her feet. "Good news, gang." Her voice was high-pitched, reinforcing her schoolmarmish demeanor. "Sales of *CRUSH for Peace* netted a hundred and twenty-seven dollars last month, giving us a total of six hundred and forty-three dollars in our bank account."

"No fuckin' way!" Doug jumped into the middle of the floor. He was about twenty-two, with close-cropped blond hair and a scraggly mustache. "I brought in almost that much myself last month."

"So what are you suggesting, Doug?" Jennifer seemed to take his remark personally.

"Somebody ain't pullin' her weight around here, and it ain't me."

Jennifer erupted in tears and collapsed onto the floor.

"Cut the bullshit!" the voice of Nicky Santangelo screamed from the kitchen. A moment later he appeared, awesome in his camouflage fatigues with ripped-off sleeves, combat boots, red bandanna around his forehead, and sheathed hunting knife hanging from his belt. "This paperwork shit is diversionary, man. Let's get down to action."

Jennifer shook her head from side to side, weeping. "If we can't trust each other," she said. "If there's so little trust—"

"I'm not bustin' my ass if everybody else is shirkin'," Doug said. "I mean this might as well be a meeting of the Young Republicans, for all the revolutionary fervor I find here."

"That's not a very caring attitude," said Maria, a short attractive woman with high cheekbones and long, straight, black hair. "We love Jennifer and accept her as she is. Not everyone is as dynamic as you, Doug."

"Jennifer works real hard at what she does," Sally said.

Alex stared at her, then at the others in wonderment.

"That caring shit's for later, man, after the revolution. Right now we need some action," Nicky said.

"The man needs action," Kenyatta said, jumping to his feet again. "The man ain't happy 'less he blowin' somethin' up. The man got dynamite for a brain. He think he still over there in Desert Storm blowin' Ay-rabs up. The man right, we need some action instead of all this candy-ass bullshit. Know what I'm sayin'?"

"We need to buy some dynamite and blow up a building," Nicky said. "Show them we mean business."

"Bombs, huh. You're whistlin' out your asshole, man," Pinto said. "Guns is what we need. We ain't goin' nowhere unless we get some money and the banks is where it's at. I move we do a job on Chase. The Castroite symbolism's beautiful."

"May I say something, please?" Jennifer had herself under control now as she wiped the last of the tears from her eyes. Everyone fell silent to give her a turn to speak. "We can't rob Chase, that's where we keep our bank account. I move we hold up Citibank instead."

"Yeah, and her daddy works at Chase." Doug sneered at Jennifer then smirked at the others. Once again she melted into tears.

"You want symbolism, Pinto?" Kirk said. "Then why don't we waste some pigs? Or maybe you're too chickenshit for that, hah? No revolutions during siesta for you."

Pinto started to lunge but Kenyatta held him back. "It's time to take a vote," he said. "I move we kidnap the mayor and hold him for ransom."

Alex couldn't restrain himself any longer. He waved his hand for silence, then took the floor. "Look, I don't mean to be negative about all this, but you're heading off in the wrong direction. I've got some experience at this, I won't say where. But I think I can put together a plan that'll bail you all out. You need money first and foremost—nobody's going to pay a nickel to rescue our dipshit mayor, and robbing banks is a tough job even for professional bank robbers. I got an idea that can net us about a hundred grand. Give me a few days to work out the details. Sally can vouch for the fact that I deliver what I say I will. It's up to you."

Sally was perhaps more surprised than anyone else present, but she wasted no time in backing him up. The talk of real money—how much did he say? A hundred grand?—ushered in an air of reverence that had them all nodding at one another like mutes. It was like Fidel himself had spoken. Like Che, like Mao. Whoever this dude was that Sally had brought to the party, he sounded like his head was screwed on the right way. The meeting broke up about four in the morning, and they agreed to adjourn for three days to consider Alex's plan.

On the way back to Sally's, through streets that were still teeming with human flotsam of every description, Sally said, "Alex, that was wonderful, the way you just . . . took control like that. It was just like what I remember about you back in California. You're a born leader, you really are. I can't wait to hear your plan."

"Plan, Sally? Come on, get real."

"What do you mean?"

"Your friends are clowns. They're misfits and psychotics. Kidnap the mayor? Rob a bank? Blow up a building? The fascist swine who run this country can sleep well tonight if this is the best the opposition can come up with."

"Alex!" Sally planted herself on the sidewalk, hands on hips, staring at him with fire in her eyes. "You can't do this to me. Those are my friends regardless of what you think of them. I vouched for you! You can't leave me high and dry. It's not fair. It's not honest."

"You can't be serious. Those . . . those idiots up there couldn't decide on what they want for breakfast tomorrow, let alone how to start a revolution. The only thing they're going to succeed in doing is getting themselves arrested, and you along with them."

"There are certain things I believe in and I thought you did, too. Look how far you stuck your neck out, out there in California. I can't—"

"I had an organization, I had financial backing. We had a shot, a slim one, but a chance to make a difference nonetheless. These jerks—"

"That's why they need you—*we* need you, Alex. You've been there. You know how to organize, how to raise money, how to get things done. You can't just say something like that to them, ask me to vouch for you, then wash your hands and walk away."

Her gaze was unrelenting, and Alex could see she was not going to back away. By taking the initiative, he had only mired himself in more deeply. Why couldn't he have bitten his tongue a while longer and allowed the meeting to disintegrate on its own?

"Okay," he said. "You're right. Give me a few days to come up with something and I'll see what I can do."

"You mean it?"

"Trust me."

She held his gaze a moment longer, and then took his arm as they continued back toward her apartment. Wonderful, Alex thought. Three days to come up with a plan for nine nincompoops to launch a revolution.

Chapter Twelve

Alex put them off for a few weeks, buying time while he pretended to be working on his Grand Plan. But as the next full moon cycle drew nearer, he began to worry more and more about his recurring wolf dreams and those blackout spells. Was there a correlation or not? He needed to have some answers, but so far his letter to Ludwig von Dracula had gone without response. Perhaps, he thought, it was madness to expect any peace-of-mind would be forthcoming from that direction. Still, he needed to take some precautions.

The following day he went to the hardware store on Second Avenue and Ninth Street and bought some duct tape. Back in his apartment, he sealed the door and windows, and sprinkled talcum powder in the area. Next he photographed his handiwork to have a record of what his surroundings looked like before any possible blackout took place.

Completely sealed in, he took a Chinese dinner from the freezer and put it in the oven to warm up. He drank a beer slowly, waiting for his dinner, when the timer suddenly went off. As Alex bent over to get his food, a sudden flash of dizziness overwhelmed him. It passed a few moments later, and Alex took his dinner out of the oven and sat down to eat. He raised a forkful to his mouth when the dizziness hit him again. As he swallowed the first bite, he discovered to his astonishment that his meal was lukewarm. Alex checked his watch—twenty-five minutes had passed since the oven timer went off.

How could that be?

As best he could recall, he had walked over to the oven to get his food, experienced a flash of dizziness, regained his balance and walked back to the table where he felt dizzy again—a transaction that should have taken thirty seconds at most. Where had the twenty-five minutes gone to? Next he was overcome by a blistering thirst unlike any he had experienced since—since the morning after his curious night with Tanya years before.

Alex went over to the refrigerator to get a beer, then thought better of it. Beer made him drowsy and he wanted to remain alert. He fixed a pitcher of iced tea instead and quickly consumed it with several large gulps. Hunger was not his problem now, but thirst. He tossed his dinner in the trashcan and filled the pitcher back up with water.

Again a wave of dizziness struck.

His head ached, he felt himself swooning. Alex grabbed hold of the back of the chair to steady himself. The aching head got worse and his thirst intensified. Aspirin was what he needed—aspirin washed down with a gallon of water. Summoning all the strength he could, he stepped toward the bathroom door and collapsed. Pushing ahead on his hands and knees he found the sink, pulled himself up and groped for the aspirin bottle in the medicine cabinet.

Again he fell.

He staggered back up, swallowed the aspirin and washed it down with a cup of cool water, but still the thirst remained and the aching in his head got worse. Alex pushed himself back from the sink and propelled himself into the living room, wobbling as he bounced from the wall to a chair to a table, and into the kitchen. Somehow he remained erect.

His thirst was now stronger than ever. He filled the pitcher brimful with water and tried to drink it down, but his stomach felt ready to burst and he barely sipped a few drips.

The pounding in his head grew worse.

Alex touched his brow; his skin was on fire. His vision blurred and the contents of his apartment melted together in a wash of color and light. He fell to his knees, then forward onto his hands, and crawled in slow motion toward the bedroom. If only he could make it to his bed, lie down and get some sleep. Inch by inch he creeped ahead on hands and knees until he was almost there. Soon he would be in his bed, fast asleep.

The threshold was as far as he got.

Alex's arms gave out from under him and he rolled onto his side. In a second, blessed unconsciousness descended upon him.

Later the same evening, Luke Fenris stepped through the revolving doors of Xanadu Towers and took the elevator to his twentieth-floor apartment. His maid Barbara was there when he entered.

"Good evening, Mr. Fenris. Did you have a pleasant trip?"

"Very productive. Did Mr. Navi take care of things while I was gone?"

"Yes, sir. There are some phone messages for you in your study. Miss Dante called to say her flight from Cancun was delayed and she wouldn't be here until tomorrow. Also, a Mr. Farlin called to confirm tonight's appointment at midnight."

"Excellent. I'll be busy with him tonight, and possibly tomorrow night. I won't be needing you for a couple of days so I've made reservations for you at the Waldorf. Charge anything you want, dinner, theater, breakfast, to your room."

"Thank you, sir." Barbara beamed. "Will you be needing anything before I leave?"

"Nothing. Enjoy yourself."

When she left, Fenris went into his study and pored through the various memos Navi had left for him. Everything was moving ahead as planned with one exception: Dan Hollings was having second thoughts about participating. He apparently had stressed out over the recent indictments of dozens of corporate executives for various securities infractions. No one was supposed to be able to back out, but Navi felt that Hollings was secure. "He can be trusted to remain silent if he has no risk," Navi had written in a memo, "but if he panics he may talk."

Fenris was not so sure. If anything goes wrong and Hollings is questioned later on, he will suddenly be at risk and might panic. Fenris decided to go along with Navi for now, and deal with the matter more thoroughly later. Pity, too. He had liked Hollings and believed he was made of sterner stuff. Hollings was a tough, no-nonsense manager. When Fenris took over Tanner-Voight a while back, he put Hollings in charge. He was a valuable employee, but not irreplaceable. Fenris dictated a memo to Tanner-Voight's board of directors, ordering the immediate dismissal of Hollings—but on friendly terms, with a handsome bonus and severance package—and named his successor.

He spent the rest of the evening revising his plan, and finished a little before midnight. When he was done he placed his notes in the top left drawer of his desk, then went over to the bar and fixed himself a Chivas Regal on the rocks. He was sipping his drink in his gray leather club chair, reading *the Economist*, when the intercom buzzed.

"Mr. Farlin is here to see you."

"Send him up."

Farlin was tall and stocky, with red hair and dark glasses.

Fenris recognized the red hair for what it was: a disguise. The man wearing it was actually General Revilo Thorn, and he was carrying a thick leather briefcase. Fenris nodded at him and ushered him inside, watching him remove the hair and eyeglasses, revealing a clear-eyed, good-looking man with close-cropped gray hair.

"Good evening, General," Fenris said, dropping the "Farlin" pretense as soon as they were alone.

"Evening to you." Thorn took in the elegant decor as Fenris led him into the living room. Thorn's name did not appear on any roster of military personnel, yet he was one of the top military leaders in the country, Commander of the United

States Ghost Commandos, a secret worldwide network of combat experts trained in espionage and guerrilla warfare. One of his assignments was to direct the assassinations of the political and military leaders of hostile nations, in the event of an attack on the U.S. Other assignments included retaliation against terrorist forces that seized American citizens and covert support for anti-Communist resistance movements. His counterpart existed in a few other nations—Russia, the former East Germany now merged with West Germany, England, Israel, and North Korea—but none had Thorn's reputation for organizational and strategic genius.

The general accepted a scotch and soda and raised his glass to Luke. "To *our* New World Order."

"Let freedom ring." Fenris sipped his own drink, and then said, "So what do you have for me?"

Thorn removed a stack of documents from his briefcase and handed them to Fenris. "Basically, the plan is proceeding well," he said. "Nkoto's a third-rate con man, always playing us off against the Japs and the Euro-weenies. Everybody throws money at him, and most of it winds up in his bank account while his people in Bruwanda starve. His value to us, and everyone else, lies in the uranium and chrome deposits, along with an outlet to the ocean.

"Bruwanda borders South Africa, and Nkoto's managed to keep the new regime there happy too. He offers them a black market trade conduit with Latin American neo-Nazis allied with militant South African whites as well as military support if civil war with white separatists should break out. His line is moderately Marxist as a sop to his ignorant followers, but he practices expediency—international welfarism with him at the receiving end. Not a bad deal for the corrupt little swine.

"Our boy there is Lomono, the sanest of a motley pack of rebels. He's Harvard educated and professes to believe in democracy, although I personally doubt that anyone who attended Harvard could have the vaguest notion of—"

"Go on, General." Luke stopped him before he launched into a twenty-minute spiel about the horrors of academia. "Just the facts, if you please."

"Yes, well, as I was saying, he's the best of the lot there. At present, the government controls about twenty-five percent of the land with seventy-five percent of the population, mostly around the capital of Nkotoville. Lomono has the loyalty of the smaller of the two big tribes in Bruwanda, and he's managed to forge a stalemate among his faction, another rebel group, and Nkoto's forces. That's the situation as it exists right now."

"Our interests rest with Lomono then?"

"Precisely. Officially, everybody's backing Nkoto only because he's still in power. But he's greedy and corrupt and nobody trusts him. Lomono seems to have some decency in him, and we've worked out a deal with him."

"What deal?"

"We provide advisers, weapons, and a substantial contingent of mercs to help Lomono seize control. In return, he'll grant us sovereignty over about thirty square miles of uninhabited territory with a narrow corridor to the ocean. In effect, we'll have our own government within the country to do as we wish."

"And if he reneges later?"

"We'll slit his throat and put a new boy in power. Once we have a foothold there, we'll be the dominant military force in the country, the tail that wags the dog, so to speak."

"How about the mercs? Recruiting going okay?"

"I've already got a hundred former Ghost Commandos to lead the assault team. We've also got thirty-five hundred support troops on line, most with jungle experience."

"How fast can we move?"

"Almost immediately, although we want to do it in stages. We don't want to tip our hand to Nkoto—or anyone else for that matter. The best course is to infiltrate slowly, keep our men dispersed while we train Lomono's army. Then, when they're ready, we bring it all together for a final strike, clean and surgical—December fifteenth at the latest, assuming you can get us the hardware on time."

"No problem. Dante doesn't know it yet, but I'll have control of his company within two weeks and get the process rolling."

"He doesn't know—?"

"None of them know anything about this part of the operation, except Navi and us. Everyone's on a need-to-know basis."

"I see." Thorn stared wide-eyed at Fenris. He hadn't even thought about that until this moment.

"Anything else?" Fenris said.

Thorn produced another report from his briefcase, handed it to Fenris and said, "Once Lomono's in control of Bruwanda, we'll have a permanent base of operations to strike out at the rest of Africa."

"Angola?"

"Mozambique first I would guess, then Angola, wherever we see a problem."

"Impressive, General. Let me see your projections for the first six months."

Thorn pointed to a section of the last report he handed Fenris. "All in there, Luke."

"This may take a while." Fenris scanned the file quickly. "Why don't you make yourself another drink and have a bite to eat in the kitchen, if you're hungry. Barbara left some turkey in the refrigerator."

Fenris lost track of time as he studied the report in detail, making notes as he went along. When he finished he checked his watch. Five A.M. Despite the hour he was wide awake. He went into the kitchen and found Thorn reading a newspaper at the kitchen table.

"You've done a remarkable job, General. I can't tell you how invaluable this is. Why don't you go home and get some sleep. I'll have Navi set up another meeting with you in a few weeks."

Thorn smiled, pleased with Fenris's reaction. "While I'm waiting I'll start getting my mercs in place. Good to see you again, Luke."

Fenris spent another hour going over Thorn's documents. The eastern skyline was beginning to show a glimmer of red when he was done.

Two hours later, the sound of the front door of his apartment slamming shut penetrated into his bedroom. Fenris opened his eyes and cocked his ears. He listened to the rapping on his bedroom door, and heard her voice call out, "Luke, sweetheart, it's me. Are you awake?"

"I'll be right there." Fenris got out of bed and walked over to the mirror above his dresser. Everything appeared normal. He tied on his blue silk bathrobe and unlocked the door.

"Darling."

Danielle jumped into his arms and kissed him hungrily. "I missed you," she said. "I don't understand why you keep locking your bedroom door. Suppose there's a fire or something? Besides . . . " She snuggled against him again. " . . . I'd like to slip in beside you and surprise you once in a while."

"You'd be sorry." Fenris smiled down at her. "I'm an ogre when I wake up unexpectedly. I might bite your head off without meaning to."

"Oh you . . . you should see what I'm like when I get up. We have to start getting used to each other you know. With all the traveling, we hardly see each other more than a couple of times a month."

"Maybe we should keep it that way . . . make love, go out to dinner once in a while, and stay friends. Marriage is the chief cause of divorce, you know."

"Not on your life, Luke Fenris." Danielle tossed an apple at him from the fruit bowl on the dining room table. "I finally got you to say yes. I don't care if we only get to see each other once a year, you're going through with it. I want a regular wedding with all the frills, even if it is my third."

"Careful. You might get addicted to them."

"This is for keeps. We have to set a date soon. Daddy keeps asking me when, and I don't know what to say."

"Soon, Danielle. Soon."

"When's that?"

"As soon as I get the nuts and bolts in place on this project . . . say by the end of November. How do you feel about a Christmas wedding?"

"Is that a commitment?"

"It's a done deal, and you know how I feel about them."

"Christmas it is then. Luke Fenris's latest merger deal. Can we go public with it, or do you want to keep it inside information?"

"I don't see why not."

"God, I love you, Luke."

She came to him and he pulled the zipper down on the back of her dress. Danielle slipped it off her shoulders and let it fall to the floor. She untied the belt on his robe and pushed it down off his body. Fenris took her hand, looked down at her with his blazing white smile, and led her back into his bedroom.

CHAPTER THIRTEEN

Peter Dante paced the ground floor living room of his Manhattan townhouse twenty blocks north on Fifth Avenue. Fenris had returned to New York the previous evening, he knew, and still he hadn't heard from him. The anxiety refused to leave. It gnawed away inside until he had reached a point where he couldn't sleep properly, couldn't concentrate on anything except where he stood with Fenris and Navi. Unable to stand the tension any longer, he picked up the telephone and dialed Fenris's number.

"Daddy!" Danielle answered on the second ring. "We were just talking about you."

"Hiya, sugar." Dante was pleasantly surprised. As long as his daughter and Fenris were an item, he felt he was secure. "Just thought I'd check in and see how everybody was doin'."

"We have the greatest news and we wanted you to hear it first. Luke and I are all set for Christmas. I finally pinned the rascal down."

"That's wonderful, darling. I'll throw the biggest bash this town's seen in years. Dante and Fenris. What a combo, a team that can't be beat."

"Luke's right here. Let me put him on. He wants to say hello."

Dante could hear Fenris's muffled voice on the other end, asking Danielle to wait in the living room so he could speak to her father privately about some business. A second later his voice was loud and clear on the line.

"Good to hear from you, Peter. How've you been?"

"Great, Luke. This is wonderful news. I can't tell you how thrilled I am."

"I'm thrilled, too, Peter. So thrilled, in fact, that I'm going to tell you right now what I want as a wedding present from you."

"Name it, Luke. I'd cut off my right arm for you, you know that."

"That won't be necessary. You're going to give me your company instead, Palliser Dynamics on a silver platter."

Dante could feel his stomach tighten and his testicles shrivel. Surely the man must be joking. "You got a strange sense of humor, Luke."

87

"I already own four and a half percent of your company on my own through open-market purchases, plus another sixteen percent through proxies. Once you sign your twenty-percent block over to me, I'll have far and away the single largest controlling interest."

"So it was you who was doing all that buying . . . you and your flunkies nibbling away at my company. You won't get away with this, Luke. I got the board on my side. I'll fight you right down the line."

"It's all over, Peter. You're dead meat floating in the water. I'm not just going to cast you adrift, though. After all, we're almost family now. You're my boy. You get to stay on as chairman, titular head of the company. Nobody will know I've got your balls in my pocket . . . unless you choose to make a public spectacle of yourself, that is."

"Fuck you, Fenris!" Dante was ready to explode. He could barely contain himself as he barked into the phone, spittle flying in all directions. "You can't get away with this! You can't just walk in and steal my company away from me!"

"You're overwrought. Your emotions are getting the best of you. Calm down and listen to me carefully. I've got enough on you and your cost overruns with the military, your deliberately shoddy quality controls on weapons programs to send you to jail for the rest of your life. I'm offended that you would accuse *me* of being a thief. Didn't Christ say, 'Let he who is without sin cast the first stone?'"

"I got leverage, too, Luke. I . . . I'll expose the plan to take over the media. I . . . I ain't gonna let you push me around."

"You can't do that, Peter . . . do you mind if I call you dad? You're already a co-conspirator yourself. I'm being generous with you, but my patience has a limit. If you turn down my offer, I'll seize control of your company anyway and throw you to the wolves. Either way I'll win. The decision is yours."

Dante slammed the receiver down in the cradle. He was so livid he could scarcely speak. He thought of calling Navi to hear his side, then decided against it. The two of them were asshole buddies, inseparable—at least until Fenris decided that Navi was expendable. The man had no shame, no spark of decency, no loyalty to anyone but himself. Dante needed to weigh his options carefully.

He poured himself a tumbler full of scotch and returned to his chair by the telephone. He sipped the scotch slowly at first, then swigged it down in large gulps. He could fight Fenris and risk exposure, possibly jail for both of them. Or, he could play hardball, take care of Fenris the same way he took care of Danielle's second husband. Nobody would ever find his body again. But that, too, was fraught with danger. Dante shuddered when he thought of what had happened to Fortunato and his boys. No one had ever succeeded in implicating Luke, but who else had the motive or the resources? The man was untouchable, almost inhuman.

Dante poured himself another drink, downed it, and then filled his tumbler again. On one hand I could fight him, and we all lose, he reasoned. If I go along I get to stay on as a figurehead, but maybe nobody will find out. I'll be taken care of and I save face at the same time. Any way he looked at it, Fenris had him by the balls—the eight hundred pound gorilla with its hand wrapped around them, waiting for an excuse to squeeze.

Dante staggered into his bathroom, succeeded finally in extracting a handful of aspirin tablets from a childproof bottle, then washed them down with the rest of his scotch. He stumbled back toward the telephone and dialed Fenris's number.

"You win, you prick." His words were noticeably slurred. "I'm gettin' too old for this shit. Welcome to the family. I hope you treat my daughter better than you're treatin' me."

"I can't tell you how much I appreciate your cooperation. Don't think of it as losing a company, but rather as gaining a warm-hearted son-in-law. Navi will draw up the papers. You'll have them in a week."

"Does Danielle know anything about this?"

"No, Dad. I'm not one of those men who brings his problems home from the office."

Dante put the receiver back down softly this time. He felt worn out, beaten, too tired to bounce back up and fight any longer. And sick inside. The combination of too much booze and aspirin on top of a heavy meal was not conducive to digestion. He stumbled into the bathroom, bent down low over the bowl, and felt the contents of his stomach bubble upward in an outpouring of food and bile.

Fenris and Danielle showered together, toweled each other dry, dressed, then left for a late dinner at Lutece. After dinner Danielle was exhausted, but Fenris insisted that they extend the festivities into the small hours of the morning. They danced, then stopped at a few popular midtown watering holes, and returned to Fenris's apartment at four-thirty in the morning, before dawn.

"I don't know where you get your energy from, darling," Danielle said. "You put in such grueling hours, then party all night long with hardly any sleep. You're incredible, Luke."

"You invigorate me, my love. I want to stay awake forever and just look at you."

Danielle wrapped her arms around his neck and kissed him. "You're sweet," she said. "Right now though, this party girl needs some sleep. I'm exhausted."

They spent the next day together, and then it was time to part.

"I can't believe where the time went, Luke. I have to get to the airport by eleven. I'm giving a speech in Austin in the morning."

"Martin's waiting downstairs with the car now. I'll ride with you to the airport, then I'm going to Asia myself for a few weeks."

"Can I meet you there when I'm through?" Danielle asked.

"I don't think so, love," he said. "Jungles, bugs, lots of nasty people. You wouldn't enjoy it at all."

"I'd enjoy being with you."

"Next time perhaps. This trip's not going to be much fun for me either, I assure you. We'd better get going now."

Martin was waiting for them with the car when they left the building. Fenris watched her board the plane, waved her off, and then returned to his apartment where he studied the Thorn reports until just before dawn. A little before sunrise, he took the elevator down to the lobby, and stepped outside onto the sidewalk.

Fenris walked down Fifth Avenue, thinking about how he always lied to Danielle about his lengthy disappearances—pretending that he was going off to distant places on business trips. He did not like lying to her; surely, it was not the best way to cement their relationship. But, for the moment, he felt that he had no other choice. Could she accept the truth yet? Was she ready for it? He thought about it a moment longer, then decided she was not. It was too early for the truth.

Chapter Fourteen

The cacophony of screaming voices and honking horns and clanging garbage pail lids lifted upward from the streets into Alex Mallum's apartment. Alex groaned, lifted the pillow from his face and listened for a long moment to the sounds of the city and the pigeons cooing on his window ledge. As he awakened gradually at first, then with a start, he noticed that the pigeons were not only on the ledge outside; half a dozen or so were sitting on the foot of his bed. He turned his face toward the window, and saw that the glass was shattered. Jagged shards stuck out from the frame like the translucent teeth of a giant shark.

"What the . . . " Alex jumped out of bed, scattering pigeons and bedclothes, and walked to the window. Splintered glass was strewn over the outside ledge and the fire escape beyond. How could that be? If anyone had broken in, the glass would be on the floor inside.

His handiwork was still intact. The duct tape was in place around the door and the window frame. The powder he had sprinkled on the floor and sill was undisturbed. Alex shook his head, clearing the remaining cobwebs. What the hell was going on? Where had he been? It was impossible that he could have gotten up in his sleep and just broken through the window like that.

As he thought, his dream of the night before bubbled upward from his unconscious. The details were vivid, alarming, more real than mere dreamlike fantasy. There was the wolf again—the wolf in his apartment leaping through the closed window. There was the sound of shattering glass. And then, there was Danielle—.

God, how he ached for her. Danielle and her thug of a father were both in his dream. Concentrate now; he needed to recall the details. A hunter was stalking the wolf. No, wait. The hunter followed the wolf, not threatening, not stalking. The setting was vague, a vast blur. He couldn't say where they had been. The wolf had charged and pounced, landing on top of Peter Dante, driving him to the ground. How good it felt. Dante screamed as the wolf's paws held him down, its face inches from Dante's throat. The wolf bared its teeth, drooling on Dante's face.

Then there was laughter, pleasant and musical laughter from somewhere in the blurry background. The wolf looked up and saw Danielle. She was kneeling beside him, hugging him around the neck, nuzzling him behind the ears. She stroked the wolf's cheeks. Then everything went blank. Alex could remember nothing else.

Alex pressed both palms against his temples. This was the first time he had dreamed of Danielle in ages. He thought of her often enough when awake. But she had never appeared in his wolf dreams before. Perhaps it was an omen that, somehow, they would get back together again. How incredible it all was. There were no footsteps in the powder. If he had walked in his sleep and punched out the window, he would have left prints in the powder and his fist would be bruised or gashed. But there was nothing, no blood, no bruise, no footprints. He had to find out what was going on before he went nuts—if he wasn't crazy already.

The alarm clock jangled on the nightstand, and Alex went over and shut it off. He had to get ready to go to work; he had missed too many days already, and his boss's patience was wearing thin. The job was menial, mostly clerical in nature, filing, sorting and delivering documents and folders, at the *New York Times*, but it was perfect for him in his new life, obscure, nonchallenging, a place to hide and make enough money to pay for rent and food. Alex was certain of only one thing as he stepped into the shower: there was a definite correlation between the full moon cycle and his wolf dreams and blackouts. That knowledge was not reassuring; it was downright alarming actually. But it was all he had to go on.

At work later that week, Alex sorted through the wedding announcements for the Sunday edition, when one in particular caught his attention. DANTE-FENRIS. Alex read it through in shock. Danielle and Luke Fenris? It couldn't be. Say it isn't so, Danielle! Anybody but Luke Fenris.

The mere mention of Fenris's name was enough to make Alex's blood boil. A week earlier a cover story in Barron's entitled, "The Mysterious Pirate of Wall Street," attempted to dissect the man and shed some light on his puzzling past and sprawling empire. That article had been no more successful than the ones that preceded it. Most of it consisted of rumor and innuendo and little if any fact. Luke Fenris exemplified—more than Peter Dante even—everything that Alex Mallum detested about contemporary America. The profile of Fenris and his business dealings had been bad enough, but buried in a paragraph toward the end was a comment that Fenris and Danielle Dante had recently been seen together at a party at Carl Navi's house in the Hamptons. The line had practically jumped off the page when Alex read it, but he dismissed it as idle gossip. Danielle, with all her faults, would never sink that low.

Now, here it was in black and white in front of him—irrefutable proof. She was actually going to marry the bastard! Alex found it almost impossible to comprehend how she could violate every principle she once stood for, and marry an amoral buccaneer like Luke Fenris. It defied credibility. He could accept the fact that she had been swayed by her father, that she had been blinded by his money, betrayed him and their marriage, and maybe even have fallen a little out of love with him. But, in the back of his mind, Alex had always attributed her defection to exasperation, not lack of love—exasperation with him and his uncompromising devotion to a losing cause. Deep inside, Alex had felt that there could possibly be a slim chance that someday they might even get back together again. He took secret pleasure over the knowledge that her second marriage had ended so mysteriously. Perhaps one day Danielle would wake up and see that her father was really as evil as Alex said he was. But, with this notice, all hope was shattered. She was marrying a man who was the exact opposite of everything Alex stood for. He had never felt so alienated from her as he did at that moment.

Tears rolled down Alex's cheeks and dripped onto the wedding announcement. The paper grew soggy, and Alex tore it into tiny shreds. "There will be no marriage!" He thought he had spoken to himself, but as he looked around at the alarmed faces of his colleagues he realized he had screamed.

"There will be no marriage," Alex whispered this time. "Because you can't marry a dead man, Danielle. And Luke Fenris is as good as dead."

Alex knew for the first time what his revolutionary plan for CRUSH was going to be.

Ludwig von Dracula sat at his desk, sorting through the hundreds, no, thousands of letters he had received since his interview. He knew he should not have gone public with his confession. The world was not ready for the truth; perhaps it would never be. Every misfit, every psychotic, schizophrenic, manic-depressive, lamebrain, kook, maniac, and moron in the country had written to tell him they thought they might be vampires. Was it always like this? Did everybody want to be Jewish, or black, or homosexual, or a woman, or whatever the new victim-of-the-month was? It was all so depressing. He had known before that the human race was really screwed up, but this was ridiculous. Space cadets! People who swore that vampires had landed in UFO's in their back yards! There was no end to the lunacy.

All he wanted to do was share some knowledge, shed some light on a forbidden topic, and let other vampires know that they weren't alone, that there was someone out there, just like them, who *cared*, It was time they came out of the coffin now and stopped pretending to be something they were not. For too long now they had lived in fear of stake-wielding religious fanatics. It was time to end their lives of silent, fearful suffering.

He didn't expect everyone to believe his story about being a vampire or of his noble heritage. But other vampires would know he was speaking from his heart and telling the truth, and possibly be emboldened to do the same. And maybe, just maybe, a few caring humans would sympathize with their plight and join them in their fight for justice. But just the opposite had happened. Thousands of maniacs wanted to be vampires themselves while the diehard bigots—judging by the hate mail mixed in with the rest—were even more hardened in their opposition to his species. One correspondent from New Jersey thought the government should ship all vampires back to Transylvania—even though many of them had lived in the United States for centuries. And an old lady in Florida had written to say that he and his people should be rounded up into rehabilitation centers—sounded like concentration camps to Luddie—for their own good.

Luddie was close to despair, almost ready to take the remaining letters and toss them unread into the fireplace. He felt his energy flagging as the night wore on, and knew he must soon get ready for a good day's sleep. He got up from his chair and went over to check the contents of his refrigerator; he was down to his last three vials of blood. He needed a pick-me-up, so he poured a few ounces into a rocks glass with some ice, knocked it back, and returned to his desk. He made a list of things that needed to be replenished—tissues, saltines, detergent, Oreos, blood, tangerines, paper towels; if it wasn't one thing it was another, always something, as cousin Emily used to say.

He was about to abandon his search for intelligent life on earth, when he came across one letter that jolted him out of his lethargy. Who was this from? He didn't give his name, but from the address and phone number Luddie could see he lived a few blocks away. A message for him from Lothar and Tanya? That could only mean that this writer had something significant to say to him, but preferred anonymity for the time being. Good Lord! He'd better check in with Lothar at once to see what it was all about.

"Yes?" Lothar answered on the fourth ring.

"Lothar? It's me, Luddie."

"Luddie! How've you been? I saw you on television a few weeks ago."

"Yes, yes. I'm sorry I ever agreed to do the interview. You wouldn't believe the crazies coming out of the woodwork."

"Tell me about it," Lothar said. "What did you expect anyway? Love? Kindness? Understanding? Nothing's changed, my boy. It's the same now as it was way back in the dark ages. But, then you always were the idealist, weren't you?"

"Yes, well, listen. I received one very disturbing letter. It doesn't say much, except that the correspondent has a message for me from Lothar and Tanya. How can this be, Lothar? Do you remember someone stopping off at your inn a while back who might have had an encounter with Tanya?"

There was a long silence on the other end, and then Lothar heaved a sigh and said, "Yes." Lothar paused for a moment, nervously nibbling at his lip. "It happened quite a while ago, five or six years now I should think. I . . . I had hoped nothing would come of it."

"Did he spend any time with Tanya?" Luddie could not keep the alarm out of his voice.

"Well . . . yes, I suppose so."

"What do you mean you suppose so?"

"They did spend the night together."

"My God, Lothar! Did Tanya bite him?"

"A little bite, Luddie. Don't get all excited."

"There's no such thing as a little bite, Lothar. You know that."

"Okay, she bit him. She bit him, all right? I prayed that nothing would come of it. Night after night for months I prayed."

"You promised me you would sedate her during the full moon periods." Luddie was almost in shock. "You know the risk."

"It was such a rainy, stormy night. Horrible, horrible weather. Who thought anyone would be out in it? It tears me apart when Tanya goes through these changes. He arrived at the inn, hurt and exhausted. Half dead. Only Tanya knew the proper medicine to use. It all happened so fast, Luddie. I didn't have the heart to stop her."

"You should have called me right away." Luddie made no effort to hide his irritation.

"I was going to at first. I swear. But when there was no news of anything unusual happening after a few months, I . . . I just let it slip."

"I'm very angry with you, Lothar."

"I never realized—"

"Do you understand what this means? This October there's going to be an eclipse of the Harvest Moon, the first full moon after the autumnal equinox."

"My word."

"The gravitational confluences could result in permanent transformation of infected males. If this particular human male is infected, we have to find out what kind of creature he becomes. If it's dangerous . . . I may have to kill it."

"Luddie, I'm so sorry. I can't tell you how upset I am by this. Please don't blame Tanya. It's not her—"

"You must keep her sedated in the future during these critical periods! She's a menace, Lothar! But we agreed to let her live because she's the last of her line . . . unless this male she bit is infected and he infects others."

Lothar was silent, properly chastised. What more could he say?

"I should be able to track him down," Luddie said. "He's obviously concerned that something's wrong with him, and he's looking for help. I only pray to God that it's not too late. I'll keep you posted."

After he hung up, Luddie checked the eastern skyline and saw that it was already too late to take any action now. Soon it would be dawn and, just as an Eskimo could discern twenty different shades of white, he and others of his species were sensitive to the delicate gradations as night yielded to sunrise. Urgent as the situation was, he could take no action until the evening.

Luddie walked over to his coffin, which rested atop a loft platform at the end of the living room. The soothing mineral-rich mud spread over the bottom was from his home village in Transylvania. Luddie mounded some of it at the top end to form a pillow for his head. Then he undressed and settled himself down inside. The early morning air was warm already, so he tossed his blanket onto a chair nearby. He pulled the lid shut above him, blocking out the grayness of the rising sun. Within moments, he dropped off into the nether reaches of pitch-black sleep.

CHAPTER FIFTEEN

"Ask yourselves," Alex said to the assembled CRUSH members, sprawled on the floor of their pigsty office like human litter in the bottom of a Dempsey Dumpster, "who personifies the corrupt establishment more than any single individual you can think of?"

God, how he hated this scene. How did he talk himself into it in the first place? If only he had kept his mouth shut last time. If only he hadn't run into Sally and been recognized in the first place. Now he was here with this useless pack of crazies, talking to them of revolution as though they possessed the power of reason.

"What is this, man?" Pinto said, scratching his filthy beard. "Twenty fuckin' questions or somethin'?"

"Yo, man. Hear the dude out," said Kirk, apparently ready for another punch-out with Pinto.

"Shut yo' face!" Kenyatta glared at everyone else. "The man say he got a plan to raise a couple o' million. I don't know 'bout you, but that gets *my* attention."

"As I said the last time, money's the name of the game," Alex continued. "At the risk of sounding like a capitalist pig, you can't even start a revolution without it."

"Tha's a fact," Kenyatta agreed.

"So what's the symbol of everything we're against? Name the one person who stands out in your mind the most."

Everyone remained silent for a moment then shouted as one voice, "Kathy Me!"

Alex rolled his eyes upward and held his hands out at the side, palms up. He shook his head back and forth a couple of times and then spoke. "Get serious. Forget about frivolous media celebrities. I'm talking about people who matter, powerful people who make bad things happen to lots of good people."

Jennifer raised her hand, the only one in the group who did before she spoke. "Peter Dante," she said quietly, as if she were waiting to be graded on her answer.

"Fuck no!" Doug yelled. "You're off the fuckin' wall as usual."

Jennifer trembled and bit her lip, close to tears.

"Any asshole knows it's Carl Navi, that slimy greaser son-of-a-bitch," said Doug.

"Greaser!" Pinto yelled, struggling unsuccessfully to hoist his bulk off the floor. "He ain't no greaser, man. He's Lebanese or Ay-rab or some capitalist prick like that."

"Chill!" Kenyatta's voice cut through the din and silence filled the room. "Let's hear what the man got in mind."

"Who's he anyway?" Pinto said, pointing to Alex. "He talks like some Social Democrat weenie. I mean, what do we really know about him anyway?"

"Sally vouched for him an' tha's good enough for me," Kenyatta said.

"Sally's got her head up her ass," said Kirk.

"Kirk!" Sally said. "I mean, like, really!"

"We need some action, man," said Nicky, the demolitions expert. "The time for bullshit's over."

"You're all being very rude," Maria said. "We invited Alex back to tell us his plan, and now you won't even listen to him."

"Right on!" Nicky said, turning toward Alex. "Go for it, man. Everybody else shut the fuck up for five minutes."

Now that he had their undivided attention, Alex tried once again to make his statement. "The one man who comes to mind more than anybody else is Luke Fenris, the so-called Mystery Man of Wall Street. Not Peter Dante, not Carl Navi. Fenris is head and shoulders above them all when it comes to the single individual who most personifies white male oppression in this country."

"Word to ya mama," Kenyatta said.

"So what're we gonna do about it?" Pinto said.

"Waste him!" Nicky said. "Blow the motherfucker's ass into a million pieces!"

"No! No!" Alex yelled, quieting them down. "We don't want to kill him. He's useless to us dead. We need to take him hostage and put a price on his head. He's worth a lot of money to us alive, not as a dead man."

"Who goin' to pay to get him back?" Kenyatta said. "The man got no wife, no family, nobody we know of who gives a fuck."

Kenyatta had a valid point, and Alex decided that he was the only one in the group with a functioning brain. There was one person Alex could think of who *did* care about what happened to Fenris, however, and he tried not to look at Sally when he mentioned her name. "Danielle Dante cares," he said. "They're engaged to be married. She'll do anything to get him back, and a million or two to her father is like nickels and dimes to you and me."

"I like it." Kenyatta beamed at him and the others. Through the corner of Alex's eye, he saw Sally regarding him with a quizzical look. "The only question is," Kenyatta continued, "is how? Man like that got to be well protected. You don't just snatch him off the street like he was Joe Blow goin' for a stroll."

"That's where Nicky comes in," Alex said. "I understand you had some demolitions training in the military."

"Just call me Boomer."

"Do you think you can rig up a little bomb? Not one big enough to blow a car and its occupants to smithereens. Just big enough to disable a vehicle that's set to go off at a certain time?"

Nicky stared at him for a long moment, hollow-eyed as though something essential had vacated the premises, then he said, "No sweat."

"This is critical. Something rigged to go off at a precise time. Low impact, enough to blow out the engine let's say, that's reliable enough to go off when we want it to."

"I said 'no sweat.' Just tell me when you need it, man."

"Three days from now."

"Three days!"

"If you can handle that."

"It's complicated, man. It's, like, a work of art, a craft. I got to rig it up, then I got to set the timer."

"Don't worry about the timer for now. Just rig it up and I'll tell you when to time it later. This will give me some time to do a little surveillance of Mr. Fenris, find out what his habits are and so on."

They made plans to convene again a few days later, and then the meeting broke up. Alex could see that Sally was troubled as he walked her back to her apartment. He took her hand, looked down at her, but she avoided his eyes.

"What's wrong?" he said.

"You're still in love with her, aren't you, Alex?"

"Who're you talking about?"

"You know who I'm talking about. Danielle. Who else?"

"Don't be ridiculous! After what she did to me?"

"I can tell, Alex. Women can tell these things. I . . . I know you're not interested in me like, you know, like you were in her."

"I find you very attractive, Sally. I really do. I'm just—just not ready to get involved again."

"It's been ages now . . . how many years? You're just not over her, Alex, that's all there is to it. Otherwise, if you found me attractive like you say you do, you'd be able to—"

"I can't even think about that right now." Alex ran a hand over his face, pressed his palms against his temples to stop the throbbing. "There are strange things going on in my life that I don't even understand right now. It's not you, believe me. If things were different I'd jump at the chance to . . . to get to know you better on a, on a more intimate level."

"I know it's a bad time for you, Alex, and I don't mean to put any more pressure on you. I just want to be sure, you know, that this plan of yours is—"

"Yes?"

"Is not just some kind of a way for you to get revenge."

"Revenge?"

"Revenge against her . . . and him, too. I read the papers about them getting married, and I know how you feel."

"Goddamnit, Sally! My personal feelings don't enter into this at all. It's perfectly logical, what I've suggested. Don't you see—?"

"It makes sense, I can see that. It's all perfectly logical. I was just curious about your motivation, that's all."

"My motivation is clear. You asked me to follow through on the plan I mentioned, not to embarrass you in front of your friends, so—"

"Okay, okay." She stroked his arm, rested her head against his shoulder. "I understand. Do you think it'll work?"

"My plan? Yeah, it'll work if your friend Nicky can do what I asked him to. Do you think he's playing with a full deck? Kenyatta's the only one there with anything resembling a human brain that seems to be working right."

"Well . . . " Sally heaved a long sigh of resignation. "We'll see I guess. Sometimes it all seems so hopeless for people like us. But we're doing the best we can. That's all any of us can do. Right?"

Alex patted her hand. He put his arm around her shoulders and pulled her closer, as though to insulate them both against the terrors of the night.

They knew before they met again a few days later that Nicky would not be able to deliver on time. The wreckage of the top floor of his apartment building was shown two nights in a row on television, and the story was on the front page of the *New York Times* (along with an inset photo of Nicky over a caption that read: If You've Seen This Man Call The Telephone Number Below).

"It blew up, man," was the way he explained it at the meeting.

"We know it blew up, Nicky." Alex tried somewhat unsuccessfully to keep the sarcasm out of his voice. "The question is, how did it happen?"

"It just went off, man. Like, I think maybe I connected it wrong."

"He could have been killed," Jennifer offered in his defense.

"Yeah, right. It was lucky I was out at the time, cleaning off windshields on Houston for spare change."

"And lucky no one else was there at the time," Alex said. "Meanwhile, your picture's all over the newspaper, which puts you and all the rest of us in danger. Where are you hiding out?"

"He's stayin' with me," Pinto said. "I got him covered."

"You better change your appearance," Alex said to Nicky. "Shave, cut off your hair, put on a suit and tie, look like you got a job down in Wall Street maybe."

Nicky just stared at him blankly. There was definitely nobody home inside, Alex decided. "Do you think you can make a bomb that'll go off when it's supposed to?"

"Of course, man. What do you take me for?"

Alex let that one slide.

"So where we at now?" Kenyatta said.

"Back to the drawing board," Alex said. "Let me see if I can come up with something that doesn't require as much . . . " He groped carefully for the right word. "That doesn't require as much—precision, shall we say?"

Chapter Sixteen

There was a message on Alex's machine from Ludwig von Dracula. Finally. His missive had not gone unanswered after all. Alex called him back and made an appointment to visit him at his loft in Tribeca, a former manufacturing center filled with old commercial buildings converted into lofts for artists and young professionals who had followed them there and driven the rents into the stratosphere.

Alex walked along the still-trendy streets, past the dirty, bleak buildings hiding spacious and well-furnished residences inside; past the renovated warehouses now converted into art galleries and pricey restaurants where the rich and famous came to be seen. Alex was turned off by the flimsy paradox, the transparent juxtaposition of the shabby and the glitzy, the tainted commingling of struggling artistry with the corrupting influence of indiscriminate wealth. Always the rebel, Alex said to himself. The knee-jerk revolutionary. Just can't get it out of my system.

The hour was approaching midnight—the hour of their scheduled meeting— and the sidewalks were quiet and empty, unlike the teeming maelstrom of his own neighborhood, which resembled a New York version of Calcutta. Alex checked the numbers on the buildings as he walked until he came to an old, shabby, five-story structure that had once been home to several electrical manufacturers. The front door was solid metal painted black, except for two small panes of cracked glass. It was locked, so he checked the panel of buzzers for a name; there were none. He rang the uppermost buzzer, which, he hoped, corresponded with Dracula's top-floor digs.

"Yes?"

Alex looked up at the face of a youngish man, obscured by shadows, poking out of a top-floor window.

"It's me, Alex."

"Step away from the building so I can see you."

Good God! Alex did as he was told, extending his arms dramatically in a supplicating gesture. "Satisfied?"

"Here's the key. I'll wait for you at the top of the stairwell."

Alex heard the object bounce off the sidewalk into a muddy pool filled with debris next to the curb. He located it with some difficulty, let himself in, and began the long climb up; of course there was no elevator, even in this relatively high-priced part of town. Out of breath and sweating he reached the top, and recognized at once the handsome young blond-haired man he had seen on television.

"Alex?"

"None other."

"I'm Luddie." He extended his hand and Alex shook it.

"How many times a day . . . er, a night do you make this climb?"

"I usually fly up," Luddie said.

Alex just glared at him. "Of course you do," he said. "What else did I expect?"

"Come on in. I'll get you a cup of coffee and we can talk."

"Actually, I'd like a Coke if you have one."

"No problem."

Alex collapsed onto the soft cushions of the sofa and rubbed his aching knees. He just couldn't get used to these long climbs no matter how many times he made them. Luddie handed him a beer mug filled with coke and ice, and sat down in a chair facing him. "I'd like to get right to the point," he said.

"Fine with me."

"You mentioned in your note that you had a message from Lothar and Tanya. Can you tell me about them?"

Alex related the entire episode of his night in the inn, his meeting with Lothar and the beautiful young woman named Tanya, and the old hag the following morning who said *she* was Tanya and that the young girl never existed. He also described the poultice she put on his injured foot, the ghastly attack in his room, and his overwhelming thirst the next morning.

"Was Tanya real?" Alex asked Luddie.

"She was real, Alex, very real. Both Tanyas, the old woman and the young beauty, are one and the same."

"Forgive me, but I find that difficult to believe." Alex felt dizzy discussing such arcane matters, which at any other time he would have found incredible, with this stranger in a calm and rational manner. Were it not for his own strange experiences and his need for answers, he would not be here in the first place.

"I'll try to explain as clearly and straightforwardly as I can. Please bear with me for a few minutes. My great uncle Victor was an expert in genetic theory. As I mentioned during my television interview, he had unraveled most of the mysteries of DNA long before modern biologists knew of such things. But his notes were destroyed when the rabble stormed and burned his castle. He escaped unharmed, but the human being he created through cloning techniques was incinerated—alive. Victor never could forget the horrible cries of pain as his creation burned to death, cheered on by the crazed mob."

"Just like in the movies, right?"

Luddie ignored the sarcasm. "The original movies were adaptations of earlier books that, in turn, were based on rumors centered in the truth. The Transylvanian government tried to suppress the entire episode, but it inevitably leaked out, as the truth often does. Mary Shelley's *Frankenstein* was loosely based on these stories, but the later films were just mass-market rip-offs and the original sources have long been forgotten. The atrocities of Hitler and Stalin have overshadowed the earlier genocides of humanity."

"This is all pretty fantastic stuff." Alex had grown visibly annoyed. "But I came here to talk about Tanya."

"It's all related, just hear me out. Uncle Victor refused to reconstruct his research after this . . . this torture and murder of his creation, but he often spoke about it to me when I was a child."

"When you were a child? You know, I'm willing to suspend belief and give you the benefit of a doubt—up to a point. But this would make you, how old?"

"One hundred and thirty. We *do* age less rapidly than you people do." Luddie preened, miffed himself. Alex could see he was not without his vanities, despite his quixotic abilities.

"Anyway," Luddie continued, "at the risk of taxing your human brain, permit me to give you a brief lesson in what modern biologists like to call the 'jumping gene theory.' Within each species is a substance called DNA, which contains complex genetic codes that determine the characteristics of living things. Inside the nucleus of every cell is a veritable library of DNA molecules—the genes. However, in the substance surrounding the nucleus of the cell, there is some other DNA contained in bean-shaped structures called mitochondria. Are you with me so far?"

"I'm positively mesmerized."

"I thought you would be." Luddie brushed back his hair and stared at Alex down the length of his nose. "Biologists have noticed that this other DNA has patterns similar to ancient bacteria and behaves differently than nuclear DNA. Somehow, an alien bacteria form has taken up permanent residence inside every human cell capable of growth. Research has shown that the genes of a cat contain patterns of rat and baboon DNA. North American skunks are born with DNA from South American squirrel monkeys. Pigs have some forms of rodent DNA. If I'm boring you, just say so, Alex."

"Look, it's after midnight, I'm tired, and you're bombarding me with some pretty heavy scientific data. I don't mean to be rude, but if we could just get to the point."

"I assure you, your patience will be amply rewarded if you bear with me just a moment or two longer. We are here for your edification, are we not?"

"I'm more than willing to be edified, Luddie. But I am a mere human after all." Alex smiled for effect. "Right now I'm just hopelessly confused."

"I'll try to keep it simple." Luddie smiled back. "Because of all this great complexity, the DNA sequences that determine many characteristics don't always jump with the full set of instructions. But, the transfer of a gene from one species to another can dramatically alter the nature of the species. Those outside genes can sit within the system for millions of years without being triggered—and then, suddenly, an explosive change in the species can take place. Many biologists now think that evolution transforms a species in a rapid leap rather than through millions of years of subtle growth.

"So you see, the vast majority of sequences in human DNA appear to be nonsensical—evidence of attempts by the DNA, perhaps millions of years ago, to produce new genes that never quite worked out but still remain within the DNA code. It's all so incredibly fascinating."

Alex merely nodded, his face a blank mask.

"The effect of a single change can be remarkable," Luddie continued. "Human and monkey DNA, for example, are ninety-nine percent identical in their letter-by-letter DNA sequence. Yet, this one percent difference produces an incredible amount of variation between humans and monkeys."

"Sort of like between humans and vampires?"

"Precisely." Luddie smiled. "I'm glad to see you're still awake and your sense of irony is still intact . . . for a human, that is. The question that concerns scientists is how the genes jump from one species to another. The answer has to do with viruses. Viruses are parasitic strands of DNA that have somehow drifted free of the cells, acquiring hard protein shells, and flit about like bees bearing pollen, carrying genes from cell to cell.

"For instance, the common cold virus attacks the body and hijacks cells, inducing them to produce new viruses and then kill the host cell as the new viruses escape through the cellular membrane. However, some viruses settle down and stay forever. It is *these* viruses that may . . . I emphasize the word *may* . . . carry the alien gene. These are known as RNA retroviruses. They approach a cell's DNA, create their own viral DNA version of themselves, somewhat like the negative of a photograph, and insert that into the cell's DNA. If that particular virus can insert itself into a reproductive cell of a species, it can become part of that species' heredity pattern for millions of years. This brings us to the matter of Tanya and—"

"Finally, Tanya."

"Tanya and, perhaps, yourself. She is the last of an errant vampire species, subject to sudden changes in her physical makeup that seem to be triggered by gravitational pulls that act as a catalyst for genetic explosions. Her saliva contains bacteria that are capable of entering another body and launching a viral attack on the genes. If, by any chance, the virus enters into a reproductive gene, the new host will become a transformed species when certain environmental factors come into play. In Tanya's case, the appearance of the full moon seems to coincide with the catalytic trigger that transforms her into a different being. When the full moon recedes, the reaction is reversed. Uncle Victor always believed that the bacterial infection can be transmitted only during the full moon phase."

"So, what all this boils down to is that I may have been infected by Tanya?"

"If she bit you during her transformation, and I'm told that she did, then you were exposed to the infection, yes. If your reproductive cells were invaded, you could possibly be subject to transformations of your own. What form that would take, I have no idea. All I can say at this point is that, based on Tanya's model and that of her ancestors, there is a tendency to transform into a kind of physical opposite of yourself."

"Like some kind of a monster, a werewolf?"

"My, how vain you are." Luddie smiled, teasingly.

"What?"

"Hmm. Perhaps you're not as quick as I thought. We're discussing opposites here. Look, the odds against this happening are astronomical. But if—*IF*—the infection invades your reproductive cells, you *could* periodically become some other form of being."

"Something monstrous?"

"Not necessarily. You could become attractive and wonderful. I did say the opposite of the real you. Just kidding, don't get upset. Tanya certainly becomes quite beautiful and desirable, wouldn't you say?" Luddie paused and smiled. "You, too, might actually prefer your altered state."

"This is so . . . so absurd, I can't believe I'm actually sitting here talking to you seriously about it. I mean, look at the time. It's practically two o'clock in the morning and here I am . . . I ought to have my head examined. Just for argument's sake, let's say there's some kernel of truth to this fantastic theory of yours. What am I supposed to do about it anyway? I mean, is there some kind of a cure? How do I find out what I turn into?"

"There's only one way I can think of." Luddie was somewhat nettled by Alex's outburst. "I would like to observe you during the next full moon. I'll see if there are any changes and photograph the results. That way you won't have to take my word for it; I'll be able to show you proof."

"Great! You're suggesting I go to sleep with a vampire in the room."

"If you came here to insult me . . . " Luddie's eyes glowed with anger.

"Excuse me. How do I know you won't bite me?"

"You're not my type." Luddie tossed his head and smoothed back his hair again.

"Well I'm certainly glad to hear that. I can't tell you how relieved I am."

"There's more involved here than just our personal vanities," Luddie said. "The full moon after the next one is the Harvest Moon. There's going to be an eclipse of that moon, and the gravitational pull of that particular planetary alignment will be sufficient to tip your genetic balance. Once the eclipse reaches the halfway point, and the moon is completely in shadow, whatever transformation takes place in you will be irreversible. There's no turning back after that."

"You can't be serious."

"Unfortunately I am. As I said, the odds are overwhelmingly against any transformation taking place. But if one does, it will be permanent. Who knows? You might prefer the new you. It might improve your disposition."

"So I'll be a werewolf forever?"

"Think of the benefits—longer life, a higher plane of intelligence." Luddie glared pointedly at Alex.

"Yes, and a fondness for darkness, coffins, and blood. Thanks, but no thanks."

"There you go with your ugly stereotypes again. Tanya's species isn't affected by sunlight and she doesn't *require* human blood, although she does prefer it to Coca Cola—ugh!—and scotch whiskey—double ugh!"

"Suppose, just suppose I turn into something dangerous, something homicidal. Don't my wolf dreams mean anything? Could I possibly be out prowling the streets, murdering people?"

"Uncle Victor's studies show that neither personality retains any memory of the other after the transformations. Your dreams are just that—dreams. Maybe you drink too much caffeine." Luddie looked at Alex's Coke.

"Well, I am relieved to hear that, I can assure you. I thought for a while that something truly horrifying was going on inside me."

"Let's not jump to conclusion. Why don't we take one step at a time? The next full moon is September sixth, about two weeks from now. I *strongly* suggest that you permit me to observe and photograph you during this period. It could be nothing at all. But, if something is taking place, both of us should know exactly what it is."

"I wonder what your uncle Victor would have to say about all this."

"Well . . . I could ask him I suppose."

"I thought, I mean I assumed he was dead."

"Not at all. He's retired and living in Greece. He's completely withdrawn from everything, given up on the whole world, just doesn't want to get involved anymore."

"With that, I'll take my leave." Alex jumped to his feet. "This meeting sure has been edifying, as you said."

"Do we have a date then for the next full moon?" Luddie asked.

"I'd like to sleep on that one a bit. I'll call you in a few days and let you know."

"Alex." Luddie rose to his feet, put his hand on Alex's arm and looked directly into his eyes. "All kidding aside, I am deeply concerned about you. I want to help you, and I'm the only one who can. Give me the chance to do that, won't you?"

Alex hesitated a long moment as he stared back into Luddie's eyes, as though trying to fathom the depths of his soul. Was Luddie a lunatic or a genuine humanitarian, for lack of a better word? Luddie would probably have preferred *vampiritarian* if he had his druthers. In the end, Alex had nothing to fall back on but gut instinct. He made his decision.

"I'm probably crazy," he said, "but I'm going to trust you. I think I should. I'll call you a few days before the sixth and we'll set it up."

The two men shook hands warmly and said goodbye. As Alex left the apartment, he could almost feel the wave of compassion wash over him as he descended the stairwell.

CHAPTER SEVENTEEN

Alex was tired and irritable at work later that morning. After leaving Luddie's, he had returned to his apartment, grabbed a couple of hours of restless, fitful sleep, showered, and then taken the subway uptown. His brain was so clogged with arcane data from his conversation with Luddie, that he had difficulty concentrating on his relatively menial job. So he decided instead to do a computer search for a suitable restaurant for his date with Sally that evening. Alex wanted Italian food, but in a real *ristorante* with flair; he wanted to make up for the way he had been treating Sally. He went over to one of the unused computer terminals and entered the key words necessary to pull up all the news articles for the last five years that included the words "assassination," "mob," and "restaurant" all in the same article. After all, it was common knowledge that big-shot gangsters ate at only the very best restaurants, or at least that was the urban mythology. The search pulled up twenty-two stories and Alex began reading. The first one was about a mob hit at a place called La Casa Nostra.

GANGLAND LEADER SHOT IN POSH RESTAURANT

"Gin Jimmy" Vincente never did get to taste the warm crusty chunks of fresh Italian bread toasted with garlic butter, a house specialty at La Casa Nostra. Instead, his head lay on a soft pillow of melted mozzarella cheese floating in a fiery pool of spicy fra diavolo sauce that topped a delicately breaded, tender veal cutlet. Vincente was the latest victim in an underworld fight for control of the numbers racket, a fight that has spilled over into one of the most exciting Italian restaurants to open its doors in recent years.

La Casa Nostra has a well-deserved reputation for its fine southern Italian cooking, and it is no surprise that a gourmet such as "Gin Jimmy" Vincente would make this the home of his unexpected last meal. "Gin Jimmy" was a regular here and his enemies knew it.

The slain gangster had been joined at his table by three associates, all of whom managed to escape harm: Tony Locaro, who ordered the exquisite

Fettuccine Alfredo in a luscious cream sauce flecked with just the right amount of freshly-crushed black pepper; Rico Angelli, who ordered the Shrimp Scampi, a school of marvelously tender large shrimps drenched in a delightful butter and garlic combination that brought tears to this reporter's eyes; and Carlo Roletti, whose serving of Lobster Fra Diavolo was clearly the table favorite.

Reliable sources indicate that Vincente had planned to order the Zuppa Inglese for dessert, an outstanding choice even among the many superb pastries available from the dessert cart. Zuppa Inglese is one of those desserts that few restaurants can produce with any degree of authenticity, and La Casa Nostra has what may be the most satisfying version in the city, with rich thick mounds of cream surmounting hearty scoops of custard and chocolate and mixed with minced pieces of fresh fruit and crisp honey-roasted walnuts. The other three diners had not yet given their dessert orders, although Carlo Roletti was heard to comment afterward that his life was saved because he had gone over to the dessert cart to examine Death by Chocolate Meringue (this reporter's undisputed favorite for New York Dessert of the Year) just before the shots were fired.

Locaro, who held the dying Vincente in his arms until the Emergency Ambulance Squad arrived, had skipped over the appetizer and ordered a simple broth with spinach and orzo, not one of the standout soups at La Casa Nostra, but as good as you are likely to find in New York. As Vincente was being wheeled out to the ambulance, a survey of critics on the scene gave a unanimous chorus of approval to the hearty minestrone soup that was thick and flavorful with enough vegetable and pasta to make a main course all on its own.

La Casa Nostra would be in the top three of any reviewer's list of southern Italian restaurants in New York City, and this reporter would rate it number one. Prices are expensive. Dinner for four, with appropriate wine selections (but not including ambulance and hospital bills), could easily run over three hundred dollars. Given the unusually large size of the main portions, you can cut the bill somewhat by sticking to just a main course and either an appetizer or dessert, and a house wine. If "Gin Jimmy" Vincente had followed that advice, who knows? He might have left early enough to still be reigning lord of the Manhattan underworld.

Police had no clues as to who was responsible for the mob assassination and promised a full investigation.

Alex's spirits improved considerably when he finished reading the review. Only in New York, he thought. Well, maybe Chicago and New Orleans too. La Casa

Nostra would do just fine, considering the state of mind he was in. He called to make a reservation for him and Sally and was about to plunge into his work for the day, when one of the *Times'* star reporters, Gus Triptolemeus, walked by his cubicle. Gus had two Pulitzers behind him already; one of them was for a story about how the mob launders political contributions, which landed him in the hospital with a concussion and two broken ribs, but also led to the resignations of a handful of state senators, a congressman, and a couple of national political leaders.

Gus was a crumpled veteran who grew up in an age of clicking typewriters, and liked to tell war stories at a local saloon and kid the young reporters about spending too much time on the telephone and at their computer terminals instead of wearing out shoe leather digging up facts. Alex liked him and respected him, and thought often about his place at the nerve center of a vast information network, capable of toppling governments and stopping armies. Alex, though he deliberately held down an obscure, low-profile position at the paper, dreamed about finding a lever in the process by which he could affect the flow of the news—a flow that would serve his own ideas, and thoughts, and his own sense of justice. Some day perhaps. But not today. Gus leaned against the opening and poked his head in.

"Hey, Alex. How's it going?"

"Great. Need anything?"

"Do me a favor, will you. Can you pull the files on Dan Hollings and Tanner-Voight Industries?"

The *Times*, of course, no longer kept actual clipping files now that everything was computerized and could be called up on the terminal. Alex shrugged. Perhaps Gus wanted to read the articles more leisurely at his desk instead of scrolling them up on the screen. In any event, having Alex pull the articles would save the reporter a modest amount of precious time, a valuable commodity for people fighting a deadline.

The files on Hollings/Tanner-Voight were thin. The CEO and his company had been in the news in connection with anti-pollution demonstrations on college campuses; then again in a joint greenmail operation with Luke Fenris when they bid to take over an entertainment conglomerate named Walnut Enterprises, then sold their eight million shares back to Walnut at a five-dollar-a-share profit. Hollings-Fenris? Interesting partnership, Alex mused. The so-called Mysterious Pirate of Wall Street seemed to have his hand in everything—several industries through control of major corporations, even Alex's life via Danielle. What, Alex wondered, was Gus's interest in this situation?

The answer to this question was sitting there at Gus's desk when Alex brought the files—in the person of Dan Hollings himself, whom Alex recognized at once from his photographs. The portly, balding executive looked ill at ease as he glanced around suspiciously at the sound of every approaching footstep, loosened his tie repeatedly, and clutched a large manila envelope tightly in both hands. Gus motioned toward it a couple of times, and each time Hollings pulled it back. Hollings looked up as Alex drew near, his eyes wide, staring, seemingly locked open in a paralysis of fright.

"Here they are, Gus." Alex handed him the files. "Thanks, kid."

Alex hovered in the area, hoping to listen in on them. "Can I get you anything else?" he said.

"That's it."

"You sure? It's no problem." Gus looked up sharply; Hollings just kept staring at him. "I mean I can—"

"That's it I said! Whatta you, deaf? Take a friggin' hike!"

Alex backed off, staring at Hollings all the while, knowing he had been out of line yet wanting to be a part of what was going on at the same time. He walked slowly toward his cubicle, glancing back at the veteran reporter and the chief executive officer of one of the largest chemical concerns in the world. Out of earshot now, Alex saw Hollings jump from his chair, still grasping the manila envelope to his chest, and rush over to the window. Gus stood up and called to him, but Hollings grew more agitated by the second. Alex saw Hollings point down toward the street, then wave his free arm wildly while still holding onto his envelope with the other hand. Gus tried to calm him down but Hollings was beyond restraint. Alex knew he should keep out of it, it was not his place to get involved, but his curiosity got the best of him. He had to know what was happening. Once again he approached the pair, just as Hollings came charging down the narrow passageway with Gus Triptolemeus in pursuit.

"They'll kill me!" Hollings screamed. "They know I'm here! They'll kill me!"

"Take it easy." Gus finally caught up with him and grabbed his shoulder.

"What am I gonna do? If I give it back to them, maybe they'll leave me alone."

"Never!" Gus said. "They know you're here, they'll never trust you again. Gi'me that before they come in, for Christ's sake." Gus wrenched the envelope from Hollings' grip and held it behind his back.

"Let me help you!" Alex suddenly blurted out. "I can help you. Trust me."

Gus stared at him for a split second, and then thrust the envelope into his hands. "Here, hide this," he said. "Put it somewhere safe an' hide behind your desk. Anything happens to me, make sure you get it to the FBI."

Gus took hold of Hollings' arm and yanked him toward the exit sign at the rear of the newsroom. Seconds after they disappeared down the stairwell, the front door of the newsroom flew open and in charged two rugged-looking men who looked as though they could have been on a secret paramilitary operation. Alex froze involuntarily, recalling the night when he, himself, was being pursued through the California night by two men who had been dispatched by the German. Alex recalled it vividly. He dashed into his cubicle, slipped the manila envelope under his chair cushion, and poked his head out through the opening to see what was going on.

Everything was happening so quickly, turmoil, commotion, people jumping out of the way, others riveted to their computer terminals. Inexplicably—Alex would review this scene over and over in his mind later to make sure he wasn't hallucinating—Alex saw, he thought he saw, no, he did see, he would swear it, one of the copy boys whose name he could never remember nod, ever so imperceptibly, in the direction of the rear door through which Gus and Hollings had exited. It was just enough to cause one of the intruders, a tall, rangy, muscular man with close-cropped brown hair, to change direction. His partner followed him as he veered to the right and came charging down the narrow passageway that led past Alex's cubicle. His first emotion was terror, fear for his personal safety. This was quickly replaced by an all-consuming outrage that these invaders, these instruments of force and violence, had forced their way into the *New York Times*, a hallowed sanctuary of lofty liberal ideals. They might as well have violated the sanctity of a church, to Alex's way of thinking.

"Fascists!" Alex shouted as he jumped into the corridor. "Haven't you ever heard of the First Amendment?"

The taller man with the long legs was in the lead. He skidded to a halt, stared down at Alex for an excruciatingly long moment, an eternity in which Alex felt naked to the bone, sure that this muscular giant was going to throttle him. Then the giant twisted his lips in a smile and said, "Yes, I've heard of it. Haven't you ever heard of the Second Amendment?"

His shorter, but equally menacing partner reached inside his jacket and pulled out something hard and metallic. He raised it above his head, and then swept it down in a long arc toward Alex's head. The last thing that went through Alex's mind—oddly enough, it wasn't the fear of pain—before he slumped to the floor was that he was going to miss dinner with Sally at La Casa Nostra, and she would be furious with him.

That was the last thing. The first thing he was aware of when he opened his eyes was the gruff voice of a uniformed police sergeant saying to him, "Can you tell us your name please?"

"Alex Maltese." The sound of his own voice seemed disembodied, somewhere out there in the middle distance not connected to this person with the throbbing head who was he.

"I understand you confronted the two men who broke in," the sergeant said.

"Uh, yeah, I guess I did."

"Can you identify them?"

"I don't know. It happened so fast. One of them hammered me before I could get much of a look."

"Would you be willing to look at some photos at the stationhouse and, maybe, talk to the police sketch artist?"

"Not tonight. My head's killing me." The last thing Alex needed was a police investigation.

"Coupla days then. Leave your number with Gonzalez here an' we'll give you a call."

Later, when things had settled down, Alex hid the manila envelope that Gus had taken from Hollings more securely down in the morgue. He breezed by Gus's desk, looking for the files he had brought there earlier, but could not locate them among the clutter of papers and notes. Alex didn't know if there was significance in that or not; they had to be somewhere. He searched back in the morgue but could not find them there either. Then he remembered the copy boy, the one he was almost positive he saw nodding at the intruders, sending them in the direction of Gus and Hollings. He searched the newsroom and did not see him among the staff. When Alex inquired, the receptionist told him the boy had gone home earlier, when Alex was still unconscious, saying he had been shaken by the episode.

Alex thought not. In retrospect, the copy boy had seemed more calm and collected than anyone else. It was something he would have to look into. Meanwhile, Alex marveled at his own combination of reckless courage and foolhardiness in exposing himself the way he did to the two men who had invaded the newsroom. Fortunately for him, he had survived the encounter with only a bump on the head. It could have been much worse, he thought, as he prepared for his date with Sally.

Chapter Eighteen

General Revilo Thorn sat in a high-backed brown leather swivel chair facing the wide expanse of New York Harbor, framed by the window in his office at TriLateral Import/Export on the eighty-fifth floor of the World Trade Center. He looked out at the stream of tiny red and white lights that silently floated across the night sky toward JFK airport, and at the colorful lights mounted on the tugs and small craft cutting through the dark, choppy waters of the harbor. In the far distance, where sea and sky blended into an unbroken gray-black vista, was the bright electric torch held high above the water in the raised arm of the Statue of Liberty.

Although he had stared through this window at the great green lady night after night, year after year, the sight never failed to stir his emotions and swell him up with patriotic pride. The Lady in the Harbor was more than just a statue to Thorn; she represented a way of life to which he had dedicated himself—a way of life that was a beacon of hope to freedom-loving people around the world. Thorn was proud to be an American, and he was proud of his role as commander of the Ghost Commandos, the only military force in existence that could truly protect his nation from foreign invasion. It could do the job without high-tech missiles and mass destruction, preserving a world worth living in.

But it was America's domestic enemies who worried Thorn the most. He felt impotent against the fifth column in government, the academics and the press, the arrogant elitists and intellectual demagogues who lusted for power, and most especially the sob-sister advisers around the president who were pressuring him to dismantle the Ghost Commandos in the spirit of détente. The Ghost Commandos! America's final and only reliable bastion of defense, made up, as it was, of volunteers (not worthless, drug-addled conscripts) who were dedicated to principle instead of a corrupt political system. Thank God that a true leader had come along, Luke Fenris, who was not afraid to utilize their services abroad and remove the fifth column at home.

The computer terminal on Thorn's desk beeped, pulling the general out of his reverie. He swiveled about, typed in his ID password, and seconds later the computer dumped a coded message onto the line printer. Thorn ripped the page off and read it: the infiltration of mercenaries into Bruwanda was proceeding ahead of schedule. Thorn smiled thinly, and fed the printout into the shredder.

He swiveled around again and retrieved a file from his desk drawer. Inside the packet was a collection of newspaper clippings that had been swiped the day before from the desk of the reporter, Gus Somebody-or-other with some foreign-sounding name. The general studied them carefully for any news that would connect Hollings and Fenris to any more than an occasional business deal. When he finished with the clippings, he called up the newspaper database on his computer for any items he might have missed. "Great," he said, audibly to himself. "Nothing out of the ordinary anywhere." Thorn replaced the file, and then pressed a button on the intercom.

"Yes, General?" a voice said over the speaker.

"Any news?"

"He just finished talkin'."

"I'll be right there."

He pushed away from his desk, and then left the office. He strode briskly through three outer rooms and arrived at a locked door with an array of buttons mounted over the doorknob. The general punched several of them in a coded sequence and, within seconds, the door rolled open. As soon as he stepped through, the door closed behind him.

The room he entered was about thirty feet square, containing a number of file cabinets and shelves stocked with assorted office supplies. Toward the rear, two of his most trusted soldiers stood alongside a chair where a third man sat slumped. The general looked at his men, who nodded at him with reassurance. They were two of his most loyal and most capable warriors, men who had served him well on many missions over the years. Thorn squared his shoulders and walked toward them. The man slumped in the chair, his face lacerated and bloody and his shirt speckled with dark brown spots, was Dan Hollings.

"Is he dead?" Thorn asked.

"Not yet," the taller man said. "We thought you would want to talk to him yourself, sir."

"Indeed I do."

Thorn turned to Hollings, cupped a hand under his chin and tilted his head back. "You were very foolish, Hollings," he said. "It was bad enough you betrayed your friends. But you betrayed your country, our cause, my cause as well. That's unforgivable."

A line of spittle ran down Hollings' chin. His lips were swollen when he opened them to speak. "Betray?" His voice was a raspy whisper. "The country's all . . . all screwed up. But what you and Fenris are doing—taking the law into your own hands—is even worse. I should've . . . should've tried to stop you sooner."

"People like you said the same thing about George Washington, my friend." He removed his hand and Hollings' face collapsed onto his chest. "Did he tell you where the reporter is?" Thorn asked his men.

"Yeah," the shorter, stockier of the two replied. "Jimmy Bones and his crew are on their way now."

Thorn nodded without speaking; he had a good deal of confidence in Peter Dante's enforcers, also a part of his team now, almost as much as he had in his own men. Thorn believed in setting an example for those who worked for him.

He reached inside a desk draw and retrieved a 9-millimeter semiautomatic from within. He placed it firmly against Hollings' left temple, stared down at the plump middle-aged executive, and said. "Peace, Dan. May God have mercy on your soul."

Hollings' eyes registered nothing, just a flat, deathly resignation. It was the last thing Thorn noticed before he pulled the trigger, dispatching the soul of Dan Hollings into eternity. He handed the weapon to his men. "Take care of this," he said. Ah well, he thought, you can't make an omelet without breaking eggs. You can't make a revolution without leaving the battlefield littered with a few dead bodies.

Gus Triptolemeus had never been so terrified in his life. His job was tracking down people to extract from them whatever stories they had inside. Now, here he was, the quarry himself, hunted, being tracked down *not* by news-hungry reporters like himself, but by violent, subversive men who had no more regard for human life than they did for that of a rat. He was holed up in this nightmare haven for derelicts, euphemistically called the Cummings Hotel, just off the Bowery. Already Hollings was two hours late, a dire omen of Gus's own chances for survival. If they had gotten to Hollings, it was merely a question of time before they followed the trail to him.

He found no encouragement in his spartan surroundings. The sagging bed, chipped-enamel sink, shelves for clothing and personal effects, all of it coated with a grimy layer of dust, looked more like the final stop for a man on the way out than for someone brimming with life. Yet, desolate though his hiding place was, he was afraid to leave it even to go down the hall to take a leak. This dingy, bleak room seemed to represent the only security he had left in the world.

Gus walked over to the window, itself nearly opaque with age-old grime, pulled the shade aside an inch or so and looked down to the street. The gun Hollings had left with him weighed heavily in his belt. Even that was a bad joke. More accustomed to hoisting beer and shot glasses than he was in hefting guns, he felt like a man with a growth on his hip. The gun, supposedly an insurance policy against a premature, violent death, was more a dead weight dragging him closer to the grave.

Suddenly, his worst fears, his darkest nightmare materialized in the street below when two cars pulled up. Three men climbed out of each, six in all, and surveyed the lineup of roach-infested hotels and fleabag rooming houses. Gus did not wait to see if they zeroed in on his. He left his perch at the window quickly, and ran as fast as he had moved in years out into the hall. There was a pay phone on the wall, and he paused long enough to pick up the receiver and dial 911. "Cop being fired on, on the roof of the Cummings Hotel off Bowery!" he screamed. Then he dropped the receiver without hanging up and ran up the darkened stairwell to the roof. There was a water tower twenty yards to the right, its graceless form deep in shadow offering the only cover in sight. Gus ran toward it, his heart thumping rapidly as though it were ready to explode, his breathing growing more labored by the second, now coming in heavy gulps, his entire body soaked in sweat. He slipped into the shadows and clung to the tower for support. Wearily, he pulled the pistol from his belt, knowing as he did it that it would not be enough, *could* not be enough to protect him against the menace that hunted him in the night.

Jimmy Bones headed up the staircase, his five confederates trailing closely behind him. Among them were the two other bodyguards who had been with Jimmy Bones when he kicked the German, shattering his jaw. The three of them were awesome enough, Jimmy with his shaved head, the second black with his fearsome Jherri curls, and the short, powerful white man built like a tank. The final three were equally impressive in their own ways, muscular with crew-cut hair, dressed in jeans, boots, and black turtlenecks despite the heat. Jimmy Bones reached Gus's room first, kicked in the door and crouched with his 9-millimeter semi-automatic aimed straight ahead.

"The man ain't home," he said.

"Look like he made a telephone call," the man with Jherri curls said as he observed the dangling receiver.

"Shit! Let's hustle on upstairs."

Jimmy led the charge up the staircase to the roof. He inched the door open slowly and whispered to the others, "Thorn said to bring him back alive. Don't forget."

Jimmy dashed out first, heading for the shadows in a low crouch as he ran, and the others fanned out in an enveloping formation around the roof. Then—a flash, followed by the report of a gun; then another. The flashes lit up the shadows around the water tower and Jimmy Bones dropped to his belly. He peered into the shadows, searching for a figure, a form, something. He fired high, hoping to frighten his quarry into the open. He heard the ping of the projectile striking metal simultaneously with the sound of sirens in the distance. The sirens were shrill, filling the night with their urgent bleatings as they came closer. Bones edged over toward the street-side of the roof and looked down. Already the police cars—three, four, five in all—were careening down from the corner of Bowery. Within seconds they were down in front, cops in combat gear leaping out with guns drawn before the cars had fully stopped. Jimmy Bones saw three of his partners leap over the edge of the roof through five feet of space onto the roof of the adjoining building. A fourth—the blocky white man— was about to jump when the beam of a searchlight from a police helicopter whirling overhead caught him in its glare.

"Stop! Drop your weapon!" The amplified voice called from above. "Drop your weapon and don't move!"

The warning was followed by a spray of machine gun bullets across the roof. Jimmy Bones, still unseen, pressed his body along the low wall at the edge of the roof, hiding himself in the narrow shadow. From his vantage point, he saw a man— the reporter they came for—dart out from behind the water tower, waving his arms at the helicopter. Jimmy could see the pistol in the man's hand, the same pistol he apparently fired when they first came on the roof. The man ran out into the open, waving, yelling, drawing attention to himself. Jimmy Bones watched as a long machine gun burst from the helicopter lifted the reporter up, twisted him in the air like a puppet being jerked on strings. Then the firing stopped and Gus Triptolemeus collapsed like a shattered doll onto the roof.

Jimmy Bones saw his blocky partner try to make the leap onto the other roof once again, but another hail of bullets drove him back. Then, instantly, the entire night came alive with a horrific roar and a blinding flash as bright as the sun at noon. Jimmy looked overhead and saw the helicopter split open like a giant hand grenade, splintering the night with a thunderstorm of twisted metal and violent debris. In a second the death-dealing whirly bird had become a brilliant fountain of yellow and orange flames.

Jimmy Bones rushed over to his injured partner, who was lying on his side near the roof's edge. "You okay?" he said.

"Jus' my shoulder. I can make it."

The man with Jherri curls appeared from out of the shadows and helped Jimmy lift their comrade to his feet. Jimmy jumped across to the other roof first, reached out and grabbed the injured man by his belt and yanked him over the open space, and then the third man landed beside them. They had already melted into the darkness when the door of the roof they had just abandoned burst open once again, and a small army of combat-ready cops dressed in midnight blue and matching bullet-proof vests fanned out over the battleground.

Down below, around the corner from the Cummings Hotel, the stench of burning debris and charred metal hung like a palpable presence in the night air. Sirens screamed from all directions as squad cars, ambulances, and fire engines homed in on the war zone. Jimmy Bones looked up and down the street from the doorway of the building. The wreckage was everywhere—buildings aflame, smoldering chunks of the helicopter littered the sidewalk and street, people struck by falling shrapnel lay whimpering with pain. But most of the commotion was around the corner, in front of the hotel. At the end of the block their car and driver waited, the engine idling and ready to go.

"Let's hit it!" Jimmy Bones leaped out of the doorway, dragging his injured comrade with him as the third man followed behind. He pulled the car door open and pushed his partner into the back seat. The man with Jherri curls jumped in beside him, and Jimmy slid into the passenger seat up front.

"Make tracks, man! Let's get outa here!"

"I'm already on my way." The car bolted forward, away from the madness in front of the hotel.

"The others get away all right?" Jimmy asked.

"Yeah, no problem. They was wonderin' what was keepin' you."

"Shee-it! This was a night to remember."

"What happened to the reporter?" the driver said.

"Dead. Done got himself all shot up like a wheel of Swiss cheese."

"Thorn ain't gonna like that."

"Oh yeah! Well ain't that too fuckin' bad, man. We're lucky he's the only one got himself killed."

Jimmy Bones looked over the back of his seat down at the rocket launcher, half covered by an old bedspread, on the floor in back. "Hey, man," he said. "You did jus' fine. That baby shoots real good, don't it?"

"Lucky for you." The driver laughed. "If it didn't, I'd be drivin' home alone tonight."

Alex read the news of Gus's death with great sorrow. He had genuinely liked the man, and respected his dedication to the job of ferreting out the truth and reporting it in the press, a dedication that was sadly enough in short supply these days. Little by little, the good guys were being killed off; soon the entire world would be populated with venal, amoral, power-hungry thugs. But, aside from his own sense of loss and his concern about the greater implications of Gus's death, Alex faced another dilemma: what should he do about the files Gus had entrusted with him? If anything happens to him, Gus had said, make sure they get to the FBI. But the FBI was about the last agency of government Alex wanted anything to do with. There would be questions, perhaps a thorough investigation into *his* background.

First things first. Alex went down to the morgue, checking every step along the way to make sure he wasn't followed, and found the manila envelope where he had hidden it. He slipped it under his shirt, ducked into the men's room, locked the stall door behind him, and settled in for what appeared to be a good half hour or so of reading. The notes were badly typed, apparently by Hollings, and they outlined an elaborate plan that belonged more in the realm of fiction than in reality. Except—it was maddeningly, frighteningly, horrifyingly real.

When Alex finished, he was soaked with perspiration. What he read was nothing less than a nightmare come to life. If Hollings was to be believed—and, evidently, he had come to the *Times* at great personal risk to reveal this plan to Gus—he was a player in a drama conceived in the fertile, but evil brain of Luke Fenris. The drama, already underway, called for the takeover—*seizure* was more like it, Alex thought—of the entire communications network of the United States, and the establishment of a *de facto* military government in Africa. What was one to make of such a plan? Was it viable? Apparently Fenris thought so, and he had the means, financial and otherwise, to bring it to fruition.

Alex tucked the envelope back inside his shirt, went over to the sink to splash cold water on his face, and was running a comb through his hair when the door of the men's room opened slowly. In stepped the copy boy—what was his name?—the kid he swore had stolen the newspaper clippings on Tanner-Voight from Gus's desk. He hadn't seen him since, now here he was edging into the men's room, glancing about furtively until his eyes locked on Alex's. Time stopped for an interminable moment as they held each other in eye-to-eye embrace. Alex broke the trance.

"You!" he said.

The boy flinched, then backed up.

"Don't go," Alex said. "I need to talk to you."

The boy turned and ran. Without thinking what he was doing, Alex dashed after him. "Stop!" he called after him. "I just want to talk to you a minute." Alex followed him up the stairs, through the newsroom without worrying about the spectacle they presented to their startled coworkers, out the door into the street.

God, this boy was fast. Alex knew he wasn't in the best of condition, but this kid had wings for feet. He darted toward the Times Square crossing and Alex lost ground. Soon the kid had opened up a block lead by the time Alex reached the south side of Forty-first Street. He zipped across Seventh Avenue, and raced west toward Eighth. At Eighth he hooked north again, back toward Forty-second when he plunged headlong into a throng of Hare Krishnas hopping up and down in their saffron robes, chanting prayers. One grabbed the copy boy by the arm and started dancing with him. Alex pushed ahead, his lungs on fire, his legs like lead. He ran out into the street, around the dancing maniacs, to cut the boy off when he finally managed to punch his way through. He was closing in fast, three or four feet away, only to see the kid hurl his dancing partner into a pushcart filled with fruit and run up Eighth toward Forty-second.

Alex saw the car first. It was out of control, or seemed to be. Then, no, it looked more like a missile with a target in mind. Its trajectory was deliberate, Alex was sure of it. "Watch it!" Alex screamed.

As the car made impact, sending the copy boy flying like a broken doll twenty feet through the air, Alex felt his heart freeze. Not another one, he thought. Not another death. Alex stood mesmerized and helpless on the sidewalk as the automobile ran across the copy boy's twisted body, then continued eastward along Forty-second Street toward Seventh Avenue.

Alex fell back into the surging crowd. The tide of people swarmed around him as he backed slowly away. In the distance, sirens cut the air. Sirens, sirens, and more sirens. Alex was vaguely aware of someone shouting, "A guy was chasing him, I saw some guy chasing him," as he receded further against the human floodtide.

Then he was running again, south down Eighth Avenue, west into one of the obscure side streets that led over to Ninth, clutching the manila envelope to his chest as he bolted along the anonymous city streets.

CHAPTER NINETEEN

Luke Fenris had to die! Alex couldn't remember when he had been so certain of anything in his life as he was of that. Convincing Kenyatta, Nicky, and the others at CRUSH that he was right should prove as difficult as telling a duck he had to swim. But getting them to execute a plan successfully was an altogether different matter. Their talents, such as they were, seemed better suited to hammering one another. Yet, assassinating Fenris—and getting away with it—was something Alex could not do alone. He needed what all successful revolutionaries needed: organization, cadre, troops committed to a cause. CRUSH may have been laughable by Lenin's standards, or even Abbie Hoffman's. But it was all Alex had to run with.

He asked Sally to call an emergency meeting, and he filled them all in on Hollings' visit to the *Times*, his meeting with Gus, their flight from the two hit men sent by Fenris and Company, the death of the reporter and disappearance of Hollings and, finally, the details of Fenris's elaborate plan and the execution of the copy boy. His entire presentation had been designed to build as strong a case as possible against Luke Fenris as the evil would-be emperor who represented everything they, themselves, opposed.

"That's why," he concluded, "we need a change in plan. Fenris has declared war on us and on the American people. Now we learn that he's closer to winning the war than any of us dreamed of. Time's running out quickly. Kidnap and ransom are out of the question now. Fenris has to die. If we chop off the head, the brains of his organization, the whole body falls apart."

"Right on, man!" Kenyatta said.

"What about that motherfucker Navi?" Pinto said. "Maybe he can pull it off without Fenris."

"Fenris first," Alex said, "then we close in on Navi."

Jennifer raised her hand. "I . . . I second Alex's motion," she said.

"Motion, shmotion," Doug said. "Let's just waste the fascist asshole and skip all the bullshit."

123

"Hold on!" Kenyatta jumped up and the others fell silent. "We still ain't heard the man's plan yet. I first and second and third my own motherfuckin' motion that we hear him out."

"Thanks, Kenyatta." If there was one person there whom Alex needed on his side, it was Kenyatta. He was the only one who could keep the other birdbrains in line. "To execute the plan I have in mind, we need to call on Nicky again. Nicky, are you with us?"

Nicky was skulking in the corner, trying to shrivel without success inside the disguise he had adopted since the bombing fiasco in his apartment building. Cleanly shaved, his hair cropped to a Ross Perot stubble, his malevolent eyes remarkably tempered by horn-rimmed glasses, attired in a pin-striped suit, shirt and tie that he had bought off the rack at Sears, Nicky could easily have passed for a Merrill Lynch stockbroker. His mother would have had difficulty recognizing him, let alone anyone who the cops or FBI had on his tail.

"Yeah, I'm here, man." His voice was a sulky pout.

"We need you to make another bomb, Nicky. A big one this time, big enough to blow Fenris and his apartment into tiny bits."

"What about other people in the building?" Maria said. "I mean like, you know, innocent people."

Alex's eyes had not glowed with such fire and determination in years. "As far as I'm concerned," he said, "there are no innocent people in Luke Fenris's building, not when half the city's living in poverty or worse, out on the streets. Besides, people die in wars and revolutions, that's a simple fact of life. Fenris started the war and we're making a revolution. His cause is evil and ours is just. Viva la Revolucion!"

Pinto was the first to shout his approval, and the others were close behind.

"Nicky," Alex said when the tumult subsided, "we need a bomb this time that blows up Fenris's apartment, not yours, with him in it. I don't want to sound as though I'm nitpicking, but the distinction is important to me—to us. Am I getting through?"

Nicky tried to sound convincing, and not altogether defensive, as he returned the stares of his fellow revolutionaries and said, "Hey, gimme a break, will ya? Accidents happen. I know what I got to do."

Later that night, Sally brewed a pot of coffee as Alex sprawled across her sofa with the cats parked on the floor near his shoes. Sally was looking trimmer these days, Alex observed, after having gone on a diet after they met and shed a dozen pounds or so. Not that she was fat before, but decidedly on the chunky side of average.

"How's it been going?" Alex said.

As though reading his mind she answered, "Great. I'm down six pounds for the month already." She touched her toes to emphasize her point. "I'm feeling better, too. Pretty soon I'll be lean and mean like you."

"I don't know about the mean part. Don't lose too much weight. You look fine the way you are."

She walked over to where he was sprawling and he smiled up at her. "Apparently not good enough though," she said.

"Shit, Sally." Alex sat up and made room for her beside him. "It's not you, it's me. I keep telling you that. It's . . . it's just the timing, that's all."

Sally sat down next to him, took his hand and traced her finger along the notches between his fingers. "If only you'd talk more, Alex. Share some of what's going on inside you with me."

"Soon, I promise."

She looked at him, the unasked questions obvious in her eyes.

"I mean it, Sally. I will, soon." Like after the next full moon maybe, when I know what's going on myself.

"It's her, isn't it? Don't hold back from me."

Alex sighed involuntarily. "I won't pretend that she's not on my mind a lot. I don't know if that means I'm still in love with her or not. But I do think about her and—and that's not fair to you if we were, you know, if we were—"

"If we were to get involved you mean? If I'm willing to take that chance, Alex, why don't you let me make that decision for myself?"

"Well . . . " He had no answer to that. Why not? It wasn't as though he were keeping anything from her. All his cards were on the table, all except the full moon card, that is. But even he didn't know what that one was. Why should he sit around moping for Danielle? She, certainly, was not losing any sleep tossing and turning, thinking about him.

"I was really surprised listening to you tonight," Sally said, shifting gears on him. "Oh?"

"I mean, I know how you feel about Nicky and the others. And there you were, all fired up just like in the old days."

"Does that scare you?"

"No. Well yes it does, a little."

"The idea of killing Fenris?"

"Not just him. That thing you said, you know, like innocent people may have to die."

"Listen to me, Sally." Alex bolted upright, took her chin in his hand, and looked directly into her eyes. "We're not playing games any longer. You joined a group that wants to make a revolution. Well, it's time to stop talking about it and to finally take some action. The future of the world—*our* future is at stake. I don't even care any more if I get caught. We all have to take a stand before it's too late. We have to take a position on one side of the barricades or the other. There is no middle ground."

"And if Nicky—if we screw up again, then what?"

"At least we will have tried. We will have put our lives on the line for a just cause. If they stop us, maybe others will be inspired enough to follow our example."

Sally looked away, took his hand back in hers. "It's scary, Alex. I just hope I'm strong enough, that's all."

"For the first time in six years, I'm in control of my own destiny again. It's . . . it's the greatest high in the world!" Alex's eyes were glowing with idealistic fervor. It was as though he had become intoxicated by his own words, transported to a dizzying, unearthly dimension.

Sally wrapped her arms around him and snuggled against his chest. She leaned up and kissed him on the side of his mouth. "Put your arms around me, Alex," she said. "I want you to hold me tight."

Pinto looked like a refugee from a Mexican fat farm, decked out in workman's coveralls, carrying a tool kit with Nicky's new bomb hidden in the false bottom. Alex and Sally, similarly attired, walked along beside him. A few paces ahead Jennifer and Doug were dressed in crash helmets, knee guards, and spandex tights in the manner of bicycle messengers. For perhaps the fifteenth time, Alex briefed them as they strode up Fifth toward Xanadu Towers.

"You've got everything straight now, right? The doorman goes on his lunch break in five minutes. That leaves only the concierge on duty behind the desk in the lobby. Jennifer and Doug go in and ask him to check the mailroom for a package they're there to pick up. That gives the rest of us anywhere from sixty to ninety seconds to get past the guard. Then we go up to Fenris's apartment on the pretense we're building maintenance workers checking the wiring, we plant the bomb in a closet, and get the hell out of there as fast as we can."

"We ain't even sure the cat's home," Pinto said.

"That's a risk we have to take," Alex said, realizing that this was the one variable he couldn't control. "He always seems to be home during the day. Maria's been watching this building for a week now and he hasn't come out once. It's almost like he's hibernating in there."

"Yeah, but what if he's travelin'? What if—"

"Look! We've come this far and we can't back out now."

Alex's words hissed through his teeth. "We'll just have to take our chances and hope he's in. If nothing else, it'll be a symbolic action for equality."

"Okay, man. Let's just do it," Pinto said.

The others waited on the sidewalk across Fifth Avenue as Jennifer and Doug entered the lobby. The wait seemed interminable as they watched them talking to the concierge. What was taking so long? All he had to do was get up off his ass and go to check a package for them. Through the glass door at the entrance they could see the concierge rise to his feet. Finally. Then he disappeared from their line of sight. A moment later, Doug half turned toward the street and stuck the thumb of his right hand up in the air. All clear. Move! Move! The three of them bolted through the traffic across Fifth and reached the lobby door in seconds. Without hesitating, Alex opened the glass door and led the way across the lobby with Sally and Pinto following closely behind. Now they were at the elevators. Waiting, waiting, waiting. Did anything ever happen quickly when you wanted it to? Five tenants waited with them—one, a youngish man with a dark, pinstriped suit and red suspenders, restraining a golden retriever on a leash. No more, please, Alex thought. It was imperative they all got on at once. If anyone got bumped, it would be one of *them*.

Mercifully, the elevator door swooshed open and everyone stepped on. It was a bit snug but nobody complained. "Mr. Fenris's apartment," Alex said to the operator. "Emergency repair."

"Excuse me."

Alex looked down into the demanding eyes of the little white-haired woman who had addressed him.

"Are you all going up on *one* job?"

"Why, er, yes. It's . . . it's a complicated procedure."

"Why that's absurd. I've been waiting a week to have my air conditioning looked at."

Alex was tongue-tied for a long, uneasy moment, but Pinto entered the breach. "What apartment you in, ma'am?"

"Nineteen East. I've been calling and calling and—"

"No problem, ma'am. We'll be right there soon's we finish."

The elderly woman's face lit up like a teenage girl being asked out on her first date. "Why, thank you. You're so kind."

Fenris lived on Twenty, the floor just above her. Alex glanced quickly at Sally who was staring at the old woman with her jaw hanging half open. He didn't have to ask to know what she was thinking: was this old woman one of the fascist swine who might have to die along with Fenris? He placed his hand on Sally's shoulder and squeezed, hoping to firm up her resolve.

The elevator stopped at six, then at seven, discharging passengers. Then, suddenly, between ten and eleven the lights went out and it halted abruptly. Darkness prevailed, and silence except for the whirring fan that wound down slowly to a stop.

"Oh no! What is it now?" asked a chubby woman in her mid-thirties.

"Don't know," the elevator operator said. "Hope it ain't another one a them brownouts, what with the air conditioners gawn full blast an' all."

"Try the phone," the same passenger said.

He opened a small cabinet above the button board and the receiver from its case. After pressing a few buttons, listening intently, he told them it was out of order.

"Oh my." The old lady was already close to tears. "Of all places to get stuck. I'm claustrophobic you know."

"It's prob'ly just a temporary malfunction," he said. "We'll be on our way in no time."

The temporary malfunction dragged on for fifteen minutes as Alex checked his watch every three minutes or so. The heat inside the car built up and the air grew stagnant and unpleasant. Perspiration flowed freely, adding to the overall discomfort. The heat intensified and the fetid air became more foul-smelling by the minute. Pinto stared straight ahead, his face an expressionless mask. Sally glanced up occasionally at Alex, but most of the time she kept looking at the old woman with an expression akin to horror on her face. Alex shifted nervously from foot to foot, working hard to tamp down his mounting frustration. Of all the idiotic screw-ups, he fumed. This was incredible. And it was no one's fault, except some great amorphous power out there. He didn't even have the luxury of being able to blame their hopeless predicament on Nicky or one of the other morons at CRUSH.

"We're going to die, we're going to die, we're going to die." The old lady was keening now, chanting repeatedly in her soft, quiet hysteria.

Alex checked his watch. One o'clock. Two hours to go.

"We're going to die, we're going to—"

"Shut up! Shut up! Shut up! I can't stand you any more!" The young man in pinstripes with the golden retriever was white with fear and rage as he screamed at the old lady. "I'm going to punch your goddamn lights out if you don't shut up! Sic her, Henry, sic her!" he commanded his dog. Henry just stared up at his master with a string of drool festooned from his mouth to the floor.

Alex raised his hand for silence. "Calm down. Let's just everybody calm down now. Panic only makes things worse."

"Tell her to shut up then!" The young man's eyes were blazing spotlights in the dimness.

"Have you ever heard such cruelty?" The old lady whimpered softly.

"You should be ashamed of yourself, talking to her like that," the chubby woman said to Henry's master. The young man's face turned red and Henry dropped his jaw to the floor, whining in sympathy with the man who held his leash.

Alex checked his watch. One-twenty. An hour and forty minutes to go before the bomb goes off.

"Why don't we all sing a song," Sally said, her eyes lit up hopefully.

"I beg your pardon," Alex said. Did he hear her right?

"When I was a campfire girl out in the woods, and it got real dark at night around the fire, we always sang songs to chase away the goblins. It worked!"

"Really, Sally?" Hang on, Sally, he thought. Don't you lose it, too. "What did you have in mind?"

"Does everybody know, Michael Rowed the Boat Ashore?"

"Fuck that, man." Pinto spoke for the first time since offering to fix the old woman's air conditioning. "How about 'La Bomba?' It's got a groovy beat, you know what I'm sayin'?"

All of them were losing their minds, Alex thought. Here we are, bomb-carrying revolutionaries trapped on an elevator, and they're talking about a songfest. "Er, why don't you lead us then?" he said to Sally.

Softly at first, then her voice strengthening as she got going, Sally began, "Michael rowed the boat ashore, alleluia. Michael rowed the boat ashore."

To Alex's utter amazement, the other passengers—the young man with the dog, the chubby woman, and the old lady—joined in the sing-along with Sally. Within moments, the voice of the old woman drowned out the others as she closed her eyes, clenched her fists at her side, and boomed out the words from deep down inside. Even the elevator operator was singing away with gusto.

Alex checked his watch. Two-ten. Fifty minutes to go.

Pinto led them next in a rousing rendition of "La Bomba," complete with gutterals and blistering, rapid-fire Spanish with just the right inflections. Soon he had the elevator rocking, the passengers temporarily oblivious to the heat and rising stench. Whatever Sally had started with her campfire girl routine, it was working like magic as they went from song to song without a break. Alex was the first to hear the thumping on the roof of the elevator, followed by the sounds of human voices. "Shhh," he quieted the others. "Someone's coming to rescue us, I think."

There was a thud from above, and then the overhead panel slid to the side. Someone stuck his head into the open space. "Everybody okay down there?"

"What happened?" Alex said.

"Citywide power failure. Just hold on a few more minutes, all right? Here's a few jugs of water you can pass around down there."

He lowered two one-gallon containers of Poland Springs water down to Alex, who uncapped them and handed one to the old woman and the other to Henry's master.

"Can you get us out?" Alex said to the man above.

"Hang tight. If the power don't come on soon, we'll lower a ladder down so youse can climb on out."

"There's an old lady down here who's ready to pass out!" the young man screamed, close to hysteria again.

"Hey, buddy!" The man said from overhead. "People're stuck all over town. Gimme a break, willya!"

Alex checked his watch. Two-fifty-two. Eight more minutes. "What time is it?" Sally skewered him with her terror-stricken eyes.

"You don't want to know."

"How much time, Alex?"

"A while yet. Don't panic."

"It's set to go off at three! Oh my God! What're we going to do, Alex?"

"Shut up, Sally!"

"I don't want to die! Can't you do something? Can't you dismantle it?"

The pinstriped man did a doubletake. "Dismantle what?"

Alex glowered at Sally, torn between rage over her loss of self-control and horror over his own impending death. "*Defuse* is the word you're looking for. Defuse, not dismantle. And the answer is no, I can't. Only Nicky knows how to do that and he's not here. Now shut the fuck up!"

"Defuse?" the young man shouted at Alex.

"Just kidding," Alex said with a sheepish grin.

"It's all over, man," Pinto said. "Say your prayers, everybody. Judgment Day is closer than you think."

Alex kicked him in the ankle. "Will *you* shut up too!"

"Whatever are you talking about?" the young man asked, more insistently this time.

"How much time, Alex? How much longer do we have?"

Alex checked his watch. Oh my God! Any minute now. Two more minutes, according to his watch. Our Father, who art in heaven . . . So it was coming to this, the sum and substance of human life. He put his arm around Sally. "Let's just hold each other tight," he said.

"I don't want to die. Daddy, daddy, daddy," Sally wailed.

Pinto reached overhead, trying futilely to reach the trap door.

Alex checked his watch and started the countdown. Ten, nine, eight, seven, six, five, four, three, two, one,—nothing! Three o'clock came and went without incident. Alex did not realize it, but he had dug his fingers deeply into Sally's shoulder and his knuckles were blanched white.

"Thank you, Nicky," Alex said. "I love you. You're a good guy, but your sense of timing leaves something to be desired."

"He did it again," Pinto said. "I can't believe it, man. Maybe he set it for three o'clock in the *morning*."

Everyone stared at Alex. "That wasn't very nice of you to scare us like that," the old woman said.

"Just a little guerrilla theater," Alex chuckled nervously.

"Yeah, you know, to relieve the tension," Pinto said.

"Well it wasn't very funny. You scared me half to death."

"I'd like to report you to management," the pinstriped man said. His suit was soaked clear through with perspiration.

"Sorry, folks," Alex said. "We thought you knew we were only kidding." If you only knew the half of it, he thought.

At three-eighteen exactly, the lights came back on inside the elevator and the little fan in the corner started to whir again. Life! Life! All was sound on heaven and earth once more. The elevator continued its ascent, discharging the chubby woman and the pinstriped man with the dog along the way. At Nineteen the old woman was the last of the tenants to leave. Crisp and pert and feisty as she had been before their ordeal commenced, she turned to Pinto as she stepped out and said, "Remember, young man. Nineteen East just as soon as you're finished." Then she was gone and the door closed behind her.

"Take us back down to the lobby," Alex said to the operator.

"What?" He was visibly surprised.

"Take us down. It's too late to go in now. We've got to check with him before we go in."

"Well—you know what you're doin' I guess."

The elevator made a slow, torturous descent to the lobby. Without glancing to the side, Alex strode briskly past the concierge through the lobby with Pinto and Sally hustling to keep up with him. The doorman, back on duty following a lunch break that he would remember for the rest of his life, tried to make conversation as he held the door for them. Alex ignored him and walked out into the streaming sunlight. The blast of light assaulted his eyes the way it did when he was a kid and spent the entire afternoon in a darkened movie house. There was a taxi idling in front of the building, with the cabby scribbling on his trip sheet after having discharged a passenger. Alex yanked the door open and ushered Sally and Pinto inside.

"Where to, mac?" the cabby said.

"Head down to the lower Eastside," Alex said.

"Sorry, Mac. Get yaselves another cab. I gotta be out in Queens by the end of my shift at four."

Alex lost it. "Do as I say and do it quickly!" he screamed. "Before . . . before I rip off your fucking arms!"

"You better do like he says, man," Pinto said. "I think you makin' him hostile."

The cabby was about to open his mouth, then took one look at Alex's eyes and thought better of it. He slipped his vehicle into gear and pushed his way into the steady stream of southbound traffic on Fifth. Forty-two minutes later they pulled up in front of an abandoned warehouse, a half block away from CRUSH's headquarters. Alex paid the cabby wordlessly, still in shock.

Upstairs the others were waiting, the radio tuned in to an all-news station as they listened for word of a bomb explosion in midtown Manhattan. They all jumped up when Alex and the others walked in the door.

"What happened?" Kenyatta asked.

Alex looked around the room for Nicky, who was slumped in the corner in his Wall Street get-up.

"What happened?" Alex answered Kenyatta, staring all the time at Nicky. "What happened is that Mister Bomb Expert over there, the Boomer, did it again."

He related the saga of the long, sorry afternoon they spent in the elevator.

"I don't get it," Nicky said when Alex finished.

"What is it you don't get?"

"I can't figure out why you're pissed off because I built a dud that didn't go off when it was supposed to an' kill you. Maybe you'd be happier if I made a bomb that blew your ass to smithereens."

"He's right," Kenyatta said. "You owe him one."

Of course Nicky was right, Alex thought. For once the man was being rational. His demolitions expertise needed a little work, or else the three of them would not be here to tell the tale. Alex erupted into a fit of giggles, and the others joined in.

"I say we all go out and celebrate," Jennifer said. "We'll drink a toast to Nicky, who—"

"To Nicky, whose great foresight saved the lives of our comrades," Doug completed the sentence.

"Yeah, I think we could all use a drink right now," Alex said. "I know I could." He went over and shook Nicky's hand. "Friends?"

"Friends."

Nicky took the toolbox from Pinto and put it in the closet. "I'll check it out later," he said.

They locked the door and walked down the rickety stairwell to the street below. In surprisingly good spirits considering the failure of their mission, the revolutionary cadre continued along the sidewalk toward the corner bar. It was almost as though an unspoken sense of relief had come upon them. It is one thing to plan the death of a leading member of the evil ruling class, and quite another to see innocent people—notwithstanding Alex's rhetoric to the contrary—die along with him.

Kenyatta was just about to open the door of the corner saloon, when his hand was arrested in place by the booming sound of an explosion. They all looked up in unison at what used to be the window of their headquarters down the street, and watched helplessly as bits of furniture and other personal effects came showering down into the street.

Pinto expressed their mood best when he said, "Shit, Nicky. You got to do somethin' about your sense of timing. You know what I mean?"

Chapter Twenty

Ludwig von Dracula woke up at the crack of night on September sixth. He tossed his coffin lid to the side, hopped out, and donned the clothing he had laid out the night before. He climbed onto the ledge outside his window, lifted his arms parallel to the ground, stared down toward the street below, and leaped off. As soon as his feet left the side of the building, his flesh and clothing melded into the hide of a bat and his body reshaped itself into the winged mammal. Luddie soared across the night sky and, in seconds, flew through the open window of Alex's apartment. The instant he hit the floor he transformed himself back to human form.

The thud of the landing caught Alex's ear in the next room. He quickly hung up the phone and came charging in to see what was going on.

"You?" he said. "How'd you get in?"

"Flew. You were expecting me, were you not?"

This is getting too weird, Alex thought. What have I let myself in for?

"It's not weird at all," Luddie said. "We discussed why we're doing this, remember?"

"How did you know what I was think . . .? Never mind, I don't want to know."

"How are you feeling tonight, Alex?"

"Fine, so far." Alex shrugged.

"Do you have your camera set up?"

"You bet I do." Alex nodded toward the bed table. "I wouldn't miss this for anything."

Luddie went over to familiarize himself with its operation. He noticed that the flash attachment was of a kind that automatically recharged after each use. The short delay after each shot might reduce the number of pictures that could be taken, but it would do.

"All right?" Alex asked.

"A bit crude, but it'll do."

"So what do we do now?" The irritation was apparent in Alex's voice.

"Do you have a deck of cards?"

"Yeah. Why?"

"Let's play gin while we're waiting. Nothing big. Penny a point, nickel a box."

"I should gamble with a man who can read my mind? Fuck you, Luddie!"

"No need to get hostile. We'll just play for fun then."

Alex got the deck and tossed it onto the table. Luddie picked it up and shuffled. "Cut for deal," he said. He split the deck in half and showed a seven, then reshuffled and slid it over to Alex who sliced out a four.

"My deal." Luddie took the cards and observed Alex as he lifted his hand and rubbed his throat.

"I'm getting thirsty," Alex said. "Can I get you something?"

"Nothing for me, thanks." Luddie dealt out two hands face down and turned one card up. "Six is the knock card." he said, watching Alex rise from his seat and go into the kitchen. He could hear him running the faucet and filling a glass, then gulping it down thirstily. He filled it again and carried it back to the card table. Luddie kept his eyes fixed on Alex as he reached for his cards, but raised his hand to his throat and massaged it instead.

"Are you feeling ill?" Luddie asked.

"I don't know. My throat's getting dry and I feel a bit feverish." Alex downed his water in a single gulp.

"Lie down in the bedroom," Luddie said. "I'll get you another drink."

Alex started to rise, lifting himself with his hands braced on the sides of the table when his legs began to buckle and his face turned red.

"Help me," Alex said.

Luddie darted around the table and caught Alex's arm as his body sagged closer to the floor. He draped Alex's arm across his shoulder and held him around the waist. With faltering steps, Luddie trundled Alex into the bedroom and lowered him onto the bed.

"I need more water." Alex's voice was weak and raspy.

"Lie down and take it easy. I'll be right back with some." When Luddie returned a moment later with the refilled glass Alex's brow was red and feverish and perspiration poured from his face onto the pillow. Luddie spilled some of the water onto his handkerchief and placed it on Alex's forehead.

"Take it easy, I'm right here," he said.

"D-don't leave me. I've never been so scared in my life." Alex's voice was barely more than a whisper.

"I'm not going anywhere, Alex." He unbuttoned Alex's shirt and removed his tight jeans.

"The pain's unbearable. I can't stand it."

"It'll pass soon, very soon. I promise."

Alex held his throat with both hands. His breathing quickened until he was gulping air repeatedly. After several moments, the pace subsided until Alex was breathing normally once again.

Luddie placed his hand on Alex's forehead and felt the fever recede. He watched as Alex closed his eyelids and fell almost instantly into a deep sleep. Luddie rose from his kneeling position beside the bed and went over to get the camera, studying Alex all the while for any signs of change.

Everything appeared to be normal for a full twenty minutes, when Luddie noticed the first stirrings in Alex's body. It occurred piecemeal at first, pulsing and bubbling like volcanic action beneath the skin in isolated areas of his body. Then convulsions spread throughout and Alex's entire being quaked violently. Portions of his frame began to expand; Luddie pointed the camera and snapped the first shot. Alex's dark hair faded, becoming lighter and lighter until it had turned completely blond. Luddie snapped away, taking pictures as fast as he could. Still Alex's body continued its metamorphosis, expanding, bubbling, throbbing.

Soon Alex's face assumed new proportions. His features twisted, changed, reformed themselves. His body stretched and grew to over six feet tall. Luddie pressed the shutter release again and then, finally, the changes taking place in Alex came to an end. The individual lying in bed where Alex had lain moments before looked nothing at all like him. He was taller, startlingly handsome, with high cheekbones, straight blond hair, and a lean, well-muscled body devoid of fat. Luddie stepped back away from the bed as the creature came alive. He watched it from the corner as it flexed its fingers, opened its eyes, then sat up abruptly and threw its feet over the side of the bed. The creature stretched its arms and yawned, stood up and yawned again, facing away from Luddie.

Luddie watched as this new Alex furrowed his brow, apparently aware that he was somehow connected to this apartment, but not exactly why or how.

When the new Alex finished dressing, Luddie stepped into the center of the room, called to get his attention, aimed the camera and shot. The flash startled the being, which raised an arm across its eyes.

"Well I'll be!" Luddie exclaimed, a shock of recognition in his voice. "Nice to meet you. Aren't you—?"

Instantly, the new Alex underwent another transformation as Luddie stopped in mid-sentence. The handsome face became a snarling, menacing visage with a long, pointed snout and a large, gaping jaw out of which two sharp fangs descended to below the bottom lip. Its nails grew into miniature, razor-sharp swords. Most terrifying of all, the creature's azure eyes now glowed with the intensity of fiery red coals.

Luddie stepped backward as a low growl rumbled from the creature's throat and it advanced slowly toward him. He put the camera down on the bureau and looked around; there was nowhere to run, nowhere to hide. Now the growl became a horrific roar, deafening and chilling in its intensity. The creature advanced a step and crouched. Luddie dropped into a crouch himself, prepared for the worst. He willed himself into combat form, transfiguring his nails into sharpened points and his teeth into elongated fangs as menacing as the creature's. The creature halted and roared, carefully measuring its transformed opponent. Luddie roared back, snarled, and circled to the side. The creature crouched lower and circled with him, then with lightning speed sliced its right claw through the air. Luddie saw it coming and caught the wrist before the claws struck home. The creature lunged with its left and Luddie whipped his head to the side, blinking as the dagger-like nails whizzed past his face.

With the creature slightly off balance after the second thrust, Luddie spun on his heels, his hand still locked on the monster's wrist, pulled it over his head and flung it to the floor. He jumped on top of the stunned form, his claws ready to strike a mortal blow to its throat, but the demon rolled out easily from underneath and catapulted to its feet. Now Luddie was at a temporary disadvantage as the creature moved in again.

Luddie thrust twice with his left, but the monster easily blocked his jabs. They each retreated a foot, searching for an opening. Suddenly, the creature rushed him. Instead of sidestepping this time, Luddie advanced as though to meet the charge, then ducked low as the monster's momentum carried him over Luddie and sent him hurtling to the floor. Luddie grabbed it around the neck and waist, lifted it above his head and spun around in dizzying circles. Then he hurled the demon against a framed Warhol poster on the wall, splintering the room with flying glass.

The monster caromed off the wall and landed on its side, lying there stunned for several moments. Luddie moved in quickly, but the creature recovered and rolled onto its hind legs to face him, growling as it did so. It crouched as though it was preparing to lunge again, its evil, fiery eyes locked on Luddie's. With blinding speed it leaped forward just as Luddie launched a charge of his own. They crashed head-on and fell to the floor a foot or so apart.

Luddie started to swipe at the monster's face with his left, but the demon charged first, catching Luddie across his legs and knocking him off-balance. The creature was over him before Luddie could recover. It grabbed him by his collar and belt, hoisted him into the air, and heaved him across the room onto a table that collapsed beneath his falling body. Luddie sat up and turned, only to see the well-aimed kick for a split second before it caught him on the temple. The second kick struck his ribs, knocking him back against the wall.

Hurt, dazed, but not unconscious, Luddie saw the third kick whipping straight at his face. He caught the ankle just before impact, twisted, and spun the monster to the floor. Seeing his momentary advantage, Luddie ignored the pain in his side and jumped to his feet. He grabbed a heavy wooden chair, lifted it overhead, and brought it crashing down on the monster's head. The chair shattered instantly. Luddie tossed what was left of it aside and rushed the beast. Again, the beast recovered quickly. It jumped up and met Luddie's advance, locking its claws on his. They struggled for several seconds, each trying to gain an advantage over the other. Luddie hurled himself backward to the floor, raised his feet to catch the beast in the pit of the stomach as it fell forward, and heaved it backward in a somersault.

Luddie twisted around and jumped onto the monster's back. He grabbed it around the throat and was about to break its neck, when the demon slashed back blindly with its right claw and ripped Luddie's face with its razor-sharp nails. Luddie howled with pain as the wound seared its way deep inside. The skin on Luddie's cheeks and forehead was flayed open to the bone; the pain was excruciating. He roared with hurt and rage. With a maddening, blind fury now, Luddie threw himself headlong at the monster's face, but the beast was ready for him. It smashed its head into Luddie's chest and knocked him to the floor. It lifted Luddie by the neck and tightened its claws against his throat. Luddie felt his strength draining out of him with each passing second. He tried to recover, tried to summon his reserve strength for one final attack, but the reservoir was close to empty.

The beast held him by the throat and brought its face close to his. Luddie could see the gloat of victory in its sizzling red eyes. Defenseless now, unable to continue the fight any longer, Luddie raised his arms slowly with the last ounce of strength he had left. He closed his eyes and concentrated all his energy into his mind. His will took over and, instantly, Luddie disappeared from the demon's iron grip. The claws closed on empty air. Luddie lifted himself to the ceiling, in bat form now, as the monster roared in frustration, searching the room for its errant foe.

Luddie circled around the ceiling, just beyond the beast's reach. He headed toward the open window but the creature, sensing the movement above its head, sprung there first and slammed it shut. The pain inflicted on Luddie's human form earlier still assailed him. His face was on fire from the slashing wounds. He needed to escape, to find sanctuary from this monster and regain his strength so that he could continue the battle another day—before the next full moon when the horrific change in Alex would become permanent. Luddie circled the room, flew throughout the apartment, looking for an exit while the beast howled beneath him, leaping and slashing its claws through the air.

Dracula grew weary, and the pain in his face intensified, rippling throughout his body. The strength in his wings diminished, and as he slowed in his flight the swiping claws of the beast missed him by mere inches. Luddie had difficulty maintaining speed and altitude, and soon fell within range of the deadly claws.

He dove, circling around the monster's waist, then ascended with great difficulty toward the ceiling. The demon swiped again, this time ripping him across a wing with the tips of its nails.

Luddie faltered, fluttering aimlessly around the living room, then landed on the coffee table in front of the sofa. It was just a matter of time now—seconds at most— before the monster closed in for the kill. Luddie needed to focus his mind for one final transformation. Concentrate and focus. Time was running out rapidly.

He opened his eyes only to see the demon glaring at him with victory in its eyes once again. The monster approached, ready to lunge. Luddie shivered with fear, and summoned his remaining strength into his mind. His final metamorphosis was accomplished with only a microsecond to spare. The beast landed claws first on the coffee table—into a puff of smoke. The claws slashed through the smoky mist that wafted upward toward the ceiling. The beast howled in frustration, battering the table until it shattered into a thousand splinters.

The mist kept rising, and stretched out along the ceiling well beyond the monster's reach. The monster leaped again and again, flailing at the drifting vapor. The vapor floated into the kitchen and the demon saw the vacuum cleaner resting against the wall. It plugged the cord into the socket and flicked the switch on. It raised the vacuum overhead and chased the mist as it sailed across the ceiling. Luddie heard the roaring machine and felt its pull, trying to restrain his movement. He soared faster across the ceiling toward the place where he remembered the door was located.

Luddie found the door on the first try, then swooped down along its surface and sailed out through the crack above the sill. The monster was just behind him and the suction tugged him back before he was completely free. There he was, so close to freedom, and now he was trapped again. He tried to regain his motion out into the hallway, but the power was too strong. He willed himself ahead with all his strength, but his strength was ebbing quickly and he felt his form being pulled back inside the apartment.

Then, abruptly, the power quit as the plug pulled loose from the socket. The suction faded and Luddie soared forward again, faster and faster, his momentum undeterred now by the vacuum cleaner. Free! Free! Free at last! Thank God I'm free at last, Luddie thought, as he flew rapidly down the stairwell and out into the night air.

As mist, Luddie was free of the pains of the flesh, and he moved comfortably through the air although more slowly than he could as a bat. His progress was slowed further by air currents to which he was also vulnerable. Allowing for an even stronger head wind than he faced at the moment, Luddie estimated that he should be back in his apartment in no more than fifteen minutes—time enough to tend to his injuries before he was required to resume his human form in approximately three-quarters of an hour.

He could easily mend his simple cuts by concentrating his mind and melding the broken skin into a seamless, unmarked surface. Minor bruises, likewise, required only brief mental exercises. But the deeper slashes and bruises to his rib cage would be more difficult to heal. He would have to enter a deep sleep for three days and allow his unconscious mind to release its restorative powers.

Luddie floated over the rooftops and contemplated the problems that lay ahead. Alex's alter ego was strong and intelligent, more powerful than he imagined it would be. He had been surprised that he was able to engage it in combat for as long as he did, and he had no illusions about being able to survive a one-on-one struggle with the monster in the future.

His choices were limited. What it came down to was that, if the demon was going to be stopped, Alex had to die before the eclipse of the moon next month. Luddie could see no other alternative. Yet, the thought of murder—the destruction of another being however demonic it was—was anathema to Luddie. Quite simply, I am not a murderer, he thought as he wended his way through the buffeting air currents. It's not for me to decide who, or what, should live or die. But what was the alternative? Alex was like the carrier of a deadly plague. It was necessary to quarantine a plague-carrier so that he did not infect others.

Quarantine, not kill. Do we kill patients, or are we supposed to treat and comfort them as best we can?

But Luddie knew in the deepest recesses of his being that a quarantine would not work in Alex's case. His change during the next full moon would be permanent. He will not merely turn into the monster for a brief interval, he will *become* the monster. Even so, do we kill the creature on the suspicion that it's evil? Isn't that what humans had done to vampires for centuries? Do I betray my own beliefs by attacking a creature I don't understand? The creature, after all, is only living according to its own nature and its own needs. It attacked me because it felt threatened itself. What about its non-beast aspect? Perhaps that part of its nature was capable of living a productive, constructive, creative existence.

Do I, Ludwig von Dracula, have the right to take the law into my own hands? Isn't that what the legal establishment was for? Could you have a civilized society if everyone struck out at someone or something they considered threatening? The answer was obvious: of course not. As justified as murder might seem to be in the case of the Alex demon, it was still unacceptable. Even if it were evil to its core, no one had a right to strike it down before it committed a crime. It was necessary to take precautions against that eventuality—but morally proper ones. Murdering Alex did not fall into that category; it was just plain wrong. Luddie would have to find another way.

Light winds buffeted the mist that was Ludwig von Dracula. He saw his building up ahead, and concentrated on negotiating the air currents as best he could to complete his journey on time. Soon he was there, and he descended to his window and entered his apartment through a crack in the sill. Inside now, he hovered two feet above the floor, and then expanded from floor to ceiling. The smoky vapor began to swirl, thickening and hardening like an increasingly opaque volcano until a human shape appeared. Luddie had returned to flesh form once again.

Instantly, the pain returned. It swamped him with a vengeance and he clutched his side to still the agonizing throbbing. His cheeks, his forehead, his entire face was on fire. He limped into the kitchen, took a vial of blood out of the refrigerator, and drained it in one swallow. Then he returned to the living room and sat down on the floor. His left leg hurt, and there was a burning sensation under his right arm where the demon had slashed his wing. The bloody gash snaked downward from his armpit to his elbow. His entire body felt as though it had been hacked and torn by sharp knives.

Luddie pressed the palms of his hands together and raised his fingertips to the point of his chin. Next he closed his eyes and mentally scanned his entire being, beginning with his head and working toward his toes. He focused on each area of his body where he felt pain. When this exercise was completed, he concentrated on the lesser injuries and could actually feel the healing taking place. He touched his face and the skin was smooth to his touch. A remnant of pain remained, but the worst of it was gone.

The bruised ribs and slashed arm would take a bit longer. His mental scanning process had revealed that there were no broken bones, and no damage to the muscles in his arm. He was close to exhaustion now, and dawn was rapidly approaching. It was time to turn in, time to will himself into a deep, deep hypnotic sleep and allow his unconscious mental forces to exercise their power. Total healing, and the complete restoration of his strength and vibrancy, required undisturbed rest for three full days.

With great exertion, Luddie lifted himself off the floor and walked over to his coffin. Rarely in the past had he felt so weary of mind, body, and spirit. His injuries, his exhaustion, his epic struggle with the demon all weighed heavily upon him. But even worse than these, there was also the question of Alex—the young human male whom he had genuinely come to like, as a human being. But what was he to do about Alex in his soon-to-be permanently transformed state? That was a dilemma with no easy solutions. That was his most terrifying nightmare come to life.

CHAPTER TWENTY-ONE

The beast that had been Alex Maltese felt pain as he looked about the apartment but stifled an angry roar. Placing a claw against one of the sore spots on his chest, he tried to understand what occurred. He had never encountered another creature such as that before. This other also had claws and fangs and the power to take on a bestial shape. But, wondered the new Alex, could I also transform into a bat or mist, like the other creature.

As the creature paced about calmly a new feeling enveloped him, fogginess, dizziness. Memories of what took place and who he was faded. "No! Not again. Don't leave me!" he screamed, his voice trailing off in frustration. The earlier encounter disappeared down a memory hole. Confusion took over, and anger. The beast looked through the window into the night and leaped head first through the panes of glass onto the fire escape. He climbed down into the alley alongside the building and receded into the dark shadows, surveying the scene ahead, trying to make sense of things. Then he collapsed.

Luke Fenris awoke, naked, and found himself once again in a back alley on the Lower Eastside. He had been in and around this neighborhood many times before but was never sure how he got there. He had no memory of what occurred, just fuzzy dreams that made no sense. Because of his past experiences, he always arranged to leave some clothes and pocket money hidden behind a false wall, a brick facade far deep in the alleyway. He dressed quickly, unaware of the bruises and marks showing on his face, stepped out onto the street and hailed a cab.

He exited the cab a few minutes later in front of Xanadu Towers. He paid the cabby, and then strode briskly across the sidewalk toward the building's entrance.

"Are you all right, Mr. Fenris?" The doorman stared at him with a look of shock on his face.

"Why yes, Matthew. Why do you ask?"

"Y-your face, sir. Were you mugged?"

Fenris rubbed his hand across his face and felt what seemed to be dried, sticky blood. There was also a dull throbbing in several places where he apparently was cut and bruised. No wonder the cabby had been glaring at him through the rear view mirror.

"Well, yes, a couple of savages did try to jump me," Fenris said, "but I boxed their ears and chased them away."

"Would you like me to call the police, sir?"

"That won't be necessary. The streets are full of degenerate swine these days. These two will just blend in with all the others."

"Are you sure, sir?"

"Absolutely. They didn't get anything anyway, except some bumps and bruises they deserved."

Fenris repeated the same fabrication to the elevator operator on the way up to his apartment. When Barbara, his maid, opened the door, she too gasped in shock.

"It's nothing, Barbara, nothing. Looks much worse than it is. Are the others here?"

"Yes, sir. They're waiting in the living room. C-can I get you something, Mr. Fenris?"

"Nothing." He waved her aside and walked into the living room. Danielle was the first to rise, and then raised the back of her hand to her mouth when she saw his face. Luke went over, kissed her, and answered her unasked question. "It's nothing, darling. Just a superficial flesh wound. It'll look like new when I wash off the blood."

"Good God, Luke. What happened?" asked General Thorn, also rising to his feet, as did Carl Navi who had been sitting beside him on the sofa.

"Couple of would-be muggers," Fenris said, making light of it. "They look a hell of a lot worse than I do right now. Give me a minute to wash up, will you? I'll be right out."

"Damn! Luke. You should be more careful. All these crazies running around. If I were you I'd start wearing a bulletproof vest. You never know who you'll run into. I'll have the agency send you one tomorrow."

"That's good of you, General." Fenris went into the bathroom and locked the door behind him. The reflection in the mirror told him everything he needed to know. His face looked as though it had been run over by a lawn mower. Poor Danielle. The sight of him had almost caused her to faint. He raised his hands to his battered visage, closed his eyes and concentrated. Within seconds he could feel the skin turning fresh and whole beneath his hands. He had discovered this bizarre healing power after cutting himself shaving once, and it hadn't failed him since. All he had to do was touch an injured part of his body, concentrate, and it made him well again.

Satisfied that he had restored the bruised and lacerated skin to its normal condition, Fenris searched his memory for details of what had transpired. He had no conscious memories of what took place before he awoke in the alleyway, just vague recollections of a strange dream in which he had become a furry, fanged beast and thrashed about with a similar creature. But few details bubbled up. He stared blankly into the mirror and studied his reflection, searching for a clue to his dilemma

Luke Fenris trembled; he felt fear for the first time in his existence, but he didn't know what it was that scared him.

"Luke! Are you all right?" He heard Danielle call him from the other side of the locked door. "Can I come in, darling?"

"I'll be out in just a moment."

There was something different about him that he did not understand. He disappeared, he knew, for weeks at a time. Where did he go? What did he do? It had something to do with the full moon; that much was evident. It must have something to do with his puzzling appearances in odd places on the Lower Eastside, but he could never remember how and why he came to be there. Why did he always appear at night? Was he an alter ego of someone with a multiple personality disorder? Perhaps a schizophrenic? What else might it be? And what about his unusual abilities, like this healing power and his sudden surges of strength in threatening situations. Most bizarre of all were his occasional transformations into a beast-like creature, like the time he ripped apart that Fortunato fellow and his bodyguards. He must be here on earth for a special purpose, he figured, a specific reason. What else could account for his genius, his staggering success, his encyclopedic grasp of financial details and the intricacies of doing deals? He had no recollection of any education that would have trained him for such a career.

What should he tell Danielle? How could he explain his mysterious absences and departures? Once they were married, it would be just a question of time before she discovered his deceptions. He had to tell her something, but what? Even he didn't know what was going on. He had no memory of childhood, of growing up, no memory of family or education. He had no recollection of *anything at all* taking place more than six years in the past. How could he tell Danielle anything that was not itself a total fabrication? And what happens when she discovers the beast aspect of my nature?

Fenris unlocked the door and went out to face his guests. "Can you excuse us a moment, darling, while we take care of some business?" he said to Danielle. "It won't take long. Then we'll go out to dinner."

She peered at him sternly, but affectionately. "Won't take long you say? It's been eternity already since I saw you last."

"I promise. Fifteen minutes, then we'll be done."

"Promise?"

"Promise."

He kissed her on the forehead, then ushered his guests into the study and closed the door.

"Gentlemen," Fenris said. "Let's start with you, General. What do you have for us?"

"Everything's in place, just as you planned, Luke." Thorn pulled some papers out of his briefcase and placed them on the desk. "The first troop movements're in the pipeline. The army'll be assembled in Bruwanda by mid-November. All we need is the go-ahead from you."

Fenris picked up the report and speed-read the first few pages. "How about your end, Carl?" he said without looking up.

"The CBS team will announce its intent to take over the network in two weeks, By December we should have control. After that we launch the CNN, NBC, and Fox actions. Eighteen months from now we'll have a pretty good media-lock on the nation. We'll control the flow of news coverage and the content. Within two years we should see a significant change in programming. The political thrust will be altered completely and, if I'm any judge of the opposition, the left wing of the political spectrum will be squealing like stuck pigs."

"Tell me about the screw-up with Hollings and the reporter," Fenris said to Thorn.

The general brought him up-to-date on the gruesome episode involving Hollings and Triptolemeus.

"Do we know the identity of the person the reporter gave the report to?" Fenris asked when Thorn finished.

"Well . . . we had a lead, one of the copy boys who functioned as our eyes and ears at the paper. Unfortunately, he bungled things, and my men got a little overanxious and eliminated him with their car before we found out who it was."

"We have to find out who he is. He's a loose cannon out there, something we don't need right now. This business with Hollings is bad enough in itself."

"We followed your instructions to a tee, Luke. Removed Hollings from the board, paid him a big bonus, everything you said. I left you a memo on it. But he panicked, that's the only word for it. He was nervous from the start and went over the edge."

"If the truth about his death gets out . . .," Fenris left his thought unfinished.

"It won't, Luke," Thorn said. "There's, well there's just nothing left to find."

"I want those papers. And I want to know who's seen them. Understood?"

"Completely."

"Then do it, General. Do it."

"We're working on it, Luke. I've got a mole in the detective squad reviewing police reports, getting the names of witnesses from the newsroom. We'll continue to check them out."

"Good, good. That's it then. Thank you, gentlemen. I've got a hungry woman waiting for me to take her out to dinner. If I don't pay her some attention soon, there'll be hell to pay."

Thorn and Navi laughed, grateful that the meeting was over and for the sudden change in mood. Fenris saw them to the door, and then prepared himself for an evening with his future bride. The rest of the night should be more pleasant than what had preceded it—although, not without a certain tension of its own.

Alex awoke under a tree alongside a hill in Central Park, once again wearing a set of ill-fitting clothes. While he occasionally found himself in his own bed after his three-day blackouts, more often than not he came to in various locations around midtown Manhattan, usually, but not always, in unrecognizable garb. On occasion, he found himself naked in embarrassing circumstances. Fortunately, when he awoke in strange attire, there was often a couple of hundred dollars in cash in one of the pockets, a small but helpful supplement to his tight financial budget. He raised himself, felt for the cash, found it, and headed to the street where he hailed a cab and went home.

Alex stood in the middle of his living room, stunned at the sight of the debris and broken furniture. The dining table was little more than a pile of splintered wood, the chairs were heaps of broken sticks, the Warhol poster had been reduced to a hole in the wall, and the coffee table was a collection of glass shards and odd-shaped fragments. The lamps that had not been broken were overturned, lying on their sides like so many dead soldiers strewn over a battlefield.

What had gone on here? What was the meaning of it all?

The last thing Alex remembered was the excruciating pain that assailed him when he started to play cards with Luddie von Dracula. Luddie! What had become of him? He had entrusted himself—his safety and sanity—to the eccentric so-called vampire, and this was the result. He had literally put himself in Luddie's hands, only to return to this—this violation of his home and personal effects. His apartment, his possessions, his very life had been trashed beyond redemption.

"I'll kill him!" Alex screamed. "What did you do to me? Why me? Why couldn't you find someone else to torment?"

He didn't know where to begin cleaning. The whole idea of sorting out this mess was enough to plunge him into a deeper pit of despair than the one he was in already. "I trusted you!" he shouted. "How could you do this to me?"

Alex was torn between rage and helplessness. On one hand he wanted to lash out and hurt whoever had done this thing to him, perhaps even kill him. On the other hand he was close to collapsing onto the floor and crying hysterically. He was saved from this emotional and spiritual paralysis by the ringing of the telephone. Trance-like, he staggered toward the jangling sound and picked up the phone.

"Yes?"

"There you are! I've been calling you day and night. Where've you been? I told you I hate it when you just disappear on me like that."

"Sally?"

"Yes, Sally. Who were you expecting? Danielle maybe?"

"Hey, chill out a bit, lady! Ease off on me, okay?"

"Why are you so upset, Mister Maltese? I'm the one—"

"Why am I so upset? I'll tell you why I'm upset. First of all, I collapsed the other day with horrible chest pains and was taken to the hospital in an ambulance. No one there could figure out what was wrong with me, so they finally released me half an hour ago. I come home and find out my apartment's been trashed by . . . I don't know, somebody. King Kong from the looks of the place. Then, while I'm standing here on the verge of a nervous breakdown, the phone rings. I pick it up and, without so much as 'How are you? Are you okay?' I'm being accused of going off on a tryst with my ex-wife. You think that's enough to get me upset? You're damned right it is!"

"Alex . . . I'm sorry. I had no idea."

"Well, maybe if you took a minute to find out—"

"I didn't mean to yell at you, Alex. It's just that I was worried about you. You said you would call me and . . . and when you didn't, I thought something happened to you. And I was right. Something did happen to you."

"Yeah, well, I didn't mean to snap at you either."

"Would you like me to come over? I can help you clean up."

"No. Thanks anyway, but it's hopeless. I don't know where to begin and I don't want to deal with it right now."

"I'm sorry I bothered you. Just give me a call when you feel like it, okay?"

"No, wait. Let's get together tonight. Dinner sound all right? Maybe a movie later once I get my head screwed on right."

"You sure? If you're not feeling all that well—"

"No. I mean, yes, I'm sure. I'll pick you up around seven if that's convenient."

"That's fine by me."

"See you then."

A night out with Sally would do him some good after this. Not that she had any answers for him. But she definitely cared about him. And he needed to be with someone who cared right now.

Chapter Twenty-Two

Dracula opened his eyes for the first time in three nights. He pressed his hand against the coffin lid and pushed it off to the side. He lay still in the coffin for several moments, and then flexed his muscles one at a time, testing them for soreness. His pain of several days before had completely disappeared. In his cursory examination, he could detect no sign of injury.

Gradually, the details of his war with the demon flooded into his mind. He recalled everything all at once: the lethal swipes with claws and fangs, the pulverizing smashes, the brutal, exhausting, and nearly fatal brush with death. The monster was terrifying, all but invincible. Somehow, he would have to find a way to stop it.

Then, almost as an afterthought, Luddie remembered why he had been there that night; the whole purpose of the visit was to observe Alex as he underwent his transformation. The task had been more perilous than he imagined, nearly costing him his life. Now that he knew the nature of Alex's infection in all its horrifying implications, he had to act at once. Luddie jumped out of his coffin and went over to the telephone. He dialed Alex's number and fidgeted anxiously as the ringing went unanswered. After three more fruitless attempts to reach him during the next ten minutes, Luddie decided to get over to Alex's apartment immediately and wait for him to turn up. He shuddered to think of what might happen if that creature survived the next full moon.

Luddie walked over to the window and willed himself into bat form. Minutes later, he landed on the window ledge of Alex's apartment. The window was broken, so he just flew through the shattered frame. Once inside, he metamorphosed back to human form and looked around at the wreckage.

The physical pain had left Luddie, but the mental anguish he experienced upon revisiting the scene of his mortal struggle with the monster immediately overwhelmed him. Poor Alex, he thought, an innocent victim in this epic saga, and yet a lethal and nearly indestructible adversary. Luddie picked his way among the ruins, shocked by the extent of the destruction. Any observer who had not been a party to the carnage would assume that a marauding army had laid waste to Alex's apartment. How was it possible that only he and one other creature had done all this? The battle had seemed endless at the time, yet it could not have lasted longer than a few minutes from start to finish. So much damage, so much devastation, so many near rendezvous with death in the blinking of an eye.

Incongruously, Luddie felt a sharp pang of hunger accompanied by a spasm of dizziness. How long had it been since he'd eaten last? He stepped over the splintered remains of the furniture and the broken glass, and went into the kitchen. Alex's refrigerator contained a broiled chicken breast neatly enclosed in plastic wrap, and a single bottle of beer—a typical bachelor's spread, not unlike his own. It was not exactly to his taste; he preferred spicier fare like Tex-Mex and Cajun food. But there was no other choice.

Luddie opened the beer first and took a long, refreshing swallow. Then he sunk his teeth into Alex's chicken breast and polished it off in several voracious mouthfuls. When he was done, he wandered through the apartment, looking for . . . for . . . there it was, just where he remembered, over by the window. The door of the camera was open and the exposed film lay beside it. Damn! Damn! His photographs—his only proof of what he had witnessed and experienced—were worthless. Then again, Luddie had not expected anything else. His situation was hopeless. How could he expect Alex to believe him in the absence of any shred of convincing evidence?

There was nothing to do now but wait. Luddie walked over to the sofa, found the remote, and clicked on the television. Thank God that, at least, still worked. He sat down and glowered at the screen, oblivious to what was on, and waited for Alex to return home.

Alex was not in the best of moods when he dropped off Sally at her apartment. She had talked him into eating Mexican food even though he despised the stuff, particularly those pasty beans and that gloppy guacamole that he believed he was allergic to. It was the only food that caused him to break out in rashes for days afterward. He was irritable and still hungry for something civilized—like a grilled chicken breast—as he mounted the stairs to his apartment. Just as he paused to catch his breath before going in, Alex thought he heard the muted sounds of voices inside. Was that Jay Leno in there, making corny jokes as usual? He could have sworn his television set was off when he left; he hadn't watched the idiot box in days.

Flinging caution to the winds, Alex decided to go in and investigate. What else could happen to him after the events of the past few days? A mugging? A knock on the head? That would be a welcome diversion. Alex inserted the key in the lock, hesitated a moment, then gripped the door handle and got ready to turn it when it flew out of his hand.

"Luddie!"

"Alex! Good Lord! You scared the life out of me. Come in already."

"What are you doing here?"

"We had an appointment, remember? I said I'd give you a rundown on everything that took place when the full moon was over. I've been waiting for hours."

"How can you . . . how can you stand there and talk to me so calmly after trashing my apartment?" The tone of Alex's voice suggested he was on the verge of hysteria.

"Don't be absurd, Alex. I didn't trash your apartment."

"You had your vampire friends in! My place looks worse than the day after a toga party!"

"Nonsense. Why would I do something like that? What kind of a savage do you think I am?"

"Well, what happened then? If you didn't party in here when I was unconscious, then what?"

"Alex, Alex. Calm down please. Let me give this to you slowly."

Alex could hardly believe that Ludwig von Dracula was standing before him, admitting him into his own apartment if you please, looking as unruffled as a British peer presiding over High Tea.

"Forget slowly!" Alex yelled. "I want to know what happened all at once. I'm a big boy. I can take it. Trust me."

"What happened, in a nutshell, was, well, you."

"Me? So it was my fault, right?"

"Yes and no. In a way, that is."

"I can't take it." Alex's patience was depleted. "I've been to dinner, I've got hives, and I'm still famished. I need a quick bite and a beer. Just make yourself at home for a minute . . . if you'll forgive the absurdity of that suggestion."

"Oh dear. I'm so sorry. I should have brown-bagged it, but then I would have had to walk over as a human, I'm afraid, and I was in such a hurry." Luddie pointed with embarrassment to the pile of chicken bones and crushed beer can on the counter.

"He eats my food, too." Alex collapsed onto the sofa in exasperation. "He destroys my home, then comes back uninvited, tells me it's my fault, and eats my food. So what's next? Maybe you want to fuck my girlfriend, too?"

"I'm so sorry, Alex. I was in a mad rush to get over here and I didn't have a chance to eat. I didn't realize it would upset you so much."

"You don't like me, do you?" Alex said. "I mean, don't deny it. Let's just get it out in the open right now."

"I do deny it. I'm quite fond of you actually, as hard as it is for you to accept that."

"Then why me? Why not find somebody else to destroy?"

"Will you listen to me for just a minute?"

"Sure. Just try to make it good. My credulity's already stretched to the max."

"You may find this difficult to believe, but I had a terrible, terrible fight with a werewolf here the other night."

"Everybody has a bad date once in a while. That's no reason to get ballistic over it."

"I'm talking serious struggle. I'm talking werewolf, Alex. Bloodcurdling, frothing, killer monster. Do you understand what I'm saying?"

"I'm not responsible for your friends, Luddie. Who told you to invite someone . . . er, some thing like that to my apartment?"

"It was you, Alex. You're the werewolf. When the moon is full you become another being . . . actually, two beings, one of which is a powerful but violent monster. That's what accounts for your blackouts."

"You told me the odds against that happening were—"

"The odds were overwhelmingly against it, against your being infected by Tanya's bite in any way. You cashed in on a long shot, I'm afraid."

"Sort of like hitting the werewolf lottery, is that it?"

"No need to get snotty about it. I'm just as upset as you are."

"Where's your proof, Luddie? You must have taken some pretty awesome photographs of all this, something fit for Ripley's Believe It Or Not."

Luddie shook his head in embarrassment, seemingly beyond belief himself. "That's the sad part, Alex. I had to flee for my life. I was almost killed. The creature is as intelligent as it is vicious. He, it, whatever, exposed the film after I left."

"So you got nothing?"

Luddie walked over to the sofa and retrieved the useless film, handing it to Alex. "Ruined. A total waste."

"How convenient for you. You come back here with the most incredible story I've ever heard and expect me to swallow it hook, line, and sinker, without a single shred of evidence."

"It's true, my friend, every word. Why would I lie to you about it?"

"I don't know. You tell me. For whatever twisted reasons you have, I suppose."

"Listen to me." Luddie's voice was firmer and suddenly less defensive. "You metamorphosed into another being. At first you appeared to be a normal, quite attractive human male. I snapped some shots of you like that, and then introduced myself. At that point you turned into a snarling, absolutely horrifying monster, complete with claws and fangs, a consummate killer. We fought, Alex, you and me, right here in your apartment, which accounts for the ungodly mess you see. You—the monster aspect of you—nearly finished me off. I was quite lucky to escape with only a few cuts and bruises and no broken bones. If we fail to do something about this by the next full moon . . ., " Luddie paused and stared at Alex for emphasis, " . . . this transformation will become permanent. Alex Maltese will cease to exist and will become, instead, this other creature."

"You say you put up a noble struggle with this . . . this indomitable monster, Luddie?" Alex sneered sarcastically. "I don't mean to offend you, but you look more like a lover than a fighter to me."

Ludwig von Dracula stepped closer to Alex. As Alex looked on in horror, Luddie's light blue eyes turned into glowing red coals. Luddie raised his hands and Alex saw his nails grow three inches longer and take on the aspects of lethal claws. Saber-like fangs dropped down out of Luddie's upper jaw, extending to his chin.

Alex backed away, too shocked to utter a word.

Without warning, Luddie plunged his claws into the wall and ripped downward, leaving four large trenches and showering plaster onto the floor. Then he went into the kitchen and smashed his fist through the wood cabinets above the sink, shattering Alex's dinnerware. Luddie was not yet finished. He came back into the living room, hoisted the sofa over his head and heaved it through the wall separating the living room from the bedroom, where it landed on the bed. Then he turned his attention to Alex who was cowering in the corner, trying to make himself invisible. He lifted Alex into the air with one hand and stared into his eyes.

"Convinced?" His voice was a rumbling growl.

"Yes, yes. Of course I'm convinced. Please put me down."

"You humans!" Luddie said. "Violence is the only language you understand."

He released Alex and dropped him to the floor. Within seconds, Alex observed the fiery eyes fade back to the friendlier blue, the fangs retract into the upper jaw, and the sharp claws shrink to normal length.

"Why is everyone always so suspicious?" Luddie said. "Is paranoia the normal condition of the human race? It's so depressing having to *prove* things all the time."

"I believe you, I believe you," Alex said, his voice still half an octave higher than usual as he struggled to regain his composure. "Tell me. You said I looked like a normal human being before you identified yourself to me. Did I look anything at all like the real me?"

"Nothing whatsoever. You were totally different in every way."

"I wonder . . . maybe there's a chance that the human me . . . before it turns into a monster I mean . . . has some redeeming qualities. If only we knew who it is."

"I know who it is, Alex. I recognized you at once."

"Anybody I know?"

"I should think everyone has heard about you in your human incarnation, if I may use the word *human* loosely. You, my dear friend Alex, are none other than Luke Fenris."

Alex felt as though he had been cold-conked between the eyes with a sledgehammer. He stared at Luddie with a look of stupefaction on his face. "Luke Fenris!"

"Yes, that's who you are after your transformation."

"But that's impossible. He . . . he's a loathsome fascist, an evil bigot with a warped mind. He represents the worst aspects of American capitalism."

"Oh, I don't know." Luddie smiled indulgently. "The extremes of right and left are equally noxious. Actually, I rather think that he and Uncle Victor would have had a grand old time together. Victor would have admired his . . . panache, shall we say? It's not Fenris, but rather his werewolf aspect that concerns me."

"Yes, well I can work on toning down his extremist tendencies now that I know who he is . . . or I am, I guess I should say. But how do I go about purging the werewolf from my nature? It'd be nice not having to worry about blackouts anymore, living a normal life, opening up more with Sally."

"Sally is your—"

"Lady friend, yes. She thinks I'm such a bear as it is during these full moon cycles."

"I don't think you've grasped the big picture yet, Alex."

"What do you mean?"

"As I've told you, there is no cure."

"So?"

"You will be permanently transformed into Luke Fenris after the next full moon unless—"

"Unless what?"

"Unless you die, my friend."

"You can't be serious."

"I'm completely serious."

"Who's going to kill me? You?"

"Do I look like a murderer to you?"

"The thought crossed my mind a few minutes ago."

"That was only for purposes of demonstration," Luddie said. "You were the one who wanted proof, remember?"

"Well if not you, who then? Who's going to kill me?"

"Do you have to ask? I should think suicide is the only decent alternative, considering the circumstances. Don't you?"

"You expect me to kill myself?" Alex was visibly annoyed, but he tried not to antagonize Luddie and risk having him turn back into that other thing again. "Try not to be so cavalier about my life, if you don't mind. I don't want to ruin your day or anything, but I don't think I'm ready to cash in my chips yet."

"Let's weigh the alternatives, Alex. It's possible that some part of your consciousness might survive in the altered state, but it would be submerged under the more powerful mind of Luke Fenris. Think of what that means. You described him as loathsome, evil, fascistic. Do you want to be responsible for unleashing him in full force against society?"

"Let me ask you this." Alex moved around the room, putting some distance between him and Luddie, who had suddenly become a bit too moralistic for his taste. "Suppose I decide to live. What action do you plan to take against Fenris on your own?"

"None, I should think. Unless, of course, he tried to make my life unpleasant in some way. If he breaks the law, it's up to the police to intervene. Otherwise, it's not my place to interfere."

"So, except for the werewolf factor, he's just another influence for good or evil in society. It really doesn't concern you what he does, is that right?"

"I'm concerned about losing you as a friend. But . . . either way, that's going to happen."

"So, looking at the big picture as you put it, on one hand I can kill myself now and end the lives of Alex Maltese and Luke Fenris."

"Don't forget the werewolf."

"And the werewolf as well. On the other hand, I get to become rich, famous, and powerful if I live. Not to mention that I also enjoy, once again, the pleasure of marriage to Danielle Dante, the only woman I've ever really loved in my life."

"That sums it up neatly." Luddie's face was grim, and slightly sad.

"It's a bitch of a decision," Alex said, "but, what the hell, I think maybe I can live with option two." He walked over to Luddie, clasped his right hand with both of his and pumped it vigorously. "I want to thank you for everything, Luddie. You've been a prince, a real brick throughout this entire ordeal. I can't tell you how much I appreciate everything you've done for me."

"What are you saying, Alex?"

"I've made my decision. I'm going to allow myself to become Luke Fenris permanently, marry Danielle, and let the chips fall where they may."

"You're overlooking the werewolf aspect. That's part of your nature, too, and it's an extremely violent, powerful, explosive, and uncontrollable force. It's evil and destructive."

"Nobody's perfect, Luddie. We all have our little character flaws."

"It . . . *you* may kill innocent people, Alex!"

"People die every day, from traffic accidents, disease, a random mugging. It's the human condition."

Luddie shook his head from side to side.

"I know you're upset with me," Alex said.

"I'm disappointed in you. There's a difference. You struck me as a man of principle, someone who was concerned about suffering and injustice. Now, here you are, permitting yourself to become an amoral wheeler-dealer who is the antithesis of everything you profess to believe in, as well as a monster that rips people apart with its own claws and fangs. I thought you were better than that, Alex."

"Well, welcome to the real world!" Alex stormed back and forth across the apartment, debating more with himself than with Dracula. "I never said I was some kind of a martyr. Besides, what good would my death do anyway? If Luke Fenris disappeared, some other corrupt, self-serving robber baron would come along and take his place. I'm not responsible for this state of affairs. I've been devoted to a cause, sacrificing my life, living like a scrounge long enough. What good has it done? To hell with that, Luddie. I've got a chance to enjoy life, make an impact, and be with the woman I love. If you can come up with a solution that doesn't require my death, I'll be happy to consider it. But, until then, my mind is made up. I'm going to—"

Alex looked up for the first time since beginning his tirade, but Luddie was gone. He felt a breeze and looked over at the shattered window. In the distance he thought he could make out a black bat winging its way through the night.

"I'm doing the right thing, Luddie!" Alex called after it. "I have no choice, damn it! Can't you see? I'm doing the right thing. I know I am!"

Chapter Twenty-Three

They met again, every night for the next two weeks, in a neighborhood coffee shop. Alex was visibly heavier as he indulged himself night after night with his favorite desserts and fried foods. Luddie sat across from him, observing him in astonishment as Alex shoveled it in.

"Why don't you just inject raw fat into your veins, Alex? Keep that up and you'll need Draino to unclog your arteries."

"None of it will matter in a couple of weeks," Alex said between mouthfuls. "This pale, puffy body will cease to exist, and in its place will stand the trim, well-muscled physique of a handsome blond superman."

"Still, one needs to maintain some modicum of balance, some sense of restraint." Luddie wrinkled his nose in distaste.

"I appreciate your friendship in my final weeks, Luddie. That night you flew off and left me alone in my apartment, I felt like such a rat, such a . . . such a sell-out."

"I couldn't bear to stay there and listen to you demean yourself with such base sentiments. I don't agree with your decision, Alex, but I do sympathize with the fear and anxiety you're experiencing right now."

"I feel so guilty, Luddie. I know I'm being horribly selfish, but I can't . . . I just don't have the courage to take my own life."

"I'll see you through the best I can. I don't know how much influence I'll be able to exert on you in your altered state, but I'll do anything I can. I called my Uncle Victor in Greece to see if he knows of any possible remedy for your situation."

"Really?" Alex's eyes opened wide and he put his fork down for the first time in an hour. "Do you think he knows of some other way?"

"I wouldn't count on it. His maid said he was away and she didn't know where he could be reached. He's quite eccentric these days, and cranky as well. Still, he's the only hope we have right now."

"But you *will* keep on trying?"

"Of course, of course. Meanwhile, what are you going to do about your friend? Sally's her name, isn't it?"

"Yes. I don't know. I haven't told her a thing yet."

"You must tell her, Alex."

"I've been trying to work up the courage. It's going to hit her hard. She's been hoping I'd get over my obsession with Danielle. Maybe I'll take her out to dinner and break it to her slowly. Or else I can tell her I have an incurable disease and I'm scheduled to die on October sixth."

"Honesty, Alex, honesty. It works best in the long run."

"In this case who'd believe it? She'll just think I'm concocting a bizarre story to get rid of her. Unless you'd like to come along and vouch for me."

"I don't think so. I'll do anything I can to help, but I learned a long time ago not to get in the middle of squabbles like this."

"Yes, well, thanks anyway. You've been a lot of help . . . I think." Alex checked his watch. "Time for me to head to work now."

"That's what I call dedication. In two weeks or so, Alex Maltese will cease to exist, but you're going to work right up to the bitter end I see."

"Just in case. It doesn't hurt to hedge your bets."

Alex grabbed the check and walked with Luddie toward the cashier by the front door. He paid the bill, and then hesitated for a moment before stepping outside.

"Can I ask you to do me one more favor?" he said.

"Sure. Just name it."

"At the risk of sounding paranoid, Luddie, I think I'm being followed. I've got nothing substantial to go on, just a feeling, a sixth sense I developed when the FBI tailed me in college."

"A feeling you say?"

"More than that actually. When I leave my apartment in the morning, there's a guy in a gray suit and a crew cut reading the *Times* on the corner . . . out of place, to say the least. And that's not all. There're little things you can't put your finger on. People rounding a corner when I turn around, the same faces for blocks at a time looking away when I stare at them. It could be me, but it's got me spooked."

"This could be serious, Alex. I'll keep an eye on you as you walk to the subway. You won't even know I'm there."

"Thanks, Luddie. I hate to keep troubling you."

"Not at all. I feel somewhat responsible for all this, and I want to help out."

"You're a credit to your species, Luddie."

Luddie smiled. "Get out of here before I lose my temper again."

He waited in the doorway as Alex left the coffee shop and headed west. He hung back and scanned the street until his eyes rested on a blocky man lighting a cigarette on the northeast corner. Simultaneously, he heard a car engine come to life and pull away from the curb, turning down the same street where Alex was walking. The smoker left his vantage point on the corner and moved briskly after the car. The automobile continued along past Alex, then slowed as though the driver might be searching for a parking space. This would not have been unusual in itself, except that the driver had just abandoned a spot no more than a block away.

Alex entered the subway station on the next corner, and the man on foot tossed his cigarette into the street and went down after him. Luddie had a quick decision to make: should he follow Alex and his pursuer into the subway, or keep an eye on the car and find out where it was going? Reasoning that Alex was only being tailed and was not in immediate danger, Luddie decided on the second course of action. He ducked into a doorway, willed himself into bat form, and flew above the car as it wended its way northward through the ever-present Manhattan traffic toward midtown. Twenty minutes later, the car came to a stop in front of Xanadu Towers on Fifth Avenue. From overhead, Luddie observed two men as they left the vehicle at the curb and entered the building.

General Revilo Thorn stormed into his office and looked at the two members of his surveillance team who were seated beside his desk. His paramilitary forces were all former combat officers and enlisted men, dedicated to him and the Ghost Commandos. These two were retired police detectives who had been good cops at one time, but not quite on the same level as those who staffed the military operations. Thorn found his patience wearing thin, and spoke a bit more harshly than he meant to.

"It's been over three weeks now and we still don't know who our man is. How much longer will it take?"

"It ain't that simple, General," the beefier of the two, the apparent leader, said. "We studied all the police reports, an' there are at least ten people in that office who coulda received it. I ordered twenny-four hour tails with backups on alla them. No one's behavin' in an unusual way. If any of them had the envelope, we woulda known about it now."

"That's not good enough, Carmody! The whole operation can be blown out of the water if those papers're in the wrong hands . . . and I definitely put the *New York Times* in that category."

"Well, supposin' I keep all the shadows active an' we keep on lookin'?"

"Supposin' you do some *finding* as well as looking," Thorn said with a note of unmistakable sarcasm in his voice. "You better have something more concrete by the time Fenris gets back next week."

He dismissed them, and then called Navi for his report. Why didn't he just go out and do everything himself, for all the satisfaction he was getting? After he hung up on Navi, he studied the clippings that had been retrieved from the reporter's desk, along with more recent ones, for any possible clues. The newspapers had been filled with stories of the reporter's death and Hollings's disappearance. So far, no one had been astute enough to connect the two events. So much for the diligence of the media. Thank God they were just as inept as he always thought they were. It was just a question of time, however, before someone established a link between them.

Thorn noticed that he had left fingerprints on the file folder with the smudgy newsprint ink. Damn it all! What kind of cheap shit did they print this stuff on these days? He got up from his desk and went into the bathroom where he soaked his hands and rinsed them clean. Then he transferred the clippings to a clean folder, taking care not to leave prints on that too. Just as he was about to feed the smeared folder into the shredder, a thought struck him. He punched a button on the intercom and bellowed, "Shapiro! Are you there?"

"Right here boss."

"Get in here a minute! On the double!"

Within seconds a short, pale, nearly emaciated man wearing dark-rimmed spectacles entered the office.

"Sir?" He saluted and stood at attention, despite his civilian suit.

"Relax. I want you to take this over to forensics and see if they can pull any prints off it. Wait until they check it out and report to me right away."

Thorn paced his office, an impatient tiger circling its cage, until Shapiro returned a half hour later.

"Well?"

"Five prints, including your own."

"I know about mine. What about the others?"

"Two prints're too smeared for proper identification. The others, a right thumb and a forefinger, are clear and identifiable."

"Excellent. Now we're getting somewhere. Run them through the FBI lab at Federal Plaza and stay on it until you have positive IDs."

For the next four hours, General Thorn entered and extracted data from his computer, bringing his other projects up-to-date. Just when he was beginning to think Shapiro had disappeared from Planet Earth, the phone rang on his desk.

"Yes?"

"It's me, General. According to the lab report, the two prints belong to one person."

"Yes, yes?" His voice was impatient, demanding.

"A party named Alex Mallum, sir."

Thorn hesitated a few seconds, breathing comfortably for the first time in hours. "Good work," he said softly, savoring the sweet taste of impending victory. "Pull the file on him and rush it over to me as soon as possible."

He hung up the telephone and began to scan the list of suspects he had in his reports. Sulzberger, Lelyveld, Raines, Becker, Jefferson, Hayes, Rosenthal, Hoffman, Maltese, O'Neil—Thorn's eyes backed up instinctively and settled on Maltese. "Maltese," he said to himself. "Maltese, Alex. Alex Maltese. Alex Mallum." Similar enough to warrant closer scrutiny. His early warning radar system was on full alert. Maybe, just maybe. The rest of the list contained no similar surprises, so he set it on his desk and pressed the button on the intercom.

"Yes, General?"

"Gail, locate Carmody and tell him to get over here right away."

Right away turned out to be twenty-eight minutes, just long enough for Carmody to roust himself out of his Queens apartment and break most of the traffic laws as he flew into Manhattan.

"Alex Mallum," Thorn called out to him before he was halfway through the door. "Does that name mean anything to you?"

"Offhand, no, General. But I can have someone check the *Times* personnel records to see if there's anything on him."

"I doubt they'll have anything there . . . if my hunch is right." Before Thorn could complete his thought, the telephone on his desk rang and he picked it up.

"Yes?"

"I can't get anything on Mallum until eight o'clock in the morning," Shapiro said. "That's the best they can do."

"Damn it all!" Thorn pounded his desk even more forcefully than he intended to, seriously bruising a knuckle. "Why do I run into snags like this when I need them least?"

"Sorry, sir."

"Well, you've done your best, Shapiro. Tomorrow it is then." Thorn hung up the telephone and turned to Carmody. "I want your surveillance team leaders here at six A.M. sharp."

"No problem, General."

Thorn sat back in his chair and heaved a sigh. "I know you and your men have done their best, Carmody."

"We have, sir. Still are."

"I appreciate that. We all just need to put out a hundred and ten percent until we get on top of the problem."

"You can count on us, General."

"See you in the morning. Go home and get some sleep now."

Chapter Twenty-Four

"I think there's someone in my apartment, Luddie." Alex was overwrought and out of breath and it showed in his voice.

"Where are you now, Alex?"

"Phone booth down the corner from my building."

"Stay there and don't go up. I'll be right over."

"I'm in no danger now, Luddie. I need a place to hide. Is . . . is it all right—?"

"Of course. I'll leave the door downstairs open for you. Just make sure no one follows you."

"Don't worry about that. But, if I'm not there in half an hour, you can send a search team out for me."

"Are you sure you're safe? I can be there in no time."

"It's better I get out of here right away. And . . . thanks, Luddie. I really appreciate it."

"Don't mention it. I know you'd do the same for me."

Alex hung up and stepped out of the booth. He searched up and down the street and almost jumped when a panhandler he recognized approached him with his hand out. He studied the man's attire—filthy torn gray jacket, matching slacks, no shirt, ripped sneakers without socks, a beat-up brown fedora—and he saw his salvation.

"How'd you like to make twenty bucks?"

The beggar frowned. "I don't go for that shit, man."

"No, no, nothing like that. I'm offering you twenty bucks and new clothes. All you have to do is swap with me."

"Whatever turns you on, bub."

Alex led the toothless derelict into a coffee shop and sat him down in a booth. He called the waitress, told the man to order anything he wanted, then sat there drooling as the hobo devoured three cheeseburgers and fries, and asked for pie and coffee.

"I envy your appetite," Alex said. "Pie and coffee after we change. Follow me."

The panhandler followed Alex into the men's room, and looked on warily as Alex took off his jacket and trousers and instructed him to do the same. The smell of the man's garments was overpowering. Alex fought to keep down the bile rising in his throat as the noxious fumes assaulted him. He paid the man with two fives and a ten, then led him back out to the booth and ordered his dessert.

"Eat slowly," Alex said, "and don't leave for at least ten minutes after I do."

The derelict grinned and shrugged. It was all the same to him. What the hell—it was the best day he'd had in years. He'd stay for an hour and eat again if Alex wanted.

The cashier nearly swooned when Alex went over and paid, dressed in the derelict's clothing. "We all get down on our luck once in a while," he said to her, before bending over like a hunchback and limping out of the shop. He saw the blocky man he had been noticing for weeks across the street, smoking a cigarette, looking as though he hadn't a care in the world. Alex watched him as he hobbled along to see if he drew his attention. He seemed all but oblivious to Alex's progress, so Alex turned the corner at the next block and searched for a cab to take him to Luddie's apartment.

The surveillance team leaders gathered at General Thorn's office at six o'clock sharp the next morning, as instructed. Shapiro was there as well, with a copy of the FBI file on Alex Mallum—two hours ahead of schedule as it turned out, thanks to some considerable arm-twisting by the general. Thorn leafed through it, looking for a photograph, which he found and passed around the room.

"Anybody recognize this man?"

The men studied it one at a time, frowning and scratching their heads, until the fourth member of the team glanced at it carefully and handed it back to Thorn. "This is Alex Maltese," he said.

"Are you sure?"

"He's aged a bit and grown some hair, but the features are unmistakable. I'd stake my reputation on it."

Thorn smiled and patted the man on the shoulder. "Finally, we're getting somewhere. Good work, good work. It's as I suspected. This is the one we're looking for. Shapiro!"

"Sir?"

"Tell us what's in the file on him."

"His real name is Alex Mallum. He disappeared from California six years ago after getting himself into some trouble with drunk driving charges. He jumped bail after trying to buy off a judge, then got himself in way over his head with some west coast gangster, Dolph Hauptmann, known as the German. His politics are way over on the left. He was active in all kinds of radical causes, even tried to run for Congress. Here's the part that gets interesting.

"Get on with it!" Thorn commanded.

"He was married briefly to Danielle Dante, Peter Dante's daughter."

"Son of a bitch!" Thorn pounded the table with his bruised fist, wincing with pain. "Damn it!" He picked up the telephone and dialed Navi's number. "Carl? Thorn here. Can you get over here ASAP? It's very important . . . yes, very, otherwise I wouldn't have disturbed you at this hour . . . no, I can't go into it over the phone, but I guarantee it's definitely worth your while."

Thorn sent one of the surveillance team leaders out for coffee and donuts as they awaited Navi's arrival. An hour later Navi showed up, starched and crisp in a suit and tie as though he were attending a ten A.M. board meeting.

"I hope this is good, Thorn," he said.

"I think you'll find it better than good. Here's our man, the one with the file. He's a one-time Commie organizer named Alex Mallum, who was married to Dante's daughter several years back. He's still wanted by the California police."

"Peter Dante's son-in-law?"

"Former. She divorced him before he left California and got himself in a pile of trouble."

Navi stared at the photograph, then looked up at Thorn. "You're absolutely sure of this?"

"It all adds up. His fingerprints were on the file, and this fellow over here positively identified him as an employee of the *Times* working under an alias. He's our boy all right."

"I guess that explains why he didn't go to the police with what he's got," Navi said. "You don't think Dante has anything to do with this, do you? Revenge possibly?"

"I doubt it, but we'll keep an eye on him just in case, at least until Luke gets back."

"I agree. In the meantime, let's pick up Mallum, find out who he's been talking to and so on. Let's make sure he hasn't compromised us in any way."

"Um . . . right now that might be difficult, sir." All eyes turned to Carmody as he hemmed and hawed and shifted from foot to foot.

"What's the problem?" Thorn said.

"Well, um—"

"Out with it, Carmody."

"We lost him, sir. He must've gotten on to us and gave the slip to Fox Team. We did our best, General, but you can only keep a tail on someone so long before . . . before—"

"The timing couldn't be worse," Thorn said. "I hate to think of what's going to happen if we haven't found him by the time Fenris gets back. He's not going to appreciate this at all."

"Sorry, sir."

"Put everybody you've got to work on this."

"Yes, sir."

"Time's our biggest enemy right now."

"I see you've shaved," said Luddie.

"Yeah. With everybody looking for the new Alex, and not hearing anything about the old Alex, I thought it was safer looking like the original me."

"Probably a good idea. Would you like Sally to stay here with us?"

"Thanks but . . . no offense, Luddie, but I don't think she'd know what to make of you, if you know what I mean."

If Luddie was offended, he gave no sign of it. "All the same, you'd better call and tell her to leave her apartment. Is there a friend she can stay with?"

"Yes, you're right. I'll call her now."

"Time's getting short. In a couple of days the full moon'll be out."

"I was going to wait until the fourth to tell her everything. The night after that is when it happens, right?"

"Actually, the night after *that*. The full moon begins on the fifth, but the eclipse will be in force during the sixth and seventh."

"Whatever. Heard anything from your uncle yet?"

Luddie shook his head from side to side. "I told you we can't count on him."

Alex picked up the receiver and dialed Sally's number.

"Well hello, stranger," she said as soon as she heard his voice.

"Sal, listen—"

"I'm happy to see you still have my number. What's the occasion? Did I forget your birthday or something?"

"Sally, please, this is important. You've got to get out of your apartment right away."

"I must say, Alex, you're original at least. I don't hear from you for days, sometimes weeks at a time. Next thing I know you call me up and tell me to get out of town."

"I'm not joking, Sal. This is serious. My life's in danger, and maybe yours as well. Can you stay with Nicky for a while? Or Pinto? Just get out of your apartment."

"This's gone far enough. Just what the hell are you up to anyway?"

"I can't explain now. Just trust me, please! I'll tell you all about it in a couple of days."

"I don't know. Why the hell should I believe anything you say?"

"Because . . . because some dangerous people are after me, and they may try to reach me through you. I care what happens to you, regardless of what you think."

"When will I see you again?"

"The fourth. Let's go someplace special, like La Casa Nostra. Remember?"

"I remember. I just wasn't sure you did. You'll call me at Nicky's?"

"In a day or two. I'll tell you everything that's going on when I see you."

"If you stand me up this time . . . " She left her threat unfinished.

"I won't. I promise."

"Who's Nicky?" Luddie asked when Alex hung up.

"I thought you could read my mind," Alex teased.

"I can, but I wanted to respect your privacy while you're my guest."

Alex laughed. "Nicky's a Class A fuckup. But he's had some valuable training, demolition, ex-Marine, Special Forces. He needs to do some work on his sense of timing. But he can put a bullet through an eagle's eye from a thousand feet away."

CHAPTER TWENTY-FIVE

Alex and Sally waited patiently at the end of the long line on Mulberry Street in front of the restaurant. Seven o'clock reservations at La Casa Nostra usually meant eight or eight-thirty, and tonight was no exception. Every ten minutes or so they shuffled forward a few inches as earlier arrivals were seated. Finally, forty minutes after the alleged time of their reservation, they passed from the street into the cocktail lounge. The circular oak bar with brass trim was packed six deep with hungry customers, and the small black cocktail tables were all occupied. As a surly hostess with lots of makeup and jewelry summoned would-be diners to their tables, others on line took their seats. Sally was wearing her usual camouflage fatigues.

"Don't you love it?" Alex said. "Making a reservation to wait on line for a table."

"Why do they overbook like this?"

"Because they can get away with it. Next year they'll be begging people to come, after some other place is written up and becomes the new hot spot."

Finally, the hard-as-nails bimbo in the sequined dress called out, "Maltese, party of two! Follow me!"

Now they trotted to keep up with her, worried that if they dawdled she might change her mind and give their table to someone else.

"Your waiter tonight is Guido," she said. "If you have any problems, bring them to his attention."

Guido took over and asked them what they wanted to drink before their rumps had hit the chairs. They gave him their cocktail order, and then stared around at the red brick walls and potted plants, and the marble knock-off statues of Roman emperors and senators in various stages of undress. Scattered around the room was an eclectic array of patrons, including rubbernecking tourists from New Jersey, and white-haired dons with pinky rings the size of ice cubes, accompanied by young bleached-blondes in abbreviated dresses.

"If you can guess which underworld figure will be assassinated next," Alex said, "the meal is free."

166

"You're such a cynic."

"Cynicism and paranoia are my first and second lines of defense."

"I'm the one who should be paranoid, waiting around for you to call me."

Guido arrived with their drinks, and launched right into a litany of specials for the evening, complete with exquisite details about the chef's lineage and regional recipes. After entertaining them for three or four minutes with elaborate descriptions of dishes they promptly forgot, Guido disappeared into the Black Hole reserved for waiters only, with a promise to return sometime before the restaurant closed to take their orders.

"What's the point of having a menu if they've got fourteen specials for the night?" Alex asked.

"Did he say the veal came with the white wine and caper sauce, or was that the grilled Mahi Mahi?" Sally said.

"I think the Mahi Mahi had a madeira-basil sauce and a medley of garden vegetables on the side."

"Are you sure? I think that was the poached salmon you're thinking of. The Mahi Mahi had a light marinara sauce and a blend of risotto and wild rice."

"Oh fuck it!" Alex said, slugging down his drink. "Stick with the veal cutlet parmagiana and you can't go wrong."

"Well you're in a fine mood tonight, Mister Maltese. It was your idea to come back here, not mine."

"I'm sorry, I'm sorry. I have a lot on my mind and I'm kind of tense about it."

"What's bothering you, Alex, as if I didn't know? Look! If you want to kiss me off, why don't you just say so and stop beating around the bush."

"Kiss you off? That . . . that's not the way I'd put it. I—"

"How else can you put it? I know you're still hung up on Danielle. You haven't gotten her out of your system yet. Don't deny it."

"It's not that. Yes, I'm still a little bit in love with her, but that's not what I brought you here to tell you tonight."

"Well, this better be good, because you've been in a strange mood for weeks now."

"Shit! Where do I begin?"

"Just come right out with it and make it easier for both of us."

"There are things happening in my life that may shock you."

Sally rolled her eyes, as if to say, "I've heard better lines than this before."

"No, really," Alex continued.

"What kind of shocking things are you talking about?"

"To begin with, there's the question of my past."

"I know about that already, Mister . . . Mister Mallum if you prefer."

"There's more than you're aware of, lots more than all the underground stuff. When Danielle left me, I lost everything in the divorce. I had no job, very little money, my political career, such as it was, self-destructed. I did a lot of stupid things, started drinking heavily and got pulled in a few times for DWI. Nothing I did was working. The last time I was arrested, some judge wanted to put me away. Some jackass lawyer I hired told me I could buy my way out of it. That option backfired on me, and set me up for even more serious charges. I lost every penny I had."

"I didn't know anything about that, Alex. But I do remember you being a man of principle who stood up for what he believed in."

"Well, I jumped bail after that and I was broke. I was virtually unemployable, the police were looking for me, so I decided to go into hiding. There was no way I was going to jail."

"I don't blame you. I would've done the same myself."

"Before I did that though, I came up with a risky scheme to raise some cash. Basically, I put a lot of money down on long shots at the track—money I didn't have. I borrowed it from a sadistic thug named the German, and blew it all. None of my picks came in. I figured that at worst I might break even, but it didn't work out that way. So anyway, the German sent two of his goons after me to either collect what I owed or . . . or else."

"Alex, how could you?"

"How could I what? I told you I was broke and needed some money."

"But to get mixed up with people like that, criminals who have no respect for anything except lining their own pockets."

"I was desperate. I didn't have anywhere else to go."

Guido came by to take their orders, but Alex waved him off and he disappeared back into his Black Hole in a flash. Alex didn't realize it, but Guido had checked his appearance out on a flier offering a $10,000 reward that was posted at the waiters' station. Had he been more alert, Alex would have observed the waiter glancing his way and comparing his face to the image he held in his hand. Convinced that he was on to something, Guido picked up the telephone and called his contact in the area.

"After I lost all the money—"

"The money you didn't have," Sally said.

Alex ignored Sally's sarcasm. "After I lost and found myself in hock to the German. I jumped in my car and raced down U.S. 1 toward the LA airport. I figured I'd better be on the next flight out of the state before he told his Neanderthals to break parts of my body I wanted to keep intact. The only thing is—"

"Yes?"

"It was a horrible night, stormy and rainy with zero visibility, and I had an accident along the way."

"Poor baby." Sally rolled her eyes upward and faked a yawn.

"I'm serious. You're not making this any easier for me. I smashed my car into the side of the mountain, then almost careened over the cliff. I could've been killed. After the impact, I wandered down the highway delirious. I was completely out of it. Somehow or other I found my way to this strange inn—very, very strange, run by this old gypsy couple. It was literally out there in the middle of nowhere."

"One has to wonder, does one not, how they manage to earn a living cut off from civilization like that."

"Sally, you've got to believe me. I'm giving this to you absolutely straight."

"I'm always willing to suspend belief for someone I care about . . . up to a point that is. So what happened to you out there that night? And what has all this got to do with why we're sitting here in Casa Nostra, spending an obscene amount of money on no special occasion?"

"The next part is . . . is almost incredible. I'm not sure you're going to believe me."

"Try me."

"Sometime in the middle of the night, the old woman, the innkeeper's wife . . . she . . . she—"

"Tell me damn you!"

"She turned into a werewolf and bit me on the neck."

"Of course she did. Now why did you think I wouldn't believe you when you told me that? It's all so logical, isn't it? Stormy night. Sadistic German. Car crash. Almost killed. And bitten by a werewolf. How could I not believe you?"

"Sally, please."

"You're such a prick, Alex Mallum!"

"Sally!" Alex looked around at the suddenly silent room, at the assemblage of startled diners who had been diverted from their exquisite and ever-so-expensive meals by Sally's penetrating shriek.

"My God, Sally. What are you doing?"

"I'm having a shit fit if you really want to know, you lousy rotten bastard!"

"Lower your voice, please. Think about what I'm saying. That's the reason for my disappearances. Why do you think you don't hear from me for days at a time? It all happens around the full moon." Alex pulled an appointment book from his breast pocket and started reading off the dates. "Remember when you took me to the Raw Shark concert? Three missing days out of my life." He held the booklet in front of her face, pointing at the entries. "And here's another time when I disappeared for three more days. And another, just about four weeks ago. Same thing. Tomorrow starts another full moon and it'll happen again."

Sally stared at him coldly, her eyes not blinking, her face paralyzed with scarcely controlled rage. Then the tears welled in her eyes and her face crumbled. "How can you do this to me? I thought . . . " She pulled out a handkerchief and mopped her face, "I thought after a while you'd, you know, get over her. I knew I was taking a chance but I didn't care. And now, you lie to me like this. You have no respect for me, Alex. It's . . . it's so fucking humiliating!"

"I'm telling you the truth. How can I make you believe me?"

"Why don't you at least have the balls to be honest with me? Why can't you—?"

"I am being honest!" Before Alex could continue, a shadow crossed the table. They both looked up and saw Guido standing there.

"Is everything all right?" His dazzling smile lit up the dark room.

"Fine, fine," Alex said.

"I'm so pleased. Do you folks live in the city?"

"Why, yes. On the Lower Eastside."

"Splendid. As a special show of gratitude tonight, we're offering our regulars free limousine service back to their residences. When you are ready to leave, I'll have a driver waiting outside for you."

"I don't know what to say. We've been here only once before."

"No matter. We appreciate your patronage and hope you return. Many, many times in the future." Guido snapped his fingers and the sommelier materialized out of the shadows, his necked weighted down with the heavy silver chain and tools of his trade. "A bottle of champagne for this lovely couple, on the house."

"At once." He clicked his heels and was gone.

"Enjoy your wine. I'll return to take your orders in a few moments."

"This is incredible," Alex said after the waiter left. "How do we rate such special treatment?"

"Making a scene works every time. And just think, it's not over yet. What else do you have to add to your incredible story?"

"In two days," Alex began haltingly, knowing she wasn't buying a word but wanting to get it over with anyway, "there's going to be an eclipse of the full moon. When that takes place, I'll turn permanently into a werewolf—actually, a part-time werewolf. The rest of the time I'll be Luke Fenris. I mean, I *am* Luke Fenris now, but only when the moon is full. That's what happens when I disappear for those three-day periods, I turn into him. He, in turn, becomes a werewolf when someone ticks him off. All this is going to become permanent, as I say, during the eclipse. Alex Maltese, or Mallum, will no longer exist. Of course I realize I have no business asking you to believe all this. It sounds crazy to me, too."

"Alex Mallum, the crusader for justice and social equality, is really a fascist swine whose only interest is looting the world for his own benefit?"

Alex shook his head. "Whoever said, 'Honesty is the best policy,' was out of his fucking mind."

"In other words, you're really a fraud. A real man of principle would never allow that to happen."

"What am I supposed to do about it?"

"Nothing, you fuck. I will! Why don't I just shoot you right through the heart with a silver bullet? I mean, if you're a werewolf, what difference does it make?"

"Don't be ridiculous."

"Don't tempt me, Alex."

"You're beginning to sound like Luddie," Alex said.

"Who's he? Another of your werewolf buddies?"

"Ludwig von Dracula is his full name."

"Dracula? As in vampire?"

"Yes, as in vampire. He's one of the most decent human be . . . I mean creatures I've ever met. He's the one who explained the whole thing to me, and he offered to spell it out for you too."

Sally stared at him in the same manner that she might regard an ugly stain on the bottom of her shoe. After a long moment she said, "Forget it. You're not worth it. You're too pathetic to even worry about any longer." She lowered her eyes to the menu. "Let's just eat up and enjoy the food, then get the hell out of here."

"You don't believe any of it, do you?"

"You're dead as far as I'm concerned. History! And you really will be in a couple of days, according to your own story. So what's the point of dragging it out further?"

"We can't just . . . just leave it like this."

"It's over. Forget it. I thought you were someone special, but you're not. You're just a creep, a *fascist* creep as it turns out. So let's drop it, okay?"

Guido returned, smiling as though they were his best friends in the whole world, and Sally proceeded to order the most expensive dishes on the menu, from appetizer to dessert as she capped her meal off with a double order of Zuppa Inglese at seven dollars a pop. Alex was too miserable to worry about the cost and ordered the "Gin Jimmy Special," Caesar Salad, Veal Parmagiano, and Zuppa Inglese for dessert, with a double anisette on the side. They sat in silence, Sally refusing to respond to his comments or make eye contact, treating him as though he were the lowliest life form on the planet. To the casual observer, they looked as though they had endured fifty years of a painful marriage and had nothing left to say to each other.

Miserable with himself, as well as with the outcome of this last night with Sally—last? My God, the finality of his existence as *himself* just hit him. Alex choked down his food without enjoyment. He felt like a man on death row with no hope of a reprieve. Yes, there was life after death, but not the kind he envisioned ever since he had learned to pray as a child. He would live again, not as a disembodied spirit reunited with his maker, but as a handsome and violent Robber Baron who personified everything that he, Alex Mallum, had fought against throughout his life.

He stared at Sally glumly as she spooned down the last of her Zuppa Inglese. "I admire your appetite," he said enviously. "I didn't think you'd manage to finish it all."

"I wouldn't talk if I were you. You look like you've been scarfing down everything in sight since I saw you last."

"What's the difference now if I'm twenty pounds overweight? I won't even be leaving a corpse behind."

Sally ignored his plea for sympathy and gathered her belongings. "Shall we go?"

"Sure," Alex said. "At least we get to ride home in style."

Alex paid the bill in cash, leaving himself with less than four dollars in pocket money. "I'd use a credit card," he said to Sally, "but I never got one, actually, because I don't want to show up in the computer bank."

Sally shook her head and rose from her chair.

As promised, a black stretch limousine was waiting for them out front. As soon as they exited into the Street, an obese man wearing a black suit and sunglasses opened the rear door for them. The driver, Alex could see, was skinny and consumptive-looking. A peaked chauffeur's cap obscured his face, and a lank ponytail hung down incongruously in back. Sally got in first and slid over against the far door. Alex followed and, to his astonishment, the fat man holding the door got in right behind him, crowding him into the middle. A third man emerged from a doorway and jumped in front beside the driver. As the limo sped away from the curb, Alex looked out the window and saw the chainsmoking man who had been following him for weeks run into the street, waving his arms frantically and speaking into a walkie-talkie. The limousine picked up speed and threw Alex against the backrest.

"What's going on? You're going the wrong way," Alex said as the driver headed toward the FDR Drive, away from their neighborhood.

"Relax," said the man in the front seat next to the driver. He grinned at Alex maniacally and pointed a semiautomatic handgun at his face. "We're takin' you an' your tootsie here on a little detour."

"What's this all about?"

"An ol' friend a yours is comin' to town in a few days, Mister Mallum. We just wanna be sure you're around to share some memories with him."

"You know my name?"

"That's right, sport. We work for your buddy Dolph Hauptmann."

"That fucking German!"

"No need to get ethnic on us. German, Italian, Irish, what's the difference? Ain't you heard we're all the same in the eyes of God?"

"Alex!" Sally said. "Don't you think you're carrying this charade a bit too far?"

The man with the gun in the front seat laughed. "I don't know, lady. First he insults my boss's ethnic background, an' now he's got you mixed up in his personal problems. Looks like you got yourself mixed up with a real loser, if you ask me."

"What do you mean you had him and lost him again?"

"Well . . . exactly that, sir. We spotted him goin' into the Casa Nostra restaurant with his girlfriend, some Amazon type all decked out like Fidel Castro in green fatigues an' combat boots. The only thing missing was a cigar."

"Get on with it, Carmody." Thorn had difficulty hiding the impatience in his voice.

"Yeah, so like I was sayin', we called in a backup team to grab him when he came out. Only—"

"Yes?"

"He got into this limo instead and shot out of there like a bat outa hell."

"The girl too?"

"Both of them, sir."

Thorn checked his watch—ten minutes past midnight. Fenris would be returning tomorrow night and the situation was going from bad to worse. "Do you know where they are now?"

"We tailed the limo to an abandoned warehouse on the Upper Westside. Castellano Olive Oil Importers. That's where they are right now."

"An olive oil warehouse no less. You can imagine who they're tied in with."

"Syndicate no doubt."

"Listen to me, Carmody."

"Sir?"

"Get all the men you have available up there now. Watch that place like a hawk. Don't let them out of your sight for one second. We may have to storm the place, and I want Mallum alive."

"I understand, sir."

"You're a good man, Carmody. Just remember—the future of your country is riding on this mission."

CHAPTER TWENTY-SIX

"A silver bullet through his heart? And the timing is critical, you say?" The connection was bad, and Luddie repeated his uncle's instructions several times to make sure he had the details straight. "It has to take place during the fifteen minutes before the full moon is in total eclipse, is that right, Uncle Victor?"

"Pay attention, boy! I said a silver bullet washed in an arsenic and cyanide solution. Why do you make me repeat myself?"

"Sorry, Uncle. This is all new to me. This is the only way to solve our problem, you say?"

"Only if the bullet penetrates the heart. The chemical infusion of the blood stream will produce the desired effect."

"I'm not very good with guns, Uncle Victor. I don't know if I can shoot that straight."

"You always were a bit of a namby-pamby, Luddie. you should get out of that degenerate city and into the country. The outdoor life, the sporting life, that's the ticket. Maybe I can get my friend Buffalo Bill Cody to help you out."

"I'm afraid not, Uncle Victor." Hadn't he heard? "Buffalo Bill's been dead for some time now."

"What a pity. One of the nicest humans who ever lived. Met him on one of his European tours. We hunted in Bavaria together. That's the problem with getting friendly with humans. They don't live that long. How about Annie Oakley?"

"Uncle, please stop teasing me. You know very well they've both been dead for years."

"You never did have a sense of humor."

"Do you know anyone else—someone who's still *alive*—who might be able to help?"

"Why do you want to get rid of this Fenris chap anyway? Seems like a decent sort to me."

"He's a cold-blooded killer!" Luddie was shocked, not knowing whether Victor was joking with him or not. "He's already attacked a good many humans without provocation."

"Serves them right. Look what they did to our people. Good, honest, hard-working vampires."

"Uncle, don't talk that way. We'll never stop this endless cycle of violence and retaliation unless we decide to deescalate the conflict, unilaterally. If we don't stop Fenris now, it's just a matter of time before humans launch a campaign to exterminate our entire species. This pattern of mutual hatred has got to be broken."

"There you go with that bleeding-heart crap again. I don't know who you take after. Not me, that's for sure. You think humans will give you some kind of a medal if you kill Fenris for them?"

"I went on television and told them who I am and what I stand for. You wouldn't believe the mail I've been getting. Very warm and friendly. Ten-to-one over the hate mail."

"That's because people who write letters to newspapers and television stations are a bunch of fruitcakes, and they think you're one of them. If they took you seriously, they wouldn't let up until they drove a stake through your heart. They'd show it on television in slow motion, with instant replay."

"You're such a cynic, Uncle Victor."

"I'd leave this Fenris fellow alone, if I were you. He's performing a public service. And, after all, your friend is making this transformation voluntarily."

"It's a judgment call, Uncle. I appreciate your help."

"Not at all, not at all. Let me know how it turns out. And, Luddie."

"Yes?"

"Try to write a little more often, will you. Despite my reservations about your political leanings, I do enjoy hearing from you."

Luddie said goodbye, then fixed himself a Bloody Mary, noting that he was down to his last six-pack of blood. Time to replenish his supply. He sat down in his rocker with the drink and contemplated his next move. He needed a shooter, a marksman he could rely on. What was the name of Alex's friend, the one who had been looking after Sally? Nicky? A fuck-up, Alex said, but one with valuable training nonetheless. Desert Storm. Demolitions. Handy with weapons. He checked his book for the address and telephone number Alex had given him, then decided to visit him in person. This was a conversation best conducted in private. Twenty minutes later he was standing in front of Nicky's apartment door, knocking gently.

"Who's there?" The voice inside was muffled, partly obscured by music from the CD player.

Luddie waited until he turned off the sound, and then replied, "My name is Ludwig. I'm a friend of Alex Maltese."

The door opened slowly and Luddie stepped inside. He sensed his host's presence behind the door, and smelled the fear and suspicion emanating from his pores. "I'm unarmed," Luddie offered without being asked.

"But I'm not. Come in slowly and raise your hands over your head."

Luddie did as he was instructed and moved carefully to the middle of the room. The apartment looked as though a bomb had exploded and turned it into a combat zone. What wasn't broken was hopelessly twisted and bent out of shape. Luddie turned and saw a wild-looking man whose hair was growing out in six directions from a recent crew cut. His forehead was wrapped in a red bandanna and he was wearing camouflage fatigues and combat boots. He waved a large pistol in Luddie's direction with his right hand, and carried a hunting knife in his left.

"No need for that," Luddie said. "I came as a friend."

"I'll decide that, motherfucker. How do I know Alex sent you?"

"Oh dear, how trying this all is. You assisted Alex in an attempt to kill Luke Fenris, but it didn't go according to plan. The would-be assassins got stuck in an elevator, and then when the bomb failed to go off on time, fortuitously sparing your accomplices' lives, you ended up blowing up your headquarters instead. It seems you have a talent for instruments of destruction, but your sense of timing needs some work. Is that accurate enough?"

"Alex told you that?"

"No, I read your mind. Of *course* he told me. How else would I know?"

"I don't believe you. How do I know you ain't some fed or some fuckin' Mafia goon who tortured Alex for the information? Where is he now anyway?"

"We have no time for this bickering," Luddie said as he walked up to Nicky and reached for his pistol. Nicky tried to pull the trigger without success, and Luddie snatched the gun from him.

"How'd you do that?" Nicky was astonished.

"I don't have time to explain. Here, hold this a minute." He handed the gun back to Nicky who, once again, tried to pull the trigger without success. Luddie took six pennies from his pocket and placed them on the wall a few inches apart. "I want you to go over there on the other side of the room and see if you can hit these pennies."

"I don't get it."

"Just do as you're told before I lose my temper with you."

"What's holdin' them pennies up?"

"Willpower, but you wouldn't . . . oh nevermind. Just get over there now before I disembowel you!"

Nicky kept his eyes on Luddie as he walked backward to the other side of the apartment. "How do I know the gun'll fire this time?" he asked.

"Because I said it will. Now, I want you to see if you can hit the pennies one at a time, a single shot for each, please."

Nicky took aim and fired five times in rapid succession, scoring clean hits on five of the coins. Suddenly, he turned in a slow arc toward Luddie and pointed the gun at his heart.

Again, the trigger locked when Nicky tried to pull it.

"Damn! How are you doing that?" he said.

"I'd be perfectly within my rights to tear your throat out right this minute. Now! The sixth penny if you please. And you better not miss or I'm really going to get angry with you."

Nicky swung the pistol back and scored a clean hit on the remaining coin.

"I'm impressed," Luddie said. "You hit it under pressure. Perhaps you're not so hopeless after all."

"What's goin' on here anyway?"

"You're going to kill Luke Fenris for me."

"What?"

"You heard me. Isn't that what you and Alex wanted to do in the first place?"

"Well yeah, but—"

"Listen to me now. I've got instructions for you and I don't want you messing up. You do know how to make bullets, don't you?"

"Sure, any kind you want." Nicky pointed at his workbench in the corner with its array of balance scales, molds, and assorted precision tools.

"Good. I want you to make as many bullets as you can fit into your most accurate pistol."

"I got boxes o' bullets over there. Why not use some of them?"

"They have to be a special kind. The slug has to be made of silver, and it must be coated with a wash of cyanide and arsenic."

"Whatta we goin' huntin' for a fuckin' werewolf or somethin'?"

"If you only knew the half of it. Unfortunately, I don't have time to explain. I'll pick you up at ten o'clock sharp two nights from now. Make sure everything is ready."

"Will Alex be comin' too?"

Luddie wrinkled his brow and frowned. "I'm not sure." He looked around the apartment. "Sally's not here, is she?"

"She went out with Alex a while ago. Why? What's up?"

"Don't mention a word of this to her. Do you understand?"

"Are they in some kinda trouble?"

"Some horrible, violent people are after both of them. The more she knows, the more danger she's in. If you value her at all, don't say a word."

"I don't know. Jeez, I—"

"Nicky!" Luddie grabbed him by the shirt and lifted him off the floor.

"All right, all right! Don't have a fuckin' conniption. I won't say a goddamn word. I swear."

Thorn walked over to the window and lowered the blind to block the morning sun. "You don't think Mallum worked out a deal with the syndicate, do you?" he said.

"It's entirely possible," Navi said.

"If he's told them anything, they'll want a piece of the action."

"How do you want to handle it?"

"I can send my commandos in to obliterate the whole bunch of them. They won't know what hit them. As far as the feds're concerned, they'll just assume it was a turf war among the families."

"What about Mallum?"

"We need to take him alive. We have to know who he talked to, how much he told them, and so on. And I don't like his connection to Peter Dante."

"I agree. Grab Mallum first, then wipe out the rest of them."

"I'll send in Cody's team for a strike this evening," Thorn said.

"He's the best you've got?"

"Damned right he is. He's got firepower and people who know how to use it."

"Are you sure Mallum's still there?"

"Carmody's had it staked out since they took him from the restaurant. Nobody could've left without him knowing."

"Well I guess that's it then," Navi said. "Nobody knows this end of the operation better than you do."

"I'll have Mallum in hand before Fenris gets in tonight. In plenty of time before the meeting."

Chapter Twenty-Seven

The fattest of the guards returned to the poker table after checking in on Alex and Sally who were tied up on chairs in the back room.

"Everything okay back there?" asked the cadaverous man with long, greasy hair tied in a ponytail who had chauffeured them from the restaurant. Underneath his jacket, an iron skull dangled from a chain around his neck.

"Yeah. The broad's mad as hell at her boyfriend, blamin' him for all the trouble, an' he's tryin' to tell her how it wasn't his fault crossin' the German like he did."

"So what else is new? Broads're the same all over. You in or what?"

"Yeah, deal me a hand."

The others sat there sullenly, staring at their cards as though they could change them into something else just by wishing it.

"Down an' dirty," said the man with the ponytail after dealing the seventh card.

"Ten bucks," said the man to his left.

"See your ten an' raise you twenny," the fat man said.

"Fuckin' bluffin'," the man who bid first said. "See your twenny an' raise you fifty." He tossed his money into the pot and winked at the others. "You ain't got no flush, not in a million years."

A yell from the back room pierced the air. The poker players looked up from their cards and laughed.

"What's he yowlin' about?" The fat man met the bidder's fifty and raised him twenty more. "Sounds like he's callin' for a glass of water."

"Fuck him an' fuck you too," the man with the ponytail said. He threw his last hundred-dollar bill into the pot. "See you an' raise you, you fat asshole!"

"Oh yeah?" The fat man met the bid and said, "Let's see what you got, pervert."

"Read 'em an' weep." The dealer laid five hearts down on the table and leaned over to rake in the pot.

"Not so fast!" The fat man grabbed his wrist and threw his cards down. "Full boat! Bite the big one, dogbreath."

179

"No, no, no!" The dealer pounded his fist on the table, scattering cards. "I'll cut you, double or nothin'."

"You ain't got no money left," the fat man said.

"Name the stake then."

"A blowjob, but only fifty bucks. That's all you're worth."

The dealer drew his upper lip tight over his teeth and sneered. "Three hundred, all the way."

"Now you're talkin'. Cut."

Again a shriek erupted from the back room as Alex called for water.

"What the fuck's wrong with him?" the fat man asked.

"Who gives a shit?" the fourth player said. "You guys bettin' or what?"

"Let me cut first," the skinny man with the ponytail said. He shuffled the deck and turned over the King of Spades, then flashed a nasty grin at the fat man. "See if you can beat that, you fat old queen."

Again, an animal roar resounded from the other room, then another and another, louder and louder than before. Suddenly, someone or some *thing* was pounding on the door.

"What the fuck!" The fat man drew his gun and rose to his feet. He walked toward the door and hesitated as a strange growling noise came from inside. Finally, he lifted the wooden plank that barred the door, pressed his foot against it, and pushed it open. The fat man stepped inside, his pistol pointed in front of him. A second later, without warning, he came hurtling back through the doorway with blood gushing from his face. His confederates ran over to him as he lay there, writhing in agony.

They all pulled out their weapons and stared at the entrance to the other room.

A blur whipped past; it charged in their direction.

Claws sliced the air and sunk into the skinny man's head, ripping it from his body. The others fell back in horror as a wild primordial beast landed on the floor in front of them, spun on its hind legs, and leaped again. This time its claws slashed into the third man's face and tore it off its skull. The fourth man stood rooted in place, a wet spot forming where the trouser legs met. He aimed his gun and fired at the snarling man-beast with the long fangs and pointed snout, but nothing happened. The beast came closer, rearing up on its hind legs. With a lightning swipe of its claws, it smashed the gun from his hand tearing his flesh and tendons. Then the monster lifted him off the ground and hurled him across the room as though he weighed no more than a ragdoll. The man's head splintered against the wall, showering the floor with blood and pulp. The body laid there still.

The beast sniffed the air, looked around, saw no movement. It walked out of the office and down the long corridor toward the window at the far end. Rearing back on its hind legs, it leaped through the closed window and landed on all fours, three stories down, in a pitch-black alley. It raised its head to the full moon, and emitted a long, deep howl against the sky. An eerie stillness filled the night. Then the beast crouched low, leaped forward again, and slithered off into the darkness.

"Good Lord! Did you hear that?" Cody whispered to Pellegrino, his second-in-command, who stood beside him on the rooftop overlooking the Castellano Olive Oil Importers warehouse. The entire twenty-man attack team was dressed in black jumpsuits, Uzis slung across their backs, munitions belts, grenades fastened to their belts on loops, bayonets, and black grease smeared across their faces. The rooftop around them was strewn with rockets, launchers, mini-cannons, bazookas, flamethrowers, rappelling ropes—enough equipment to take over a small country.

Again the howling chilled the air, and Pellegrino turned to Cody and said, "Probably just some crazy dog in heat."

"Foster, Goldstein," Cody called to two men behind him.

"Yes, sir."

"Get over there and find out as much as you can—how many men they've got inside, how well they're armed, where they're located, you know the drill."

Without hesitation, the two men dropped over the side of the building into the pit of blackness, tethered on ropes. Cody and the rest of his team waited on the rooftop in total silence. Sixteen minutes later, Foster and Goldstein reemerged out of the blackness as quietly as they had left.

"I don't like the looks of it, sir," Goldstein said.

"What's the problem?"

"The place looks deserted. Lights on all over the place and no sign of movement or anybody inside."

"Deserted!" Pellegrino said. "It can't be. Nobody's left since they went inside."

"Could be a trap," Cody said. "We'll move in in two waves through random entry points to see if anybody can draw fire. The second wave will wait until we've identified the fire points, then move in next. C team will cover us from the rooftop. I'll take the first wave in, and Pellegrino will lead the second. Let's move out."

Cody and seven of his men pushed off over the side of the building on ropes. They rappelled down in wide arcing leaps, then pushed off the side of the building over the roof of the warehouse, landing on silent cats' feet. They scattered across the rooftop, peering down over the side for windows. They anchored grappling hooks onto the ledge, then swung over and lowered themselves, each one stopping at a different window. The eight of them worked as a single entity, individual parts of a whole functioning with a central brain.

The brain was Cody, and he controlled his unit with quick gestures or a nod of his head.

The men clung to their ropes with one hand, and readied their Uzis with the other. With flawless timing, they kicked off the wall in unison, swung out away from the building, then crashed feet first through the windows on the swing back in. Glass shards imploded into the building throughout the warehouse. The attack squad hit the floor, rolled over quickly, and ducked for cover. Amazingly, not a shot was fired from anywhere. The entire warehouse was bathed in stillness.

"Cody here," the commander called into his walkie-talkie. "No hostile fire here. Report in."

One by one, the members of his team called in to report the same results. No fire. No people. Anywhere. Nothing but silence.

"Fan out and secure the premises," Cody said and clicked out.

Five minutes later, with his men all assembled in the main storage area, Cody called for Pellegrino and his team to join forces with them. Within moments, sixteen men clad in black were ripping open carton after carton containing five-gallon drums of imported olive oil, stacked ten feet high from one end of the warehouse to the other. Except for one carton against the wall, hidden behind a wall of cartons blocking it from view—this one contained large plastic baggies filled with white powder.

"That's over ten million bucks worth of horse you're looking at," Cody said. "Burn it before we leave."

"Commander!" Goldstein's voice crackled on Cody's hand radio.

"Cody here."

"I'm on the third floor, sir. You'd better get up here right away."

Cody hit the stairwell running, and bounded up three flights of stairs without pausing for breath. Goldstein was there waiting, staring grimly at the carnage around him. He didn't speak. No words were necessary; no words could have described adequately the stunning still life Cody had been called to witness. A huge fat man lay dead with his face ripped to shreds. A head with a ponytail rested in the corner, while a headless carcass—obviously the body it had once been attached to—lay in a heap fifteen feet away. A third body, its face flayed away from the skull, sat smashed and broken near an overturned card table. A fourth man, his head split open like a melon, was crumpled against the wall.

"Good God Almighty!" Cody said.

"Not even he can help these guys," Goldstein said.

Miraculously, the man with the split head was whimpering softly. Still alive! Cody went over to him and nudged him with his steel-toed boot.

"Where's Mallum?" he said.

"Who?" His voice was a pathetic sob.

"Your hostage. You know who I'm talking about."

"I guess the German's got him now."

"The German!" Goldstein shouted. "So he's the one who's in on this."

"Thorn'll have a fit," Cody said. "I can't believe he got to Mallum first."

"Thorn and Fenris both."

"Did you check the other room?" Cody asked.

"Yes, sir. Nothing at all. Looks like somebody was tied to chairs in there, but it's empty now."

"Well, we better get out of here and report back."

"What about him, sir?" Goldstein nodded toward the whimpering man who was writhing in agony.

"I can't imagine who—or what—is responsible for this." Cody aimed his Uzi and put a short burst directly into what was left of the man's brain. "Not even a punk like this should have to live that way," he said.

Chapter Twenty-Eight

Sally waited a full half hour after she heard the last of the footsteps leave the room outside, and then crawled out from behind the steel file cabinet. She had slithered over and wedged herself behind it after Alex had turned into a raging demon right before her eyes, and burst the ropes that bound them to the chairs. If she had not seen it for herself, she would never have believed it—not if she lived to be older than Methuselah.

Who could believe it?

Her Alex, the man she loved and thought she knew and understood, howling with unearthly screams for a glass of water as though he would die if he didn't get it. And then—and then what happened next was like something out of a Stephen King novel, or one of those old horror films. She saw him, she actually saw him with her own eyes metamorphose into a demon, a snarling, raging, vicious monster with blazing fire in his eyes and claws and fangs like she had never seen before. Could it be that all those incredible things he had told her during dinner were really true?

Sally inched her way to the door, then tiptoed through the carnage in the outer room. The sheer horror of what she saw held her riveted in place. Could Alex possibly be responsible for—Good God, no! The very idea chilled her to the bone. The place looked like a slaughterhouse where humans were butchered for the market. Alex? Mr. Social Consciousness himself! A raging beast capable of doing this! Impossible! The whole idea was unthinkable.

She had to get away. She slipped into the hallway and listened for any signs of activity. Nothing, just darkness and silence. Sally quickened her pace and headed toward the stairwell. She fairly leaped down the stairs, taking them three and four at a time without pausing. On the ground floor she saw an exit door, leading into a massive garage. She ran through and ran abruptly into a tall, muscular, blond-haired man with tattoos carved into both arms. His hair was long and greasy and he stared down at her malevolently. Beside him was a short, slim man with jet-black greasy hair, and behind him stood another blond with a crew cut, glinting ice-blue eyes, and a thick scar running down his cheek.

"Looky here," the tall man with the tattoos said to his buddies. "We got ourselves a guerrilla lady all dressed up for combat."

"Better watch your ass, Cowboy," the short one said. "She looks like she can kick some butt."

"Eat me, Greaseball," said the tall man. "Before I sic her on you."

"Who you callin' greaseball, you sack a shit? Maybe you—"

"Enough!" shouted the man with the crew cut, apparently the leader. He stepped between the others and said to Sally, "Who are you?"

"I . . . I just delivered a pizza," she said.

"Take her back inside," he said.

The one called Cowboy grabbed her arm and yanked her back inside the warehouse.

"Take your hands off me, you creep," Sally said.

"Listen to her," the short man said, laughing at his partner. "You sure you can handle her by yourself?"

"Fuck you, midget!"

"What are you doing here?" the man with the crew cut said.

"I just murdered four people. If you don't believe me, go upstairs and see for yourselves."

"Go up and check it out," he said to his two lieutenants.

"Your name wouldn't be the German by any chance, would it?" Sally said when his two goons had left.

"You know who I am?"

"Don't tell me. They call you the German, you come from California, and you beat people up for a living."

"Where did you come by that information?"

"I can't believe this." So far everything Alex had told her was checking out. "You wouldn't be looking for somebody named Alex, would you?" Sally said.

The German fixed her with one of the most evil smiles she had ever seen. "Well, well, you do know quite a bit, don't you?" he said. "You know who I am and you're obviously a friend of Alex Mallum. And where might I find Mister Mallum now, if you don't mind my asking?"

"You're too late, I'm afraid. Some hoodlums kidnapped Alex and me and tied us up in a room upstairs. Alex got real pissed off after a while, so he broke through the ropes and ripped them all to shreds."

"Don't toy with me, you fat bitch!" the German said.

"It's true. He killed them all and he's coming after you next."

Cowboy and Vinnie Raposo came charging down the staircase, their faces drained of color. "You wouldn't believe it!" Raposo said. "Four stiffs up there tore to shreds like . . . like a . . . a pack of wild dogs went on a rampage."

"See!" Sally said.

"Alex did that?" the German asked her.

"I told you. I mean, they did piss him off!"

"Where is he now?" The German's face was a scarlet blur.

Sally hesitated just a moment. "Why, I believe he told me he had a dinner date with Luke Fenris," she said.

Alex was awake. At least, his mind was fully conscious but when he tried to sit up he had no control over his body. He looked around at his surroundings, but a shroud of darkness covered everything. *That damned Luddie never told me I would be blind.* His mind was alert but Alex could only hear. He listened intently for some clue that could tell him where he was. There was breathing nearby, then a voice. *Her* voice.

"I'd like to watch the eclipse, Luke."

Danielle, is that you? I'd recognize your voice anywhere. Come closer, my love. Hug me. Kiss me.

"What eclipse, sweetheart?" a male voice said.

Could that be Luke Fenris?

"Haven't you heard? There's going to be an eclipse of the moon tonight. I think it's already started."

Alex heard footsteps, and then the sound of drapes being drawn. Suddenly he could see as moonlight flooded the room. He looked around and saw the tops of buildings and, high in the sky above, the full blood-red harvest moon with a small piece missing from the rim. He was completely aware of his environment; he was not blind after all.

I seem to be in an apartment, looking out a window.

A woman appeared in his line of vision, a beautiful woman whom he recognized. Danielle! She was just as gorgeous as he remembered, dressed in a clinging silver lame dress that reflected the moonlight, a necklace of diamonds and other glittering stones, and large earrings with diamond-studded webbing covering both ear lobes. She moved toward Alex, slowly, seductively, an erotic smile on her pouty lips. *Danielle. My love. Come closer. I want to hold you in arms once again.*

She looked into his eyes and sat down on the edge of the bed. "Luke darling, I love you so much," she said.

Luke? What do you see in that slimeball? Alex saw a hand reach out toward Danielle but it didn't appear to be his. What's goin' on here? Where's my body?

"I love it when you touch me. And I love running my hands over you, feeling your breath on my neck, making love with you, feeling you hard inside me."

Forget I asked.

"Soon now, my darling, we'll be together all the time," Fenris said. "I'm going to make you forget all about those other men you were married to, particularly that Mallum fellow."

We had some great times together, didn't we, Danielle? Remember that night in Carmel? You'll never be able to duplicate that with him.

"Alex? I can't imagine what I ever saw in him," Danielle said. "He was like something out of a different lifetime."

What!

"You had your politics in common at least."

"I was a rebellious little jerk back then. I wanted to get a rise out of my father, make him pay more attention to me. Alex was a campus hero who represented everything my father hated. At first I thought it was romantic, Peter Dante's daughter married to a revolutionary, a crusader for social and political change. I guess I was using Alex without even realizing it at the time. After a while the novelty wore off. I grew up and Alex didn't."

That's not the way it was at all! You loved me! Tell him, Danielle!"

"We all have our youthful flings," Fenris said. "What was it Churchill said? Whoever is not a socialist at twenty has no heart; whoever is not a conservative at forty has no brain."

Tell him the truth!

"It was adventurous at first. My father was incensed. We shared the excitement of protest. But Alex refused to grow up, to see the other side of things. He was . . . fanatical! A didactic left-wing ideologue who jumped up on his soapbox every chance he had. It got so boring after a while. Drove me absolutely nuts."

Danielle, you hypocrite! You were as committed as I was until your father blinded you with his money. It wasn't like that at all! We had fun, too! And lots of sex all the time. You were insatiable, and I couldn't get enough of you.

"You must have cared for him a little," Fenris said.

"Hah! To top it all off, he was lousy in bed. Nothing like you, Luke darling."

Oh, Danielle. You really are a cruel, coldhearted bitch after all.

"Why are we talking so much about him? You never asked about him before."

"Strange as it seems," Fenris said, "Mallum has recently intruded into my business affairs. I want to know all I can about him before I take countermeasures."

Try and find me, you bastard! Have I got a surprise for you!

"Alex? Is he here? In New York?"

"Possibly. I needed to know how you felt about him before . . . well, before I take appropriate measures to eliminate him, shall we say."

"Are you going to hurt him, Luke? Kill him?"

"Does it matter to you?

Danielle filled the bedroom with her rich laughter that sounded like music to Alex's ears. "Matter? Not in the least. Whatever you have to do to protect yourself is perfectly fine with me, darling."

Danielle! He wants to kill me and all you can do is laugh!

"Come, darling," Danielle said. "Let's watch the eclipse together."

"You stay and enjoy it if you like. Our guests are arriving for dinner any minute, and we have some important things to discuss."

Danielle looked at him and pouted. "They see you more than I do, Luke. I'm jealous."

"Bear with me a little longer, sweetheart. I just need to tie up some loose ends and then things will be different. We'll spend a lot more time together. That much I promise."

CHAPTER TWENTY-NINE

Alex understood now that he was looking out at the world from behind Luke Fenris's eyes while still maintaining his own separate consciousness. But he was unable to exercise any control over the body that he inhabited. Not yet, anyway. Two men in the dining room whom he recognized from television and the newspapers—Carl Navi and General Thorn—were seated side-by-side across from Fenris. A third man was occupying another chair further along, even though the spaces between him and the others were empty. As Alex squinted to see him clearly, he was horrified to discover that this other guest was none other than Dolph Hauptmann, the German.

What the hell are you doing here? What did you do to Sally?

The table was laden with exotic dishes steaming in their individual bowls. The steamy vapors wafted upward, although Alex could only fantasize about the variegated aromas. He could see and hear, but he could not smell. Could he taste? He would find out momentarily whenever Fenris decided to take some food.

"Barbara is a magician in the kitchen," Fenris said. "Wait'll you taste her shredded beef in garlic sauce. Better than anything you've ever tasted in a restaurant."

Alex looked on as Navi passed a platter to the general, who spooned a generous helping onto his plate. Navi helped himself, and then held the dish up to the German who waved it away contemptuously.

"Try the shrimp and pork as well," Fenris said. "You won't find anything like it anywhere. How about you, Mister Hauptmann? Don't you care for Oriental food?"

"Do you have anything without all this garlic?" the German asked.

"Knowing Barbara, probably not."

"Forget it then," the German said.

"Since you don't care to eat, why don't we get right down to business? You said there was something you wanted to discuss with me."

"I won't pull any punches. I know you've got Alex Mallum, and I want him."

Interesting trick. Let's see you try to pull this one off.

"Why do you want him so badly?"

189

"Let's just say I want to send him on a permanent vacation."

"What makes you so sure I have him?"

"Because she says so, and she oughta know." The German nodded over his shoulder, and Alex felt a tingling sensation running down the length of his spine—yes, he could feel, too!—as his eyes traveled across the room and landed on Sally who was wedged between Cowboy and Vinnie Raposo.

You're alive! Thank God! I didn't know what this creep had done to you.

Standing directly beside them were men whom Alex didn't recognize—Cody and Pellegrino—and a third man whom he did, Carmody, the chain-smoker who had been following him for weeks.

"So, young lady," Fenris said. "You told Mr. Hauptmann that my men cut Mallum loose and brought him here?"

Sally nodded yes.

"But you know that's not true."

Sally didn't respond.

"Why did you lie to him?"

"Because," Sally said haltingly, "it was kind of true and, if I told the real truth, he wouldn't have believed it and he would have killed me."

"What is your name?"

"Sally Milano."

"Well, Sally," Fenris said. "I give you my word that nobody is going to kill you."

Right on, Luke! It's you and me together now.

"Just a fuckin' minute!" the German shouted. "She's my prisoner, and I'll decide what happens to her."

"Sit down!" Fenris said. "And please don't mistake my hospitality for weakness, not if you care to walk out of here under your own power."

Cody went over to the German and pointed to the chair. The German glowered back at him for a long moment, then sat down reluctantly.

"Tell me now, Sally, what the truth really is," Fenris said.

Sally gulped audibly and visibly. "I don't think you're going to believe me either."

"Let me be the judge of that."

"Well, Mister Hauptmann here had us kidnapped when we left the restaurant the other night. These men picked us up in a limo and drove us to a warehouse where they tied us up."

"Is that true, Hauptmann?"

"Yeah."

"Continue, Sally."

"They kept us prisoner there till the next night when . . . when—

"Yes?"

Sally was on the verge of tears. "Mr. Fenris, I'm not even sure what happened next. Only I saw it with my own eyes."

"Tell me everything you remember."

"Alex told me ahead of time it was going to happen, but I didn't believe him. I thought it was just his way of breaking up with me. He . . . he turned into a wild beast, a werewolf or something. He howled like one anyway, then broke the ropes and attacked the guards in the other room outside."

"That explains the wolf howl," Cody said.

"What howl?" Fenris asked.

"Remember that howl?" Cody said to Pellegrino.

"I'll never forget it."

"What kinda crap is this?" the German said.

"Quiet!" Fenris said. "What are you talking about, Cody?"

"Just before we went in, there was this wild howl, just like a wolf. We figured it was probably a dog, but it didn't sound like any dog I ever heard. We had other things on our mind, so we kind of just dismissed it."

"Why did you tell Hauptmann that I had Mallum?" Fenris asked Sally.

"I was hiding in the back room when your men came in. I heard them say they worked for you. When Mister Hauptmann and his creeps over there caught me sneaking out, I had to think of something. I knew they wouldn't believe me if I told them what really happened. I just made up the first thing that came into my mind."

"You're a fat lying bitch!" the German said, rising from his chair.

"Watch your tongue," said Fenris, and Cody pushed him back into his seat.

"There was another reason, too," Sally said.

"What was that?" Fenris said.

"I . . . I believed that Alex really was . . . is . . . here with us.

"How can that be?"

"This is the most farfetched part of all. Alex told me he had been infected by a vampire bite. When the moon was full, he changed into something, somebody else. You! He said that after tonight, after the eclipse, the change would be permanent. He would disappear into you and you . . . *you* would remain as you are right now, a blend of Alex and yourself, until you died. I know it sounds crazy, but that's what he told me."

"You ain't falling for this bullshit, Fenris, are you?" the German said.

Silently, Fenris wondered if this strange story had anything to do with his own mysterious problems. The idea that he could have some sort of connection to that whiny Commie clown sent a shiver through his body. He studied Sally silently for a long breathless moment, and then said, "I'm not sure I believe it, but I do think she does. I'll tell you what I really think though, Hauptmann."

"What's that?"

"I think Mallum had a big secret, one he thought would be worth a great deal to you, so much in fact that he hoped it would get him off the hook with you."

"What kind of secret? Nothing Mallum knows could save his ass."

"I think he told you his secret," Fenris continued, "but you weren't sure he was telling the truth. So you decided to sound me out about it yourself and make up your own mind, and maybe cut yourself in for a piece of the action. Only somebody else grabbed Mallum from you and you went to the warehouse to get him back. You were too late, though. He was already gone by the time my men arrived."

"You're just as wacky as this crazy broad over there. I had enough of this talk about vampires an' werewolves for one night. Come on, boys, let's get away from these fruitcakes before they make us as crazy as they are."

Cowboy and Raposo started to leave, but Cody and the others had their guns out first. They looked toward the German for direction, and then sat back down when he did.

"Tell me, Sally," Fenris said. "Did Alex have a secret about me that he may have told you? Something that could be somewhat valuable, shall we say, if it were passed along to the wrong person?"

"Well . . . " Sally was perspiring, wrestling with her own troubling thoughts.

Tell him the truth, Sally. It's better that way.

"Tell me what you know," Fenris said.

"Alex hated you," Sally finally blurted out. "First he wanted to kidnap you, then he wanted you dead. He said you were dangerous, that you had this secret plan to, well, to take over the government and run things your own way. But he couldn't prove it, not after his reporter friend was killed. He said, coming from us, it would just look like we made it up. That's why he said the only way to stop you was to kill you. Oh! Oh my God!" Sally started to cry.

"What's wrong?"

"You have to kill me now, don't you? You have to kill us all since I told everybody your secret. I can't believe how stupid I am!"

"You're not a problem for me, Sally," Fenris said. "As you said, who'd believe you? I'm not going to kill you. These fellows here are a different matter, however."

"I didn't know anything about any o' this stuff," the German said, his eyes bulging as though they would pop. "I swear to God!"

Way to go, Luke. Sally will play along with us since she knows I'm you now. I wasn't lying to you, Sally. I was telling the truth. I . . . I really love you, not that vicious bitch in the other room.

"Maybe you didn't know it before," Fenris said, "but you do now."

As though on cue, Danielle emerged from the bedroom, glowing radiantly. "Isn't anyone else interested in the eclipse?" she said. "In a moment the moon will be all blacked out. It's absolutely breathtaking."

As she passed in front of the German on her way toward Fenris's side, he grabbed her by the hair and bent her head back at a sickening angle. "Nobody move or I'll snap her fuckin' neck in half," he said.

"Freeze!" Fenris shouted. "Don't anyone move a muscle."

"You want this bitch alive," the German said to Fenris, "do everything I say. Boys! Collect all the hardware."

To hell with her, Luke. She's no good. Sally's the one we have to save.

Fenris stood motionless as Cowboy and Raposo relieved his men of their weapons, and handed a pistol to the German who pointed it at Danielle's head.

"Ain't it something, Fenris," the German said, "how a man can be down on his luck one minute, and ridin' high the next? Just one a those little quirks of fate I guess. Let's go, boys. We're taking the broads along with us."

Stop him, Luke! Don't let them walk out of here with Sally!

"Luke, help me, please," Danielle whimpered as the German backed her toward the door.

No one noticed as Fenris's fingernails grew into razor-sharp claws as he held them at his side, and his teeth began to inch slowly down the sides of his mouth.

"Go get the maid in the kitchen," the German said to Raposo. "Make sure she don't call the cops."

A moment later, Raposo came out of the kitchen with Barbara in tow. "She was on the phone when I went in," he said. "I think maybe she called them already."

Do something, Luke. You're a wolf. Shred him to pieces. To hell with Danielle. Save Sally.

"Anyone blinks the wrong way an' this one's dead," the German said, his weapon still aimed at Danielle's head. "The next one is for you, Fenris. Come on, boys. Let's get outa here."

Suddenly, the air was rent by a piercing howl.

"What the fuck was that?" Raposo asked.

Attaboy, Luke. Rip him apart!

"Don't worry about anything," the German said. "As long as we got his girlfriend here, nobody'll try anything."

The German took another step backward toward the door when a deafening explosion rocked the room. The front door of the apartment imploded inward, slamming into Hauptmann and the others, knocking them to the floor. Alex looked up and saw Nicky standing in the doorway, with an automatic in his hand. He had adopted the standard police crouch, and Luddie was standing beside him.

"Nobody move," Nicky yelled. "Everybody against the wall. Luddie, see if Sally's all right."

Luddie helped Sally up first, and then offered his hand to Danielle. She smiled at him in gratitude as Luddie checked her out thoroughly, favoring her with his most dazzling smile. Luddie walked over to Fenris next and stared deeply into his eyes. Alex looked out, trying to yell, to get his attention and tell him it was all right, it's me in here, Alex, but he could not speak. Fenris sensed something familiar about Dracula, but he couldn't identify what it was. His eyes began to glow like red coals as he glared back at his former adversary.

"Who are you fellows?" General Revilo Thorn spoke for the first time since their arrival.

As Luddie went over to pat him down for weapons, Thorn exhaled deeply into his face. Luddie felt himself grow faint as the general's garlic-powered breath washed over him.

"What . . . what did you have for dinner?" Luddie asked.

"Beef in garlic sauce, I believe it was. Quite delicious. As I was saying, I don't know who you fellows are, but you arrived just in time. We . . . "

He hesitated in mid-sentence as Luddie staggered from the impact of the garlic and toppled over onto the floor. Thorn reached out to arrest his fall, but held himself in check when Nicky told him to freeze. Sally was standing by the wall near the door, and Nicky told her to move to the side. Then Nicky turned to Fenris and pointed his weapon at him.

"Now, Fenris," he said. "It's time for you to die."

God no, Nicky! What are you doing? You kill him and you kill me too. Just get Sally out of here and run. Wake up, Luddie! This is all your fault. Wake up and stop him!

Nicky started to squeeze the trigger, then hesitated a second. As he stared into Fenris's eyes, he saw his face transform with fangs growing down to his jaw. Everyone else was staring at Nicky who seemed to be the only one who noticed what was happening to Fenris.

"No!" Sally yelled. "That's Alex in there. Don't shoot him."

"What are you talking about?" Nicky said. "He's not Alex."

Fenris's transformation was nearly complete when Nicky pulled the trigger at the same instant that Sally lunged into him, sending him sprawling. The recoil knocked the gun from Nicky's hand and the round missed its target. Suddenly, chaos ensued as Cody and his men and the German, Cowboy, and Raposo all dove for the errant weapon. Cody landed on top of the pile of guns the German's men had confiscated from them, and came up with a .45. He fired a round into the ceiling and everyone halted in place. Fenris's visage returned to normal, and all eyes turned to Cody. Everyone had frozen except Nicky who reached beneath his jacket and pulled out a grenade. Nicky removed the pin and held the handle tightly against the outside of the explosive.

"If I let this go, we all die," he said. "Sally, back out slowly."

"Not so fast," Cody said, his own pistol aimed at Sally. "I've got time to put a bullet into your lady friend before that thing goes off. Just bring it over here. Slowly, or else she's dead. You've got to the count of three before I shoot."

"Alex," Sally yelled at Fenris. "If you're in there I want you to know I love you and I forgive you. You had no choice."

I love you, too, Sally. Give him the grenade, Nicky. He won't hurt Sally.

"One," Cody counted.

"Run, Sally," Nicky said. "He's bluffin'."

"Are you sure?"

"Yeah." Nicky released the handle and tossed the grenade into the middle of the room, near where Cody was standing. Nicky grabbed Sally's wrist and bolted toward the open doorway as everyone jumped for cover. The German saw Nicky's gun—the one he arrived with that Sally knocked from his hand—lying on the floor near the sofa. He dove for it, picked it up on the fly, and then leaped behind the sofa.

They all waited for the explosion from their various positions. Moments passed, then nothing. "It's a dud, a dud!" Cody yelled. "All clear."

The German rose first, aiming Nicky's gun at Fenris. "Nobody fucks with me, Fenris!" he said. "Nobody, not even you." He fired twice, both rounds smashing into Luke's chest, one bullet thudding directly into his heart. Instantly, Fenris's white shirt was soaked with blood. Danielle started toward him, and then stopped abruptly as Fenris emitted bellowing, thunderous, roaring cries of pain.

Oh, the pain! The pain! You didn't say anything about the pain, Luddie! Wake up and help me!

The room swirled all around him as Alex clutched his wounded chest and lurched away, down the hallway into the bedroom. He shut the door behind him and collapsed onto the floor beside the bed. Already his body was undergoing subtle transformations as darkness enveloped him, obliterating every last trace of light.

CHAPTER THIRTY

The police arrived thirty-five minutes later.

"We came as soon as we got the call from your maid, Mister Fenris," Detective O'Sullivan said as he looked down at the body of Alex Mallum in Fenris's bedroom. Sally knelt beside the body, cradling Alex's head in her lap while she wept disconsolately. "Can you tell me what happened?"

"That man," Fenris said, pointing at the German who was handcuffed, along with Cowboy and Raposo, between two policemen, "broke into my residence with his thugs there while I was dining with my friends, and shot my good friend Alex Mallum. Through the heart. I believe it had something to do with an old gambling debt."

Both General Thorn and Carl Navi stepped forward and confirmed Fenris's statement.

"That gun at his feet is the one he used," Fenris continued. "It's got his prints all over it."

"What about these other two?" O'Sullivan asked, nodding toward Sally and Nicky.

"She's the deceased's fiancée. As for him," Fenris regarded Nicky for a long, silent moment, "he was one of my guests for the evening."

Detective O'Sullivan took in Nicky's Rambo outfit, unlikely dinner attire to say the least, and then looked at Fenris and shrugged as if to say, "Well, if you say so. Anything that simplifies my job's okay with me." Nicky stared at Fenris in astonishment; the man he had come to kill had just eased him gently off the hook. In the confusion, no one noticed the black bat out on the window ledge, alternately looking at the blacked-out moon in full eclipse and the commotion inside Fenris's apartment. Danielle hung back in the corner, looking back and forth between the body of her ex-husband on the floor and the man she had planned to marry, now restored to his former beauty.

"If you don't mind, Detective O'Sullivan," Fenris said, "this has all been quite an ordeal for my friends and me. If you'll take these men and book them, we'll be along in few minutes to give our statements."

"Of course, sir, if you'll instruct your guests not to touch anything. I'll have the forensic unit here within the hour to take care of the body and wrap things up."

As soon as the police had left, everyone turned to Fenris and spoke at once. Thorn's voice rose above the others. "I don't get it, Luke. I saw you take a bullet in the heart."

"Thank God for that bullet-proof vest you gave me. It saved my life."

"But?" Thorn pointed down at Alex's body, the head still cradled in Sally's lap. "Is that really Mallum? How'd he get here anyway?"

"The German got to him first. Did us a favor actually. He dumped him in here before I got home, and then tried to blackmail me for a piece of the action. Only he didn't count on our friend Nicky barging in and getting his fingerprints all over Nicky's automatic. There's a bullet in Alex's chest right now that'll match perfectly the round fired from Nicky's weapon."

"What the hell are we supposed to tell the cops, Luke?" Navi said. "I'm still not sure what happened myself."

Fenris flashed his most dazzling smile and said, "Why, just tell them the truth, Carl. We all will. Hauptmann barged in here with his goons looking to collect the money Mallum owed him, and then shot him dead when he resisted. Simple. Why don't you head over to the precinct now, and I'll be by shortly. I want to console this poor woman here before her heart breaks completely."

Danielle stepped forward awkwardly, her face a welter of confused emotions. "D-do you want me to stay here with you, Luke? Or . . . or—?"

"Why don't you run along with Carl and the general, my sweet? Mustn't keep the police waiting now."

"Will I see you later, then?"

"Possibly. Who knows? Take Barbara to the Waldorf and stay with her. I'll call you there later."

Fenris saw them to the door, and when he returned to the bedroom, Luddie was standing there beside Nicky and Sally. He turned to Fenris and said, "Congratulations, Alex. I'm so happy to see things worked out well after all."

"Yes, well I'm glad you're happy. Maybe now you'll tell me exactly what happened before I have a nervous breakdown or something."

"I spoke to Uncle Victor just before the eclipse. He told me how to trigger a chemical reaction that would destabilize your genetic pool and cause the body to split into separate beings. We knew the electronic matrix of your brain would remain in the surviving body. The only thing uncle couldn't be sure of was which body would survive. The whole thing was risky, but under the circumstances I don't think we had any choice."

Nicky stared at the man who looked like Fenris in astonishment, and Sally rose to her feet and approached him cautiously.

"What's goin' on here?" Nicky said. "You're talkin' to him like he's Alex."

"Are you really Alex now?" Sally said.

"Indeed he is," Luddie said. "Oh, how complicated life can be sometimes."

"Well if he's Alex," Nicky said, "then who's that layin' there?"

"It's an empty shell," Luddie said. "The shell that used to be Alex's body, but Alex's memories, his soul, and his feelings are all inside this body now. I must say, Alex. You've come through this better than anyone would have expected. You've survived intact, for all intents and purposes, with far superior physical attributes. Oh dear! No offense intended."

"None taken," Alex said. "It helps to know one's limitations."

"I can't believe it," Sally said, looking imploringly into his eyes. "Is it really you in there, Alex?"

"Yes, it's me all right." He reached out, took her hand, and pulled her close. "The old me almost lost you. The new me's not going to make that mistake. I love you, Sally. I know that now."

"I love stories with happy endings," Luddie said with genuine tears welling in his eyes.

"No more Danielle?" Sally asked Alex.

"No more Danielle. She's history. Frankly, I just don't give a damn about her anymore."

Luddie came closer and squeezed Alex's shoulder. "Um . . . since you're through with her, Alex. I mean . . . I don't know how to say this, it sounds so awkward—"

"Be my guest, Luddie. She's all yours. I just hope you know what you're getting into."

"I still can't figure out what the frig is goin' on," Nicky said.

"Why don't you come along and I'll explain it all to you," Luddie said. "I think Alex and Sally would like some time to themselves right now."

CHAPTER THIRTY-ONE

"I can't believe the size of this apartment, Alex," Sally said after circumnavigating the entire place the fourth time. "I mean, to think that one person lived here while thousands, tens of thousands of people are homeless. Fenris may have been an evil swine, but he sure knew how to live."

"Do you think you could get used to it?"

"Try me."

"You'll have to learn to be superficial like Danielle. Go to all the society affairs, summer in the Hamptons, be seen at the right clubs."

"Superficial is easy. I'll just start reading *New York* magazine."

"There's a good start. Just imagine. We've got all the money we'll ever need. We can donate as much as we want to our favorite causes, maybe do some real good now."

Sally stared in the mirror at her attire. "The first thing I'd better do is get out of these. Do you think Danielle has a *peignoir* lying around that would actually fit me?"

"Don't even think about it. We'll get you fixed up with a new wardrobe first thing tomorrow."

The telephone rang and Alex picked it up on the second ring.

"Luke? Carl here. Glad I caught you in."

Alex covered the receiver and rolled his eyes at Sally. "What can I do for you, Carl?" he said.

"I've bad news I'm afraid. The Feds are coming down with insider trading charges against you. My contacts tell me that indictments are coming down any day now. Tomorrow they're moving in to slap liens on all your bank accounts and revoke your passport."

"What are you saying?"

"Luke, it's all over! The game's up. If you don't get out of the country soon, they're going to throw you in jail. They're coming down hard."

Alex swallowed hard and ran a hand through his lush blond locks. He was rich and handsome now, but once again he was a fugitive. "Thanks, Carl," he said finally. "I'd better act fast."

He slammed down the receiver and called out Sally's name.

"Just a moment, darling. I'm changing into something a bit more exotic."

"Hurry! Pack a bag! We're getting the hell out of here!"

Sally ran back into the room. "What are you talking about?"

"It's all over. Back to square one again. The federal government knows all about Luke Fenris and his illegal attempt to take over the media. They'll be closing in on me sometime tomorrow, which means we'd better get the hell out of here tonight."

Sally spun around on her heels with her arms extended and said, "And give up all this you mean?" Then she burst out laughing, and Alex joined in with her.

"Pack up everything we can carry now while I search the apartment."

"Search for what?"

"I can't believe that someone like Luke Fenris doesn't have an emergency stash around here somewhere—for just such an emergency as this."

Thirty-five minutes later, Alex found exactly what he was looking for; it was mostly fifties and hundreds, packed tightly inside a three-suiter. Alex did a rough count and estimated that it came to at least a million dollars—walking-around money for Luke Fenris in the event he had to do a midnight flier. As he lifted his eyes skyward to give thanks for his good fortune, Sally wheeled two large valises bulging at the sides out of the bedroom.

"Since none of Danielle's clothes fit me anyway, I decided to take them all and starve myself into them. Oh yes, I did squeeze in a couple of suits and a change of underwear for you."

Alex smiled and patted the bag at his feet. "We may be homeless," he said, "but we're far from broke. Call Nicky and tell him to meet us at JFK in an hour, in that butterfly-shaped building where you charter airplanes."

On their way out, Alex slipped the concierge a fifty and said, "We're going to the Hamptons for a few days. If anyone comes by tomorrow, tell them we'll be staying at Mister Navi's estate."

"Thank you, Mister Fenris." The concierge looked quizzically at Sally, then turned back to Alex. "Shall I call for your car, sir?"

"That won't be necessary. I've a taxi waiting for me outside. We'll manage the bags ourselves. See you in a few days."

The concierge pocketed the fifty and went back to his newspaper, knowing when he was being told, ever so politely, to mind his own business.

The traffic was light, and they arrived at JFK in forty-two minutes. Alex made arrangements for a chartered flight, paying in cash no questions asked, when Nicky arrived in a taxi dressed as though he was ready for combat.

"Yo, Sally," he said. "Hey, Alex, is that you?"

"Who'd you expect?"

"I still can't get used to you lookin' like that. What's up anyway?"

"Maybe you can get used to this though," Alex said, handing Nicky a shopping bag stuffed with cash. "There's a hundred grand in there for the gang to carry on the struggle, just like I promised them at the meeting. Don't spend it all on bombs. Invest it in the future. Oh, and here's an extra fifty thousand just for you, Nicky, for being such a . . . well, for just being Nicky . . . and, for saving our lives."

Nicky's jaw fell perceptibly as he stared back and forth from Sally to Alex. "Where . . . where did you guys—?"

"Don't even ask," Alex said. "You don't need to know what's happening right now. It's better that way."

Nicky swallowed hard, his Adam's apple bobbing. "Well, shit, thanks. What can I say?"

"We've got to be off, Nicky. You'll read about it in the papers soon. We'll be in touch with you—just as soon as things calm down a bit."

Sally hugged him tightly and kissed him on the cheek. "I'm going to miss you," she said, "all of you guys."

Alex shook his hand and squeezed his shoulder. "You'd better head back to town now. It's better if you don't know where we're going."

"What do you want me to tell the others?" Nicky said.

"Tell them we love them," Sally said. "We wish them well and we'll be thinking about them . . . and about you, too."

Tears rolled freely down Sally's cheek as Nicky's taxi whisked him off into the darkness. "He's good people," she said to Alex.

"They're all good people," Alex said. "The best thing they can do with the money is open up a restaurant, hire Barbara to be their cook, and keep Pinto in an endless supply of food."

"God love them."

"God love all of us." Alex checked his watch. "Say goodbye to New York now, darling. It's time to hit the road."

CHAPTER THIRTY-TWO

Six months later, Ludwig von Dracula drained a cold glass of blood and picked up the telephone. He let it ring a few times, and was about to hang up when someone answered.

"Hello," a woman's voice said.

"Hi. Is this Danielle Dante?"

"Yes."

"My name is Luddie. I don't know if you remember me. We met a few months ago at Luke Fenris's apartment. The night of the shooting."

"Luddie? Hmmm, let me see . . . yes, you were the cute blond guy with the garlic allergy."

"Right. I was wondering if you would like to go out to dinner next Saturday night. I know this really wonderful Indian restaurant where they never heard of garlic, and they have some lovely live sitar music. There's a patio where you can sit in the moonlight and dance."

"I'd love to. Sounds divine. So tell me what you've been doing with yourself all this time?"

"Senator Dante," the reporter from ABC called out, "your deceased predecessor, whose unexpired term you're filling, had a strong interest in foreign affairs. Do you plan to continue in his footsteps?"

"I hope so, Sam. The people sent me to Washington to do a job, and I'm going to give it my best. I've always had a strong interest in foreign policy going back to my days at Palliser. The people voted for change when they swept out the old regime and elected people like me, and I intend to put my experience to good use for them. Yes, Dan?"

"As the man who broke the Bruwandagate story, do you have a particular affinity for African concerns and the plight of the people there?"

"Yes, Dan, I do. I intend to seek a seat on the Foreign Affairs Committee and move Africa right up to the top of the agenda. I'm especially encouraged by the recent appointment of Carl Navi as Undersecretary for African Affairs."

"Senator, do you think the government will ever catch up with Luke Fenris?"

Senator Peter Dante stroked his chin in the manner of the Elder Statesman and said, "I don't know, Tom. General Thorn, our new FBI Director, has extensive experience in international intelligence, and I'm sure if anybody can catch up with Luke Fenris, it's Thorn. I see I'm out of time now and have to rush off. Thank you all for coming. I look forward to continuing an open and active relationship with the media. Our freedom is in your hands. Keep on digging for the truth. That's what the First Amendment is all about."

Kenyatta stood behind the bar of the gang's new Sino-Carribe Restaurant, checking the glasses one final time for spots before the doors opened for their first-night crowd. Pinto fidgeted with the buttons of his blue tuxedo jacket near the door, and Maria straightened his collar. In the kitchen, Barbara, chief chef and half-owner, made one last pass by the stoves to make sure the cooks had everything under control. Satisfied that they did, she joined the others in the dining area.

"Another half hour," Maria said.

"I'm so nervous," Barbara said. "This is my first business. I enjoyed working for Mister Fenris. He treated me very well."

"Yeah, well, if your cookin' is half as good as I think it is, we got no problem."

"Jus' remember, Pinto," Kenyatta said, "twenny percent of the profit goes to charity, so you better control your appetite."

Two hours later the place was packed. The crowd was six-deep at the bar, waiting to be seated. At ten o'clock a tall fat man led an entourage of eight through the front door.

"Your name, sir?" Pinto asked.

"Maury Cesare."

Pinto gulped audibly. Cesare's name did not appear on the reservation list, but Pinto knew who he was. Cesare had replaced "Gin Jimmy" Vincente as boss of bosses in New York's top underworld family. Pinto had a decision to make, and he came down on the side of personal safety. "Yes, sir. Maria!" he called. "Show Mister Cesare and his guests to our best table please."

Marie reached for a stack of menus and smiled brightly at Maury Cesare. "Follow me, gentlemen. I have our big circular table ready for you."

The crowd at the bar glared in their direction, wondering who these dignitaries were who could just walk in and be seated so quickly. The time passed smoothly until eleven-thirty, when two strange men entered the restaurant and walked over to Cesare's table. Cesare rose to his feet, smiled broadly and extended his hand. "Tony Locaro! Rico Angelli!" he said. "What a surprise. Sit down and have a drink with us."

"I don't think so," Locaro said. "We brought a message from Mister Vincente."

"Vincente's dead," Cesare said."

"In that case, you can give him a message from us." Before Cesare's men could respond, the two intruders pulled pistols from beneath their jackets and emptied them into the boss of bosses. Screams filled the restaurant and patrons ducked beneath their tables for cover. Within seconds Locaro and Angelli had raced out the door, with Cesare's men following closely behind.

As Barbara came running out of the kitchen to see what all the excitement was about, she bumped into Kenyatta. "What happened?" she yelled.

"Maury Cesare just got shot in the dining room. Looks like he's dead."

"How awful."

"Yeah, awful." Kenyatta's grin stretched across his face. Barbara stared at him in alarm, until she finally caught on. She, too, grinned from ear to ear. "You realize what this means?" she said.

The two of them raised their fists in the air and then slapped their palms together. "We're a success! We're a success! We're a success!" they shouted in unison.

Mr. and Mrs. Alex Maltese sat in lounge chairs, gazing up at the full moon from their oceanfront retreat along the Costa Rican coastline. Alex's hair was dyed black as was the full beard he had recently grown, but it was impossible to hide the finely crafted features and compelling blue eyes that had once belonged to Luke Fenris. Sally was wearing one of Danielle's old bikinis and looked ravishing now that she had shed twenty-five pounds and started exercising regularly.

"Another gorgeous night," she said.

"I feel like I've died and gone to heaven. Want to catch a movie later?"

"Maybe. I'm not sure Tom Cruise does it for me dubbed in Spanish. Hey, did you read about Barbara and the gang in the Times today?"

"You mean about their new Sino-Carribean restaurant? Isn't that great? Some Mafioso was shot there last week while he was eating some of her jerk chicken, and now they can't keep the crowds away. They're making money faster than they can count it."

"If they're not careful," Sally said, "they'll turn into regular capitalists."

"You sure you don't want to take in a movie?"

"Let's see if Nicky wants to join us," Sally said. "He's been working too long in his gun shop lately." Suddenly, she looked over at Alex who was rubbing his throat and frowning. "Are you all right, honey?"

"My throat's a little scratchy and I'm thirsty as hell. A glass of water'll fix me right up. God! I can't believe how beautiful this is. Have you ever seen such a magnificent full moon in your life?"

ABOUT THE AUTHORS

Gary Greenberg is the author of several popular works on biblical history, including *101 Myths of the Bible*, and *The Moses Mystery*. His books have been published in many foreign editions. He is also the author of numerous articles on history, libertarian politics, law, and personal computers. One of his essays, *Legal Systems under Anarcho-Capitalism*, frequently pops up on libertarian web sites. In 1978 he was the Libertarian Party candidate for Governor of New York. He has also appeared on numerous radio and television programs and served as a consultant to National Geographic Television's *Science of the Bible* series. He maintains a web site at www.bibleandhistory.com. He works as a criminal defense attorney in New York City.

Jerome Tuccille is the author of 25 books covering a wide range of topics-true crime, biography, fiction, and personal finance. His best-selling, widely acclaimed biographies include *Gallo Be Thy Name; Dillerland; Trump; Alan Shrugged; Rupert Murdoch;* and *Kingdom*. Tuccille has also written a true crime memoir, *Gallery of Fools,* dealing with a major New York City art heist. His novels include *Wall Street Blues* and *The Mission*. Tuccille is a vice president of T. Rowe Price Investment Services, and in 1974 he was the Free Libertarian candidate for Governor of New York.

PERE/ET PRE//

THE MOSES MYSTERY
The Egyptian Origins
of the Jewish People
by Gary Greenberg

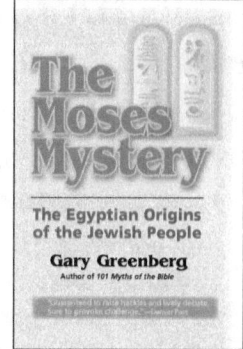

What do history and archaeology *really* say about the origins of ancient Israel?

Although the bible says that Israel's formative history took place in ancient Egypt, biblical scholars and Egyptologists have steadfastly refused to explore the role of Egyptian history and literature on the origins of Jewish religion. *The Moses Mystery* attempts to set the record straight. Based on extensive research into biblical and Egyptian history, archaeology, literature and mythology Greenberg argues that the first Israelites were Egyptians, followers of the monotheistic teachings of Pharaoh Akhenaten.

Some of the many intriguing revelations in *The Moses Mystery* include:

- Ancient Egyptian records specifically identify Moses as Akhenaten's chief priest and describe the Exodus as the result of a civil war for control over the Egyptian throne

- Abraham, Isaac, and Jacob were characters from Egyptian mythology

- The Twelve Tribes of Israel never existed

An ingenious comparison of Biblical and Egyptian history.– St. Louis Post-Dispatch

A must read for those interested in biblical scholarship. – Tennessee Tribune

Insightful and valuable. – KMT magazine

Also by Gary Greenberg

King David *versus* Israel: How a Hebrew Tyrant Hated by the Israelites Became a Biblical Hero

101 Myths of the Bible: How Ancient Scribes Invented Biblical History

The Judas Brief: Who Really Killed Jesus?

Manetho: A Study in Egyptian Chronology

PEREƩET PREƩƩ

KING DAVID VERSUS ISRAEL:
How a Hebrew Tyrant Hated by the Israelites Became a Biblical Hero
by Gary Greenberg

In this controversial biography of one of the bibles most revered figures biblical historian Gary Greenberg challenges the conventional image of King David as a much beloved hero of the ancient Israelites. Originally published as *The Sins of King David: A New History,* the author has re-edited the manuscript, refined some of the arguments, and added many additional biblical citations.

I heartily recommend this substantial volume . . . [It] is a worthy addition to the library of first-rate and challenging books on [King} David.
—DR. DAVID NOEL FREEDMAN, EDITOR OF THE ANCHOR BIBLE DICTIONARY AND THE ANCHOR BIBLE PROJECT

Placing these texts into their historical, political, and geographic setting, Greenberg is able to separate much historical fact from biblical fiction. . . Greenberg shows David to be an ambitious mercenary, ruthless politician, unjust tyrant, and military imperialist. —LIBRARY JOURNAL

Gary Greenberg will make you think. He might even make you angry. In his latest book he paints a portrait of a ruthless, deceitful, corrupt leader who was a traitor to Israel. —GREEN BAY PRESS-GAZETTE

Also by Gary Greenberg

The Moses Mystery: The Egyyptian Origins of the Jewish People

101 Myths of the Bible: How Ancient Scribes Invented Biblical History

The Judas Brief: Who Really Killed Jesus?

Manetho: A Study in Egyptian Chronology